The Faithless Fool

The Gareth and Gwen Medieval Mysteries:
The Bard's Daughter (prequel)
The Good Knight
The Uninvited Guest
The Fourth Horseman
The Fallen Princess
The Unlikely Spy
The Lost Brother
The Renegade Merchant
The Unexpected Ally
The Worthy Soldier
The Favored Son
The Viking Prince
The Irish Bride
The Prince's Man
The Faithless Fool

The After Cilmeri Series:
Daughter of Time
Footsteps in Time
Winds of Time
Prince of Time
Crossroads in Time
Children of Time
Exiles in Time
Castaways in Time
Ashes of Time
Warden of Time
Guardians of Time
Masters of Time
Outpost in Time
Shades of Time
Champions of Time
Refuge in Time
Unbroken in Time
Outcasts in Time

A Gareth and Gwen Medieval Mystery

THE
FAITHLESS FOOL

by

SARAH WOODBURY

To Deborah

Cast of Characters

Gwen—Prince Hywel's investigator, Gareth's wife
Gareth—Prince Hywel's steward, Gwen's husband
Llelo—Gareth and Gwen's son
Dai—Gareth and Gwen's son

Conall—Ambassador from Leinster
Godfrid—Prince of Dublin
Caitriona (Cait)—Godfrid's wife, Conall's sister

David—King of Scotland
Stephen—King of England
Maud—Holy Roman Empress, rival to the English throne
Henry—Maud's son
Hamelin—Henry's half-brother
Ranulf—Earl of Chester
James Carr—Scottish nobleman
Margaret Carr—James's wife
Douglas MacGregor—King David's commander
Æthelwold—Bishop of Carlisle
Father Dunstan—Priest at Carlisle Castle

1

Carlisle Castle

22 May 1149

Day One

Gareth

King David of Scotland placed a naked blade on the shoulder of his great-nephew, Prince Henry, who was kneeling at his feet, and recited the words of chivalry in a commanding voice that carried throughout the hall.

"Au nom de Dieu, je te fais chevalier." *Be thou a knight in the name of God.* Then he stepped back and made a motion with his hand. "Avance, chevalier." *Arise, knight.*

As Prince Henry rose to his feet, stamping, shouts, and applause filled the hall. Henry was sixteen years old, exactly halfway in age between Gareth's boys, Dai and Llelo, who were fifteen and seventeen respectively. Both sons had stopped cold at the sight of the prince receiving his knighthood from the King of Scots.

Envy was plain in their faces, prompting Gareth to put a hand on a shoulder of each. "Your time will come. Never fear. The prince is young to be knighted, but he is also a prince and may one day be King of England. Do not begrudge him his day of glory." He paused a beat before adding in a low voice, still in Welsh and for their ears alone: "The next one may be a long time coming."

The arrival of the Welsh party had been delayed, thankfully not by a storm in the Irish Sea, but by the slowness of the journey through the estuary at the mouth of the River Eden and then up the Eden to Carlisle Castle. With all the rain they'd been getting, a continuance of the rains of the winter, the river was running high and fast, so they'd been rowing upstream against a heavy current. At times, walking would have been faster, except they hadn't wanted to stop along the way. Although this area of Scotland had once been Norse—and British before that—now it was populated by people who cursed the sight of a Viking longship. And not without reason, given the centuries of Danish conquest and warfare.

That the ship flew the white flag of peace and was helmed by none other than the mighty Godfrid, Prince of Dublin, was beside the point. The people on shore didn't know who he was, nor that he had Conall of Leinster and Gareth of Gwynedd beside him. They saw only the round shields of Vikings hung on the sides of the ship and armed men at the oars.

Still, none of the locals had attempted to stop them, not only because a second look had reminded them of the folly of taking on Danish warriors, but also because the ship carried women and children—Gareth's wife, Gwen, and their children, of course; and also

Caitriona, Godfrid's wife (and Conall's sister). Thus, they had reached Carlisle in one piece, found their lodgings at the cathedral guesthouse in the town, and then hastened to the castle. As it turned out, their timing had been perfect, and they'd entered King David's majestic hall just in time to witness his bestowal of knighthood on Henry.

Having received a hug from his uncle and general congratulations from the other noblemen in his vicinity, Henry descended from the dais and made a beeline towards the Welsh party. Then, to Gareth's utter surprise, Henry didn't stop a respectful distance away but walked right up to him to embrace him. "I'm so glad you are here!" Pulling back, he seemed to realize that the hug had perhaps been slightly beneath his dignity. Clearing his throat, he added, "Welcome to Carlisle."

"Thank you." Gareth bowed gravely back.

"Were you in time?" Henry accepted everyone else's obeisance and then raised them up with an impatient gesture. "Did you see?"

"We did, my lord," Gareth said. "Congratulations. The honor is most deserved."

Henry made a face, again revealing himself to be sixteen and, in truth, no more (or less) mature than Gareth's own sons. "I am not a child begging for a sweet. I would not besmirch my uncle's action by suggesting that I am undeserving of the honor, but we all know that I have led few men in battle up until now—and those with little success."

"I think you underest—"

"What did I just say?" Henry cut Gareth off with another gesture.

Gareth bent his head respectfully. "Of course, my lord."

"Then again, now that you're here," Henry rubbed his hands together, "the task of taking back my mother's throne can begin in earnest!"

2

Day One

Gwen

Henry's gleeful comment was another reminder, if Gwen needed one, that their partners in this alliance were taking the inclusion of the Welsh seriously. Henry truly wanted them there, and his desire to see them appeared to stem from a true affection that went far beyond politics. What's more, he'd specifically asked for the presence of not only Gareth, but Gareth's entire family. Llelo and Dai were as integral to this delegation as their parents. Even Taran and Tangwen, left behind tonight at their lodgings, had been wanted. It seemed that, for Henry, their alliance was not merely a means, as it undoubtedly was for Earl Ranulf of Chester, to keep King Owain Gwynedd from attacking his lands.

While the bargain couldn't have been offered simply because the young prince wanted to see them all again—and to share with them the moment of his knighting—Gwen had to wonder how much his hero-worship of Gareth had played in the proceedings.

This journey had been nearly six months in the making. Once King Owain had agreed to Prince Henry's offer of a treaty last December, discussions had been underway as to the best method to confirm their alliance. Not since the days of the great High Kings of Britain had anyone attempted to unify the powers of Wales, Scotland, and England, as Henry had proposed to do, should he go so far as to actually depose King Stephen as King of England. Everyone wanted the ceremony worthy of the historic occasion.

So while discussions had been lengthy, they hadn't actually been contentious. King David had made clear from the start that this treaty wasn't Prince Henry's alone, that he had the full support of not only David but Earl Ranulf as well, and they genuinely wanted to see King Owain at Carlisle.

Still, generations of distrust between Gwynedd and the Normans remained a significant barrier to an actual in-person meeting. More than anything else, this had been a difficult matter to overcome. In the end, in fact, it had been an impossible matter. King Owain's advisers believed that no member of the royal family could possibly venture into Chester, which was just over the border of Wales into England, much less all the way to Scotland, out of fear of being played false. Gwen felt that fear in her own heart. Even Prince Henry couldn't deny that it had happened before, and that there was nothing he, King David, or Earl Ranulf could promise that would make Owain certain it wouldn't happen again.

It was one thing for these three other great magnates to unite against their common enemy. It was quite another to include King Owain, who shared no family connections with any of them. While blood ties were certainly no barrier to war—after all, King Stephen and Empress Maud themselves were cousins—sometimes they helped keep the peace. Why else would kings marry their daughters to their enemies? King David and Maud may not have been blood kin, but he was still Maud's uncle, since her father, King Henry I of England, had married David's sister, Edith.

At the moment, King Stephen seemed far more concerned about the power of King David than that of Henry, who, as he himself had just admitted, had so far accomplished very little with his acts of rebellion. And really Stephen's concern was legitimate. David of Scotland had stepped into the breach created by the death of Henry's uncle, Robert of Gloucester, and was daily encroaching farther south into England. By the terms of this treaty they were signing this week, Henry, once he became king, would cede all of Northumbria to his uncle.

The fact that Henry and his allies had also made overtures towards Dublin and Leinster only added to the significance of the event. It was King David, in fact, who'd asked Godfrid to sail to Wales to collect Gareth and Gwen—as well as Conall, who'd been acting as ambassador to Gwynedd. King David had arranged this for his own purposes, not knowing what close friends they all were, and during the journey they'd decided to keep their attachment to themselves, at least until they knew more about what they were walking into.

Now, within moments of Prince Henry's greetings, his eyes went to Llelo and then to the sword belted at his waist. "I see you still wear it!"

Llelo's sword had come from the hand of Henry himself, in the course of events at Bristol Castle the last time they'd seen him.

"Of course, my lord." Llelo bowed low. "I count myself a lucky man every single day that I was in the right place at the right moment to act, and I remain humbly honored that you would bestow such a magnificent weapon upon me."

It was a fine speech, and Gwen would have patted her son on the back at how well he'd done if it wouldn't have disrupted the proceedings and called attention to him in a way he wouldn't want. Dark-haired and dark-eyed, nearly as tall as his father, though thin as a rake, Llelo was growing into his position as his father's apprentice, not only in regards to assisting with investigations, but also by learning to be diplomatic.

Henry smiled. "I hope you know that if I had been a knight myself when I gave it to you, I would have knighted *you* on the spot."

He hesitated. And then, in the pause that followed before Henry's eyes lit, all those watching him, except perhaps Llelo, saw the thought that came into his mind as if it were written in the air above his head. Spinning around, Henry strode towards his uncle, who had remained near the dais in conversation with several noble men and women.

King David broke off to greet Henry, bending close to hear what he had to say. Though his hair was entirely white, compared to Henry's tight red curls, King David was unbowed by age. He was also taller than Henry, who was short and stocky. Even so, the set of their shoulders was similar, and Gwen thought she could see the uncle in the nephew, despite not sharing blood. Henry admired David so profoundly he looked to emulate his mannerisms.

After a brief consultation, King David lifted his head to look over Henry's shoulder and, for the first time, openly inspected the newly arrived Welsh contingent. His eyes narrowed for a moment in what Gwen saw as calculation, and then he patted Henry on the shoulder. Whatever he said made Henry spin around, a grin splitting his face, while the king himself made a magisterial gesture from behind the young prince, summoning them all forward.

Gareth led the way, followed immediately by Conall and Godfrid, as was their right, with Gwen and her two boys close behind. As he waited for Gareth to reach him, the king slid the sword by which he'd dubbed Henry into its sheath with an air indicating he was accustomed to its use. His hand had been steady as he'd made his great-nephew a knight, but upon closer inspection, David's face was thinner than was perhaps healthy, whether due to age or illness, Gwen didn't know. Nonetheless, his eyes were nearly as bright as Henry's as he looked over his guests.

"I couldn't be more pleased to finally meet the great Lord Gareth." His eyes were assessing but not critical. "Prince Henry speaks of you often—as well, of course, of the bravery of this young man."

Llelo straightened under the king's gaze, realizing it was to himself the king was referring. "You honor me with your kind words, my lord."

"How old are you, son?"

"Seventeen, my lord."

"Older men have been knighted for far less than saving the life of the future King of England." A low rumble came from within the king's chest.

"My lord, that isn't what happen—" Llelo began to explain, but the king overrode him.

"In our tradition, each candidate for knighthood must spend the night in the church, as Henry did last night, praying and asking for forgiveness for his sins, so that he might be reborn anew as a knight. It is, in a sense, another baptism, if the priest would not think such a comparison unholy. Are you willing?"

In a matter of a quarter of an hour, they'd gone from huddled together in the doorway of the great hall, feeling awkward and uncertain about their welcome in this strange castle, to being offered an honor beyond Llelo's wildest dreams. Or rather, it was an honor straight out of Llelo's wildest dreams.

From Llelo's expression, he could hardly believe his good fortune—though, in the heartbeat before he replied to the king, he shot a glance in his father's direction, worried perhaps that there was a diplomatic reason he should decline, or that the knighting was taking place under false pretenses. Like Gwen, however, Gareth had been there when Llelo had stopped a killer who'd drawn a knife in the prince's presence, albeit to murder another. He gave the briefest of nods.

In response, Llelo straightened his spine that was already straight as a poker, and, as with Henry, his thoughts were plain on his face before he spoke them: "Yes, my lord. I am ready."

Even with his burgeoning maturity, the excitement of what lay before him was too immediate for Llelo to understand the true significance of what he was being offered. Gwen didn't think Prince Henry understood either. She was quite certain, however, that King David was fully aware of the symbolism behind the gesture. The pause between Henry's query about the possibility of knighting Llelo and David's approval had involved a brief assessment of the consequences of knighting a young Welshman as one of Prince Henry's first acts as a full-fledged knight himself.

Everyone, even Prince Henry and Gwen's boys, were very aware of the momentous nature of bringing Gwynedd into this pact between England, Scotland, and Chester. To do so was to acknowledge Gwynedd's power and authority as a kingdom equal to any of the others. In that light, knighting Llelo was no small thing. Gwen had seen David come to the conclusion that he could not regret tying Gwynedd more closely to Henry, and thus to David. In fact, the tighter the better.

Gareth had brought the precious document, signed in the proper place by King Owain, who had already accepted the cost that would arise from it: allowing Cadwaladr, his treacherous younger brother, back into his court. By comparison, aiding Henry, Ranulf, and David in overthrowing King Stephen seemed a minor matter, even if on the surface it was a bold step and not one to be taken lightly.

Nonetheless, it was one to be taken. David, Henry, and Ranulf had to have known it too, even as they sent Cadwaladr back to Owain. They either wanted very badly to get rid of him (perfectly possible given how odious he was) or they truly wanted Owain on their side. Even with this lovely welcome into Carlisle Castle by Prince Henry, Gwen couldn't help thinking that the former still outweighed the latter.

And yet, the truth could not be gainsaid: as long as King Stephen remained in the ascendancy and retained the English throne, whatever these great magnates were agreeing to, and whatever alliances they made, were just words. For over a year, the war had been at a standstill, if not a stalemate. Just that spring, Stephen had failed to take Worcester from Queen Maud's allies, even as he built two castles nearby in an attempt to counter the alliance's power. So far, it was only King Owain who'd made any real concession.

Meanwhile Dai, from his position slightly behind his brother, was practically dripping with jealousy. Despite the envy, which not a single soul here could blame him for feeling, he put his hand on his brother's shoulder and said in a loving way in Welsh, "If anyone deserves this, Llelo, you do."

"But wait!" Henry was practically bouncing on his toes. "He shouldn't do this alone, Uncle."

Gwen's heart broke to see the sudden joy and hope in Dai's face in the heartbeat between when Henry said those words and when he cupped his hands around his mouth and called across the hall, "Hamelin!"

3

The young man at whom Prince Henry had shouted had been listening intently to a nobleman with a thick beard and an expansive manner, judging by the way he was gesticulating broadly. At Henry's summons, Hamelin made his excuses and hurried over. His red hair was almost exactly the same color as Conall's own—and Henry's own—though Conall wore his clipped to almost nothing, and the young man's was more of a mop on his head.

As Dai's expression shuttered, Conall moved to his side, but didn't touch him. To do so would mean acknowledging the range of emotions Dai had experienced in an astoundingly short period of time. Conall was nearly three times his age, but that didn't mean he couldn't remember what it was like to *feel* so fully.

Hamelin appeared to have missed the entirety of the conversation between the king, his half-brother, and Llelo because he strode across the room with an expectant air but not one that expected anything in particular. Gareth and Gwen had met this illegitimate half-brother to Prince Henry during their investigation in Bristol, and from his cheerful expression, he was having no trouble remembering all of them.

He stopped a few feet away, made a respectful bow, and then reached out a hand to Llelo. "Welcome! I saw you come in, but I couldn't get away from old Carr sooner."

Llelo clasped his forearm in return, unable to keep the outsized grin off his face. "It is marvelous to see you here!"

For his part, King David said, "Hamelin," in mild rebuke.

Hamelin bowed more fully in his direction, but while his words were apologetic, his manner was insouciant. "My apologies, my king. Please forgive my slip of the tongue. My thoughts were entirely focused on how happy I was to see an old friend."

He said the word *old* this second time completely without irony. When one was nineteen, the year and a half he'd known Llelo *was* a long time.

David made a motion accepting the apology, and Henry nodded indulgently, since all three of them seemed to be in agreement that nobody enjoyed being cornered by *old* Carr, the man to whom Hamelin had been speaking, who didn't appear to be as old as the name implied either. He was fifty, perhaps, but not ancient.

And then Hamelin listened with widening eyes as Henry explained what he planned for Llelo, and added, "I'd like to knight you and Llelo together."

Conall had never seen a man look more astonished than Hamelin did in that moment. Henry's smile broadened to see the impact of his words. He was Hamelin's younger but legitimate half-brother, and for him to offer Hamelin the chance at knighthood, on the heels of his own ascension, was almost too much to take in.

Nonetheless, Hamelin managed an eager nod of acceptance, followed by an even lower bow. "Thank you, my lord."

"I'm thinking the vigil should be at St. Mary's this time," King David said.

"We'll go now." Hamelin grabbed Llelo's elbow and set off with him, heading down the great hall towards the main door, all the while motioning with his free hand and talking animatedly. Llelo hastened to keep pace, nodding that he was listening, in that diplomatic manner he'd learned from his father. That didn't mean he wasn't still grinning madly.

Dai watched them go with as neutral an expression as Conall had ever seen, even on wizened diplomats. He was apprenticed to become a member of the Dragons—Prince Hywel's special force of highly trained men—in whose service he had already performed great deeds. But today was not to be his day, and he was struggling with the disappointment at the loss of an honor he hadn't known moments before was even a possibility.

Conall had no children of his own, so he was hardly one to counsel another man's son, but he liked Dai and didn't enjoy seeing him suffering. Leaning close, he said under his breath in Danish, which Dai spoke fluently, "I wasn't knighted until I was ten years older than you, and I'm a king's nephew. Your time will come."

Though Dai's expression remained more wooden than was typical for him, his breathing settled. "Father was in his twenties too."

Meanwhile, Gareth was talking to the king. "I apologize, my lord. I don't know Carlisle well. Is St. Mary's another name for the cathedral? As perhaps you know, we are staying in their guesthouse."

That was where Conall's sister, Caitriona, had chosen to remain rather than coming to the castle that evening with the other adults. She was pregnant with her first child and unwell with the whole process—even as she was overjoyed that she'd been able to conceive. She hadn't produced a child during her first marriage, and she and Godfrid had gone into their union knowing that natural children might never be forthcoming.

Godfrid's brother, Brodar, who was also the King of Dublin, had at one point questioned Godfrid's decision to marry Cait at all, given her apparent barrenness. Godfrid had held up Gareth and Gwen's example of adopting two sons as an option if natural means of producing an heir failed. In the Danish world, as in the Welsh one, the only relevant factor in a child's inheritance was the acknowledgement of the father.

It was as if Caitriona had been holding herself together just until they arrived in Carlisle, at which point she'd collapsed into bed. Any one of them—Gwen, Godfrid, or even Conall—would have stayed at her side if they hadn't been shooed away by Cait's own maidservant, as well as by Cait herself.

"St. Mary's is the church located within the outer bailey of the castle," Prince Henry said. "I did spend last night and much of the day at the cathedral, since the Bishop of Carlisle saw fit to oversee my vigil, but at this hour Hamelin and Llelo will be better off at the castle's church. We've disrupted the cathedral's schedule enough this week." Then his brow furrowed as he turned his head towards the doors, through which the pair had disappeared. "Hamelin did hear you, didn't he, Uncle?"

For a castle to have its own church was not unusual, especially a castle as large as Carlisle. When they'd arrived, they'd had to traverse a portion of the outer bailey in order to reach the inner gatehouse and then the great hall. Conall had never seen a bailey that encompassed as large an area as Carlisle's palisade, which even now the king was rebuilding in stone. Conall guessed the line from the southeastern corner to the northwestern one was nearly two hundred yards.

"Dai can steer them aright." Gareth motioned to Dai and switched to Welsh. "Follow them, son. Before they begin their prayers, they will need to wash their faces and hands, which they may not remember, anxious as they are to begin. Thank goodness Llelo put on a clean shirt at the guesthouse before we came here. Make sure they both have what they need, including your support in word as well as deed."

"Yes, Father." Dai had recovered enough to nod vigorously and then was off like an arrow from a bow after his brother and Hamelin.

Gareth then turned to face the prince and king. "Thank you, my lords. This is an entirely unexpected honor. We are grateful beyond measure."

"All the better for being unexpected." The king smiled, and Conall thought his pleasure was genuine, since his eyes twinkled too.

Gwen, in turn, laughed, even as she shook her head in disbelief. "This was not how we thought we would end the day when we began it. I'm so pleased for Llelo." She looked at Prince Henry. "Thank you, my lord."

"It is the least I can do." Henry frowned. "I am not unaware that I have left your other son out, but he is only fifteen ..." His voice trailed off.

"A little suffering could be good for him." Conall took the liberty of stepping in. "You are right that he is disappointed, but also right that he is young. You can already see that he is rising to the occasion."

"It isn't in victory that the mettle of a man is made clear, but in disappointment and defeat." King David gestured to the high table. "Have you dined?"

"No, my lord." Gareth put a hand to his breast pocket. "I have the signed docu—"

"There will be time enough for that. Suffice that you are here. You shall eat with us." King David patted Prince Henry on the shoulder. "My nephew is hanging by a thread. He was given water and bread, but otherwise hasn't had any food since yesterday. It would do nobody any good to have him expiring within hours of his knighting!"

Since the ceremony had ended, the table on the dais had been rearranged such that chairs lined both sides, seating upwards of twenty people. Some regulars to King David's court had to be displaced with the arrival of Conall's party, but he saw no disgruntled faces among the onlookers. All appeared well in King David's domains—at least on the surface. Conall's uncle, the King of Leinster, had charged him with the task of ferreting out any unpleasantness going on underneath. Rivalries, conflict, and outright betrayal were endemic to Irish royal courts. Conall had heard no rumor of similar proclivities in Norman or Scottish ones—barring the war for the throne of England, which overshadowed them all.

King David was still smiling. "Here at the end of my life, I find myself valuing the simple pleasures: good food, great wine, and companions to go with them."

Conall bent his head. "I must say that I agree, though you are not that much older than I, my lord."

The king's lips twitched with amusement. "I *am* old, Lord Conall. I will see a few more winters; that is all."

"Are you ill, my lord?" Gwen asked.

King David turned to her, but before he could answer the question—if, in fact, he had been going to answer it—Dai returned to the hall.

Although he'd skidded to a halt in the doorway, and his urgency was unmistakable to anyone who knew him, he managed to make his way somewhat more sedately to the dais where his parents were standing. By the time he reached them, he had himself fully under control and spoke in Welsh, so as not to make an announcement to the whole hall, "We found a body in the church. And before you ask, it definitely isn't where it's supposed to be."

4

Day One

Llelo

Someday Llelo was going to head up an investigation all by himself, but he wasn't sorry that the moment for that particular ascension wouldn't be today. He had his hands full with the woman who'd found the body. To Llelo's mind, the woman's response was a far more difficult thing to have to deal with than the body itself.

To his utter and complete horror, she was currently sobbing uncontrollably in his arms. In the dim light of the candlelit church, her manner appeared entirely genuine, completely overcome by the shock of seeing the decayed and dirt-covered body reclined in the priest's chair next to the lectern.

So far, that a body had found its way into the chair, a place it absolutely should not be, was all he'd been able to determine about the crime scene. Somehow, it had fallen to him to hold her in his arms. He longed to get closer to the corpse, as Hamelin was doing.

He was sorely tempted, in fact, to call Hamelin over and make him take her. After all, Llelo was the investigator, and Hamelin was an older Frenchman. He knew all about women!

More than anything, Llelo felt it was his task to have a better idea of what they were facing *before* Dai returned with his parents. He would have liked to be able to tell his father when he arrived a litany of details about the scene, ones Llelo had already elicited from both the body and the woman. But all he had managed to determine since he found her in the church porch, opening her mouth to scream for help, was information he himself could see just as easily.

While he knew from experience that hearing her true thoughts when they were fresh would save time later, so far, the woman's own story was a nearly impenetrable mix of tears, recriminations, and anguish, all said in French with a broad Scottish accent that was hardly more than mush in his head. He'd spent most of the time he'd been holding her simply trying to soothe her and stop her (unsuccessfully) from soaking his shoulder with tears.

Finally, he was able to seat her on a bench against the wall, shielded from the body by a pillar and the altar. The woman was thin, almost angular. If he'd had to guess, given the lines around her eyes and mouth and touches of gray in her hair, she was in the vicinity of fifty years of age.

"Madam, if you could just tell me what you know, I would be most grateful." Llelo was crouched in front of her, far enough back so that he wasn't touching her anymore. Thankfully, she'd pulled a handkerchief from her waist and was dabbing her eyes with it.

"I came here to pray as I often do in the evening. Once the knighting ceremony was over, I saw no reason to stay in the hall." Her voice firmed slightly. "I knew my husband would be well entertained with the other nobles and their wives, and he gave me leave to depart. I first refreshed the flowers by the front door and afterwards started my prayers. But then I noticed this *horrible* smell wafting towards me from beyond the altar, and then I saw that—that—that *thing* in the priest's chair only a few yards away from where I was kneeling. How could I not have noticed him sooner? How long has he been just—just—just *sitting* there?" These last comments were accompanied by stuttering and renewed sobs.

As the woman's tears began again in earnest, Dai returned with their parents in tow—*and* Prince Henry and King David. Llelo took a few steps away from the woman in order to bow. "My apologies, my lords, for disturbing your evening."

He might have added, *I also didn't intend for my brother to fetch you too* along with a warning glare at Dai, but Llelo was going to be knighted (he hoped, provided the appearance of the body didn't change what Prince Henry wanted), and he needed to be careful about chastising those beneath him, as Dai had suddenly become, especially when the situation was hardly his fault.

The thought was a revelation. By Welsh law, Llelo had become a man at fourteen, but he'd known it for the lie it was. Now, however, whether or not he really felt himself to be an adult inside, he needed to make it so.

And Llelo supposed it was inevitable that the king and prince would want to see the body for themselves. Even if Gareth had come alone, he probably would have had to fetch them. It was the king's church after all.

King David motioned with one hand, in a manner Llelo had seen him use several times already in the short while since they'd met. "It was necessary."

Gareth halted next to Llelo. "Summoning us was the right thing to do. While we didn't actually come to Carlisle to investigate the whys and wherefores of an unexplained body, it seems inevitable somehow that one has come for us anyway."

A burst of sobbing came from the bench where Llelo had left the woman. In those brief moments of normalcy, he'd genuinely forgotten her.

"My dear Margaret." King David moved towards her. "I am so sorry you had to see this. Would you like me to send for your husband?"

Margaret's tears ended abruptly, and she gave a vehement shake of her head. "You and I both know that Lord Carr is averse to unpleasant smells and even more to unpleasant scenes." Then she flung out her hand in a dramatic gesture to point in the direction of the priest's chair, which she couldn't see from where she sat. "Just look at him!"

None of the others had been immediately cognizant of the body that had brought them here in the first place. Hamelin, who was the only one who had so far approached the corpse, was almost invisible in the shadowed church. He hadn't initially come forward to greet his brother and the king, leaving such formalities to Llelo.

Now, he took a few steps away from the body, such that his white face and the blonder highlights in his red hair reflected some of the candlelight that was working ineffectively to light the church. "It's over here." He bit his lip. "Just as a warning, it's an ugly sight."

Llelo hovered between where the king now looked down at Margaret sitting on her bench, and the corpse, which he wanted to see up close. Whether his father saw his hesitation and took pity on him, or had simply decided the way things needed to go, he looked at Llelo's mother, canting his head in Margaret's direction as he did so and raising his eyebrows questioningly.

Gwen didn't quite roll her eyes at Gareth, but her aversion was plain on her face. Llelo felt bad to be foisting Margaret on his mother. But not bad enough to deal with the noble woman again himself.

His mother knew what he was thinking, as of course she would, and her mouth twitched as she passed him. "Don't feel guilty, son. I didn't need to see a body today anyway." She spoke in Welsh too, for his ears alone, and then she smoothly transitioned back to French as she approached Margaret, who was now sobbing in the arms of the king. "Perhaps it would be best if you came with me? I'm sure a cup of wine wouldn't go amiss."

Margaret agreed, to the relief of the men in the room, even if they'd maintained their concerned façades up until now. Once Gwen successfully guided Margaret down the nave to the door, there was a general sigh of relief around the room. Everyone became more matter-of-fact, eased by the familiar stoicism of the men around them. It was an attitude Gwen had run up against time and again as she'd taken part in investigations. Many men wanted to treat all women like fragile flowers and became patronizing in their presence. Sadly, Margaret's hysterics had done nothing to challenge the attitude or expectations of these men.

The women's departure did give Llelo the opportunity to finally approach the body alongside the king. The church was arranged similarly to every other church Llelo had ever entered, though it was larger than most, as befitted the grandeur of Carlisle Castle in general. Twice as long as it was wide, the nave was divided two-thirds of the way down its length by a dais upon which the altar, the lectern, and the priest's chair rested.

Parishioners were confined to the western two-thirds of the church, while the eastern portion was the domain of churchmen. This area included choir stalls and another altar on the eastern wall, immediately beneath a glorious stained-glass window, designed to let the light of the morning sun flood the church.

"This is not what I expected." The king came to a halt within view of the body but not crowding Gareth, who was crouched in front of it.

And *it* was a good description. It was still a body, but it barely looked human, other than being dressed in military gear: a padded coat such as a common soldier might wear and that once might have been blue, a wide belt at the waist upon which a sheathed knife still rested, and high boots. The face was desiccated and also waxy, with a yellowish sheen to it, while the hair was half gone, like a dog with mange. The man had been dead for a long time. It would be up to his father—and thus Llelo as well—to determine how long.

"My apologies, my lord." Dai's eyes were wide, since it appeared he was getting a good look at the body for the first time too. "I-I-I myself didn't realize—"

Gareth put out a hand. "You came running, as you needed to. Though I suppose, given how long ago this fellow died, walking would have made no difference."

5

Day One

Gareth

Gareth suddenly realized he'd taken charge. Turning to the king, he said, "My lord, excuse my impertinence."

"Have you been impertinent? If so, I hadn't noticed."

Gareth swallowed, giving himself time to consider how to explain what he was apologizing for. "I have some experience with death, my lord, as I suppose you know, but I have no desire to usurp the role of your principal investigator. I would be happy to assist him if he desires my help—or to bow out entirely."

"A dead man has appeared in my church!" The king gestured to the body. "I need to know how and why as quickly as possible."

"I did not come here to investigate an unexplained body."

King David let out a little laugh. "I am sure that there are men within my court who might put themselves forward in that regard, but I am also well aware that I have no investigator with your experience or expertise."

"Be that as it may, I am also not a member of your court—"

Prince Henry cut in. "You weren't a member of my uncle's court, nor mine either. And yet I summoned you, and you came."

"I did." Gareth bent his head in the prince's direction.

"I certainly have no regrets on that score." Henry was being completely serious.

"By all means," the king made another motion towards the body, "carry on."

Gareth still wavered. "I would, of course, be happy to give my opinion, but if you change your mind, please don't hesitate to replace me."

"Perhaps I wasn't entirely clear." King David now spoke with a tinge of exasperation in his voice. "Unexplained death is rare enough in my experience that few have ever encountered it, much less an unexplained body." Then he laughed outright at the disbelieving looks directed at him by everyone else in the room, none of whom was a Scotsman. "Don't get me wrong! A Scot is as hotheaded as the next man—more so!—but that is all the more reason few go about their business in the dark. They certainly don't leave months- or years-old bodies in churches! When a Scotsman murders another man, he does it openly and with a hot head."

"As you wish, my lord." Gareth gave way, even as he remained skeptical of the king's assertion. More likely, Scots were getting away with murder because the king had nobody qualified to investigate. Still, Gareth had to admit that this particular situation was unprecedented in his experience, even if it wasn't the first desiccated body he'd seen. "Can you tell us what you know, Llelo?"

Llelo gave a little jerk at being addressed so suddenly, but immediately rose to the occasion, clasping his hands behind his back and speaking in a clear voice that didn't tremble at all. "Lord Hamelin and I arrived at the church door just as the woman was about to call for help. She told me she'd come to pray, as she usually does at this hour, and then noticed the body. I was unable to learn any more from her than that."

"Her name is Margaret Carr," King David said. "She is wife to one of Hugh de Morville's men, James Carr. They are in my court at Morville's behest. You may have noted him in the hall just now."

"We discussed him earlier." Prince Henry's ebullience of before was gone, replaced by a mature solemnity. "Margaret is right that he would not have added to the scene. He is quicker with his tongue and his opinions than perhaps is currently needed."

King David didn't question Henry's not-very-complimentary assessment, unlike Hamelin's earlier in the hall. Instead, he gave a low grunt that might even have been of agreement. Henry was not Hamelin, and if Henry was going to be a good king, or even a great one, a clear-eyed perspective on every one of his underlings was called for. "Can you tell how long he's been dead?"

For that, Gareth would have to get closer, and everyone seemed happy to leave him to it, since it had apparently become his job. By now, the reek of dirt and decay was pronounced throughout the nave. The only reason Gareth hadn't suggested opening the front door and letting in some air was because someone walking in the bailey might wonder what was happening inside and seek to satisfy his curiosity. The last thing they needed were residents of Carlisle Castle wandering into the church before they'd had a chance to move the body.

Gareth made a gesture, not meant to be dismissive so much as clarifying. "If you'll excuse my reticence, my lord, I'd prefer not to draw any definitive conclusions as yet for fear of biasing the investigation before we've even started. I can tell you, however, that from the condition of the body, he died more than a month ago, maybe as many as three or four, was buried, and has been recently unearthed."

"So ... not years?" Prince Henry asked.

"I wouldn't say so."

"How can you be sure?" King David said. "It looks to me as if he could have been dead a decade, as Henry just suggested."

"If you don't mind my asking, are you sure you really want to know? The explanation is quite detailed, and a little grim."

"Please." King David sounded curious more than anything. He would have seen death often, of course. And truly, the situation *was* curious. Gareth had offered to step aside, but his cursory examination of the scene had even him wanting to know more. Really, if he was honest, which he invariably tried to be at all times, he'd started investigating death all those years ago out of curiosity and a strong sense of rightness that would not let him be. In the intervening years, little, at least in that regard, had changed.

So he gestured to the corpse's face. "Do you see the waxy substance that coats him?"

"Yes." That was from the king.

"It forms when a body decomposes in a warm, moist environment, such as would have been found these last months in this region of the world, particularly if the burial was hasty and kept him within a few feet of the surface of the earth. The very fact of being buried slows decomposition and prevents certain types of insects from getting at the body. If Carlisle's weather was similar to what we experienced in Gwynedd, where we have had an excessively wet and warm spring, I would not be surprised to see him in this state after three months."

"It did rain a great deal, even if it hasn't rained as much recently," the king agreed. "In fact, if we saw the sun even once in a week, we felt ourselves blessed."

"I don't know why the body decays this way nor the physical process by which it happens, but I believe it is a result of oils in the body coming to the surface and congealing, somehow, in response to continual soaking. The effect can occur as early as three weeks after death, but it happens more commonly closer to three months. Initially, as with this body, the oils are yellow and soft. Eventually, they will turn white and brittle.

"We are lucky, really, that it happened at all, because it has preserved the form of the face such that someone who knew him might be able to recognize him. If he died of an injury, such as a stab wound or a beating, that might be preserved as well." Gareth looked back at the king. "I'm afraid I can't say anything more about the circumstances of his death until I get him to the laying-out room where I can inspect him fully. Before that can happen, I need to examine his surroundings and, as you indicated, determine if he was buried close by."

"He had to have been," Henry said. "The guards surely would have noticed someone bringing a dead body through the front gate!"

"Not if he was buried under a pile of hay," Gareth said gently.

"Or let in through the postern gate." King David was looking thoughtful.

Gareth nodded. "As you say, my lord. It is too early to judge anything as yet."

King David gave something of a scoff. "You know quite a bit already."

Gareth merely smiled politely. What he didn't tell the king was that this knowledge came from a mix of personal experience, since he'd spent far too much time over the years with dead bodies—mostly animals of late, thankfully—and conversations with anyone who knew anything at all about death and the natural process of decay.

"I'm thinking he could have been buried in our own churchyard," Prince Henry said. "He might even have a gravestone."

"*Our* churchyard." King David gazed at the prince before swinging around to Gareth. "You did say, *unearthed*?" His expression indicated extreme offense at the idea.

"I did, and the adjacent graveyard is the first place we will look, I assure you. But, in that case, we would have a very different investigation on our hands."

"Different ... how?" King David said.

"If he was buried legitimately, then likely he wasn't murdered—" Gareth was forced to break off his explanation as two men strode into the church, one dressed in a military tunic showing King David's colors and the other in the robes of a nobleman. Both wore intent expressions, which immediately smoothed to something resembling concern at the sight of the king and prince standing in the middle of the nave.

The nobleman, whom Gareth recognized now as Lord Carr, the man who'd been speaking earlier to Hamelin in the hall, hurried up to the king. "My lord, I am concerned about my wife. Is she here? She mentioned that she was going to the church, and now I hear—" He stopped, his hand to his mouth, having spied the man in the chair.

The second man had noticed the body by now too, and he swallowed hard. "Pardon, my king, for our intrusion. Your steward said that there was trouble here, but he didn't say what it was." This newcomer had a voice that resonated well, and from the way he was dressed, in full mail and with a sword at his waist, he was a knight—and likely a high-ranking one, given the confidence with which he addressed the king.

King David was still looking at Lord Carr. "She was here, James. She is in good hands with Lady Gwen, Lord Gareth's wife."

Gareth had been taken aback by the arrival of Lord Carr, who seemed as ineffectual as Hamelin had implied, but Douglas seemed cut from a sturdier cloth. "May I inquire as to your name, sir?"

"Douglas MacGregor." His eyes were still on the body.

King David flicked out a hand. "Lord Douglas is one of the commanders of my forces, most recently in Worcester. Douglas, this is Lord Gareth of Gwynedd."

Douglas finally appeared to come to himself and wrenched his eyes away from the body. Turning to Gareth, he bent his head. "I am honored, sir. I was unaware you were with the king and apologize again for my intrusion. I have only just returned from Worcester and have not heard any news but this."

Earlier in the spring, Empress Maud had taken the city of Worcester from King Stephen. Since then, her forces had held off Stephen's men, who'd fortified two castles in the vicinity in response. This was the first mention Gareth had heard that King David had sent his own soldiers to bolster the garrison there. Worcester was truly far out of the king's range, being a full two hundred miles south of Carlisle and a mere thirty miles north of Gloucester, the former seat of the empress's deceased brother, Robert. Robert's son William held the west of England for Maud now. If he couldn't muster enough men to hold Worcester without David's forces, then it was no wonder Gwynedd's men were needed, and Henry had sought this alliance.

"You did not offend." The king motioned towards the body. "You might as well have a look at him since you're here."

"Of course, my lord." Douglas immediately squared his shoulders and looked intently at the corpse, his eyes moving over the body. "His coat and armband identify him as your man, my king."

"I noticed that," King David said. "It was my thought he was a member of the garrison here at Carlisle."

Gareth was somewhat embarrassed that he hadn't noticed the armband as of yet, filthy as it was, not to mention loose around the sleeve of the dead man's desiccated arm. It was something of a miracle that it hadn't fallen off, but he could believe that oils, age, time, and whatever else had been in the ground with the body, had permanently affixed the band to the sleeve of the man's coat.

"Is anyone missing from the garrison?" Gareth asked.

"Yes and no." Douglas hesitated before clarifying his cryptic remark, adding reluctantly, "We did lose a man as we left Carlisle, though at the time we didn't think he'd died. Three months ago, as we began our march south to Worcester, one of our soldiers failed to appear as commissioned."

"I was not told," King David said.

"My lord, it is not so unusual an occurrence, and I haven't thought about him in months." Douglas waggled his head in apology, or perhaps impatience, now looking at Gareth as he explained further. "I arrived back in Carlisle only this afternoon, having been gone all spring." Then he turned to Prince Henry. "I apologize for missing your knighting ceremony. I needed to speak to the families of the men we lost in Worcester before they heard about the losses from someone else."

It was a noble task, and Gareth was beginning to hope Douglas really might be helpful going forward. "Would it be wrong to assume it would be common knowledge among the local people that this man was missing?" He asked in a mild tone, not to be interpreted as a judgment on Douglas's inability to keep track of his men. Gareth had served in an army, and Douglas was right that desertion, though warranting harsh penalties at times, was common nonetheless.

"To the contrary, it would not. The company's commander thought little of his absence initially, since he was a local boy. At first we assumed he would be among those we collected directly from his village as we marched through it. He had a mother and betrothed there. But then he wasn't there either."

"Nobody looked for him?" Gareth said. "Neither his mother nor his betrothed?"

"Not that they said, and none of his companions remarked upon his absence either, at least to their captain, until we were well away from Carlisle. Apparently he wasn't much missed, being dumb as a post and hardly capable of carrying out the simplest orders." Douglas put out a hasty hand. "This is from his captain. I myself didn't hear of his desertion until days later, at which point we'd lost two more the same way." He shrugged. "It happens. Not all men, especially when they are young, are built for war, and some do not discover this fact until they're already committed."

"I would ask this man's name," Gareth said.

Douglas blinked, perhaps not realizing he hadn't yet given it. Gareth himself had only just realized it too. "If this is the man I fear him to be, he was called Aelred."

The name was very Saxon. "So he was English, not Scottish?"

"His father was English. Because his mother is still alive and Scottish, I always thought of him as a local boy, despite his name."

"Was his family one of those you spoke to today?"

"No." He paused, looking thoughtful. "Since he never joined us, as I said, I had no cause to think he'd died."

"Can you tell by looking that this body is that of Aelred?"

Douglas leaned in closer, his nose wrinkling as he concentrated—or maybe that was just in response to the smell. "He might be the right height. The uniform is right. The hair is the right color, what's left of it." Douglas shook his head. "I'm sorry. I can't say for certain."

"Where is his captain now?" King David said. "I assume he remains in Worcester?"

"His residence there will be permanent. He died of dysentery last month."

They all looked at the unearthed body for a moment, and then Douglas tsked through his teeth. "What did this poor bugger do to have died before we'd even started?"

6

Day One

Gwen

Margaret allowed Gwen to guide her steps back through the gatehouse, into the inner bailey, and then into the kitchen, located next to the great hall.

From the looks of surprise on the faces of the kitchen's occupants, Margaret's presence was an uncommon event. The hour was late, but the kitchen was still full, mostly due to preparations for tomorrow's meals, though many people remained in the hall and needed continual feeding.

Gwen gave the cook, who was standing behind his work table, a rueful smile. "Lady Margaret has had an unsettling experience, and I felt the hall was an inappropriate place for her to recover."

Without waiting for permission, she then guided Margaret to the corner bench and table, standard furnishings in every castle kitchen from Dover to Aberffraw to Edinburgh. Once Margaret and Gwen were seated, a servant brought over a carafe of wine and two cups without needing to be asked. Gwen poured wine into a cup and placed it between Margaret's hands. She drank without appearing to notice she was doing so.

Gwen resented just a little bit the role Gareth had assigned her. While the men conferred over the body, she was tasked with appeasing the witness who'd discovered it, who just happened to be a woman.

At the same time, and as she'd said to Llelo, Gwen didn't have a strong desire to examine a body that even from a cursory inspection she could tell had decayed almost beyond recognition. The smell alone was foul enough to make her nauseous—and she had barely recovered her stomach from the journey by boat to get here. Even if it had been a relatively calm few days on the sea between Aber and Carlisle, and Godfrid had acquired a potion from an apothecary in Dublin that mostly worked to keep Gwen's nausea at bay, she had no desire to renew the feeling of queasiness so soon. She remained grateful that the Danish prince had appeared on the beach in front of Aber, with his broad smile and expansive hugs, to ensure the safest and easiest journey possible. That he'd brought Caitriona with him only added to the joy.

It was Caitriona who had done more poorly on the journey, less because of her stomach, which was enviously made of iron, than from exhaustion. She was among those left at the monastery, and while Gwen completely understood why she had preferred to sleep rather than endure an evening in Carlisle's great hall, the two of them had become friends enough that Cait's presence would have lightened the burden of a dead body in a church. Not that Cait would have enjoyed the smell any more than Gwen.

"I don't understand." The shock in Margaret's voice had not lessened. "Who would do such a thing?"

Several servants had moved closer, a matter of taking a few steps to the other side of their worktables. And even for those farther away, all eyes were now on Gwen and Margaret.

Margaret had spoken in French, which some of the kitchen staff appeared to understand, even if for many Gaelic might be their first language. Scottish Gaelic was a tongue very similar to Irish, Conall's native language, which Gwen spoke distressingly poorly. There were hints in both of Welsh, as if the three languages had once been one and the same but had diverged from each other long ago.

That so many people would be able to understand and over-hear—and that they would be the center of attention—had absolutely not been Gwen's intent in coming to the kitchen. Now she was wondering if she should have taken Margaret somewhere else. Normally, that place might have been the church, clearly off limits in this instance, or a guesthouse common room. Since Gwen herself was not staying at the castle, she didn't feel right about invading that space, and she didn't actually know where Margaret's rooms were or the women's solar, if this castle had one. It might not since King David was a widower. It wasn't as if Margaret was in any condition to help either. At least Gwen had had the sense to avoid the great hall, which must be a hotbed of rumor and speculation by now.

Gwen also would have preferred to speak a language the kitchen staff didn't understand. She herself spoke three with some fluency: Welsh, English, and French. Carlisle Castle, however, had always been a crossroads of many nations, and that was equally true since King David had made it one of his primary fortresses. David himself had a Saxon mother and had been married to a Norman, not to mention had spent many years living (and fighting) in and against England. Thus, he and his close companions knew many languages too. It might be that the only language Gwen and her family were safe in speaking, one nobody here would understand, was Welsh, their native tongue.

But even that notion was immediately dispelled by the arrival of another servant, this one bringing a fresh loaf of bread and a block of cheese. "Mae'n ddrwg gen i, ond dw i'n meddwl bod well iddi hi fwyta." *I'm sorry, but I think she'd better eat.*

Astonished, Gwen looked up at the young woman. She was younger than Gwen, perhaps not even twenty, and her eyes were bright with intelligence, which shone from her smiling face. She knew she'd surprised Gwen. "My name is Bronwen, and my family is from *Dùn Breatann* for twenty generations."

Gwen understood immediately what Bronwen was telling her: though located a hundred miles to the north of Carlisle, Bronwen's ancestors and Gwen's were the same. Today, what had once been the British Kingdom of Alclud was hardly more than a barren rock with a few ruins perched on top. And yet, at one time it had been a British stronghold and supported one of the mightiest fortresses in the north. *Dùn Breatann* or Dumbarton, which was what the English called the place, meant *fort of the Britons.*

"I'm Gwen."

"I know, my lady." The woman put a hand to her heart. "May I assist you further in any way?"

Before answering, Gwen glanced towards Margaret. Having already ripped off a piece of bread and stuffed it into her mouth, she was now slurping her drink around it. Given how unladylike her behavior had become, Gwen was starting to think that the two cups of wine she'd consumed in Gwen's presence were not her first of the evening. Maybe not even her fifth. Gwen couldn't blame Margaret for being upset and saw no harm in giving her another moment to collect herself—and allow the bread to absorb some of the wine already in her stomach.

Gwen also had some questions that Bronwen might as well be the first to answer. "Did you hear what happened?"

Bronwen pressed her lips together for a moment, clearly a little worried about how Gwen would react to an answer in the affirmative, but then she wilted under Gwen's calm gaze. "One of the servers overheard that a dead man had been found in the church. The hall was emptier than during the ceremony for the prince, but the people left can discuss nothing else."

"My son spoke in Welsh—" Gwen broke off at Bronwen's rueful face.

"I am not the only one in Carlisle from Dumbarton. Besides, someone also overheard King David telling his steward why he was leaving. Anyway, it was impossible to miss the sudden departure of the king and prince."

Gwen supposed she shouldn't have been surprised that the king couldn't go anywhere—or leave anywhere—without attracting attention. And while many would have wanted to rush right over to the church to see for themselves, King David's control and authority were sufficient to have prevented that from happening. "I suppose I might as well tell you the gist of things, since rumor is already widespread. Better it at least be accurate: the body of a man *was* found in the church. He has been dead for some time, though when I left, few conclusions had been drawn as yet as to how or when he died."

"By some time you mean ..."

"Months."

Bronwen put a hand to her mouth. "He couldn't have been in the church all this time!"

Gwen had wanted to keep the explanations to a minimum, but she should have known it would be impossible not to answer questions once she appeared willing to be forthcoming at all. "No. From the dirt on his clothing and skin, he was buried and unearthed very recently."

"Unearthed?" The word came out very loudly in Welsh.

Nobody else in the kitchen reacted immediately to what Bronwen had said, beyond a concerned glance in her direction. Even if they had understood, Gwen couldn't regret giving Bronwen the information. It was no less than the truth as well as, Gwen hoped, just salacious enough to keep the gossip-mongers happy for a time.

"Over the next hours and days, we will likely be asking questions of everyone in the castle as to what they know about the matter."

"We?" Bronwen blinked. "Oh, of course. Your husband is Lord Gareth. He will be leading the investigation."

"That is up to King David, but yes, at the moment, my husband is in the church."

"Do you suspect someone here?" Her question came out slightly breathless, more shocked by that idea than by the body in the church.

"Someone moved him from wherever he has been all this time." Gwen made an appeasing motion with one hand. "But that isn't really what I meant. Our hope is that someone will have seen something, at some point, even if they didn't think it was significant enough at the time to report."

"Like a man carrying a dead body over his shoulder?" From her dry tone, Bronwen was recovering from her initial surprise. "Can you at least tell me who it is that is dead?"

The girl's comment had prompted Gwen to shoot her a smile, appreciating the young woman's quick wit. "I don't know, and it would be wrong of me to speculate."

"Would it be helpful if I made some inquiries for you among the kitchen workers?"

Gwen canted her head. "Perhaps less that, since I know my husband will want to make his own inquiries, than for you to keep your eyes and ears open. If you learn something, anything, in conversations with those around you—because we know everybody will be talking about nothing else—please come find me. We are staying in the cathedral's guesthouse."

"Yes, my lady." Bronwen bobbed a curtsey and moved away.

Even five years married to a knight, who was now the steward to the *edling* of Gwynedd, Gwen didn't feel very much like a lady most of the time, but she saw the value of the authority being a lady gave her. Gwen had given Bronwen more information than she might have done had they not shared a Welshness, but otherwise, Gwen was less interested in being allied with those she encountered in this foreign castle than being treated with respect by them. If she and Gareth were going to get at the truth, the people here needed to believe in their competence.

It was time to return to Margaret. Only a few fingers of wine remained in the carafe, and Gwen poured the rest into Margaret's cup. At least this time, although Margaret picked the cup up right away, she sipped the wine instead of downing it in a few gulps. The conversation with Bronwen had gone on long enough that Gwen was worried Margaret would be too drunk to talk. Plying a witness with drink could be a good way to soften them for questioning, but it could equally lead to gloom and belligerence.

"Please tell me what happened. Take your time."

Margaret's elbows were on the table, and her hands clutched around her cup. "You know my father died last week."

"I'm sorry, I did not."

"We were very close." She started to tear up. "And now this!"

Gwen reached out a hand. "Take your time."

Margaret took a last sip of wine, set the cup down, and met Gwen's eyes for the first time. Despite having consumed an entire carafe of wine by herself, her gaze was steady. "Every evening, once the meal is over, along with the pomp, I retire to the church to pray. On my estates, we have a private chapel for my particular use. We don't have our own priest," she hastened to say as Gwen opened her mouth, though that wasn't what she had planned to ask, "but the village priest comes every week, or more often at my request."

"I understand. Please continue." What Margaret did at home seemed irrelevant to the issue at hand, but now that the woman was talking, Gwen didn't want to interrupt the flow.

Margaret made a gesture with one hand that could have been dismissive. "That is all. I was on my knees before the altar, deep in prayer, when I noticed a disturbing smell. The church was very dark, so I assumed it was empty. Empty is how I prefer it, and I confess I took it for granted that I was alone."

"So you didn't see anyone else, either on your walk to the church or once you entered it?"

"No. Not even the priest." Margaret smiled slightly in a manner that was almost condescending. "He knows my routines, and he understands my needs. I am usually in the church for half an hour at most, and I try to come early enough to accommodate his own desire for private prayer. Even if he were moved to come at the same time as I, he has a little place in the vestry for himself, or he could be alone in the chancel past the altar where laymen do not go."

Again, so as not to stop the flow of information, Gwen did little more than nod, and Margaret understood the motion to imply encouragement.

"The smell made it so I no longer could remain on my knees. I stood and followed my nose to the lectern, and then to the priest's chair behind it." She put a hand to her mouth. "It was so awful. If it hadn't been nighttime, I would have seen him right away. I confess I screamed and ran for the door, at which point it opened to reveal Lord Hamelin and another boy—your son, is he?"

"Yes. That's right." Gwen canted her head. "Do you know who it is that's dead?"

"No!" Margaret's eyes went very wide. "Why would you think I did?"

"You said *him.*"

"He was wearing King David's colors. I could see that even through the dirt." Margaret shook her head. "How could anyone do such a thing?"

Asking questions instead of answering them was a noted practice of someone with something to hide or who wasn't telling the whole truth. Margaret's questions seemed innocuous, however. Really it was too soon to judge anyone or their motives.

Gwen also thought, but didn't say, since it would be impolitic so soon into the investigation, *do you mean how could anyone murder someone, or how could someone disinter a body and leave it in the church?* Both, probably.

"So you're saying you go to the church every evening?"

"Yes." Then Margaret frowned. "Though, I was later than typical, what with the knighting ceremony starting so late. I watched Prince Henry receive his honor and then left immediately thereafter."

Margaret really hadn't wanted to spend any more time in the hall than she'd had to. Again, however, Gwen kept her private thoughts private.

"Had you been in the church earlier in the day?"

"No."

"Do you know how often the church is used?"

"Often enough, I would say. The priest could give you a better answer. If what you're wondering is how often the church is empty and available for someone to leave a body in it, I wouldn't necessarily know."

"Do you know if anyone routinely comes to the church after you?"

"Again, that would be the priest."

"And after he leaves, who uses the church at night?"

Margaret frowned. "No one that I know of. Not until he says mass at dawn. Even in winter, that can be too early for me."

"Would you say your habits are common knowledge among the residents of the castle?"

"I suppose so, though again, I was later than usual tonight." Margaret's eyes went wide. "Do you think I could have just missed the man who did this? He-he-he could have been hiding in the vestry! What if he thinks I saw him? Do you think I'm in danger?"

Gwen was taken aback at this sudden fear in Margaret's eyes and was sorry she didn't have a good answer for her. "I genuinely don't know, but perhaps, until we know more, you shouldn't wander about on your own."

All of a sudden, Margaret appeared quite sober, and her eyes were thoughtful. "I will take myself to the hall and then to bed."

"That's probably a good idea. Thank you. You've been very helpful."

From the other side of the room Bronwen made a motion as if to suggest she could refill the carafe, but Gwen gave her a slight shake of her head. Margaret could seek out more drink on her own, but Gwen wasn't going to facilitate further consumption. As it was, she counted herself lucky that Margaret's thoughts hadn't yet gone as far as Gwen's. Namely, if the church was empty all night, why not leave the body during the darkest hours? Why risk moving it when so many people remained out and about—unless the person who left it had a very specific reason for leaving it in the church when he did?

7

Day One

Gareth

Before any further work could be done, Gareth decided he needed to clear the church of onlookers, which was going to be tricky when one of them was the King of Scots and the other a potential heir to the throne of England. Both had been very friendly and welcoming to Gareth's entire family, but they were also very certain of themselves and used to getting what they wanted at all times.

The need was clear, however, so he turned to face the men before him, spreading his hands wide as he did so, with an overtly apologetic expression on his face. "While it seems I may have a long night before me, there is no reason for anyone else to stay if they have pressing duties to attend to." Specifically he bent his gaze on Prince Henry. "If I am not mistaken, my lord, you have been awake for two days and a night and have not eaten properly in that time. With what's at stake with the coming campaign, you don't want to do your-self an injury by not caring for your health sufficiently."

He'd spoken as diplomatically as he could, intending his manner to be that of a father or kindly uncle, but he was telling Prince Henry what to do, and the prince could still take offense. At the same time, one of the first things he'd learned in his efforts to be-come a diplomat in the service of Prince Hywel was that the only thing he could truly control was himself. How other people reacted was their responsibility, not his. That said, it wasn't a lesson he'd ex-actly mastered.

So he almost laughed when it wasn't Prince Henry who react-ed badly but James Carr. The Scottish nobleman had said very little up until now, perhaps uncharacteristically if Hamelin's assessment was correct. Now he drew himself up to his full height. "Who are you to make such a suggestion?"

Gareth had no interest in defending himself, and it was hardly the first time a stranger had questioned his right to investigate a body. He was opening his mouth merely to say his name again when King David intervened and said it for him: "As I said earlier, this is Lord Gareth. From Gwynedd." His tone was very dry. "He is the great Welsh investigator, here at my request. We are lucky to have him."

Lord James settled back a bit on his heels, his jaw still tight and indicating he wanted to argue but knowing there was no possibil-ity of doing so.

Gareth merely canted his head at the king, accepting the acco-lade—not so much as if it were his due, but because he could no more argue with the king than James could. For another few heartbeats

James continued to look fierce, but then he subsided entirely and turned to face Gareth instead of the king. "Even so, I am happy to be of service, as always, in any way I can."

"That is a generous offer, and I am grateful," Gareth said, working on his diplomacy again.

"What Lord Gareth means to say is that he could use your help, but not just in this moment." King David was still speaking in that dry, amused tone. "Do not fear, Gareth, that Prince Henry or I are offended. We are not experts in unearthed bodies. Thankfully, few are. We are happy to leave the investigation to you."

Gareth took in a quick breath. "I appreciate your confidence, and I'm sure I will need assistance. There *will* be much to do in the next hours and days, not the least of which is questioning everyone who may have been about the castle tonight, to see if anyone saw anything suspicious near the church that they didn't think to mention at the time." He directed his gaze back to James Carr and with sudden inspiration added, "It would be most helpful, my lord, if you could return to the hall. By now, I'm sure it is rife with rumor, and many have heard—or misheard—what has transpired. A few words from someone of your stature and authority might go a long way to soothing those troubled by these events. Your lady wife might be there as well. I imagine she will need some comforting." He had laid on the politeness and deference with James even more thickly than he'd done with the king.

"Not to mention guidance." James's comment came out as a growl.

While that wasn't quite the effect Gareth had hoped to have, James no longer seemed opposed to leaving. Turning to the king, he bowed and said, "Anything to assist, my lord."

"Thank you, James. As always, your wisdom is of great comfort. Perhaps you could also send word to Father Dunstan that Lord Gareth has need of him in his church."

"Of course, my lord."

Gareth hadn't forgotten about the priest, but he could focus on only so many things at one time.

That left Lord Douglas. He had watched the proceedings from beside the king and had been all but glowering at the body without respite the whole time Gareth had been conferring with James. While both men were sure of themselves and accustomed to ordering others about, Douglas commanded men in battle. Dead bodies would not be in any way new to him.

Now Douglas managed to unstick his eyes from the body long enough to direct his attention back to Gareth. "May I also assist in some fashion? I admit dead bodies in churches are a bit out of my experience, but there must be something I can do to help."

Gareth was impressed that he would admit ignorance to a total stranger, and he was beginning to see why King David had elevated the man to his current commanding position. "As a commander of the king's forces, and because you may know the man, if peripherally, you are better suited than I to make inquiries among the men under your command."

Douglas gave a sharp nod. "Of course. I will proceed with the questions immediately and find you again as soon as I have something to report." He took a step towards the door, to all appearances looking as if he intended to begin immediately. Then he turned back and made a gesture that might have been apologetic. "I have heard of you, of course. Please forgive my rudeness. This is all very unsettling."

"It is forgotten." Gareth had no difficulty being gracious. It *was* unsettling. "I appreciate your assistance and would appreciate even more any information you discover, no matter how insignificant it appears at first. I might also suggest, when you question your men, that the fact they know nothing or remember nothing is also helpful. If nobody saw anything, that tells us something too."

"In my experience, when soldiers say they know nothing, they are lying. Only when the punishment starts does the truth come out." And on that ominous note, which was the opposite of what Gareth had intended to convey, Douglas gave the king another bow and set off down the nave to disappear a moment later through the door.

King David watched him go and then said to Gareth in a soft voice, "He is a hard man, but a good one. He knows what he is about. And although James too has presented himself in a somewhat less than salutary light, he has the confidence of many of my lesser nobles, as well as, of course, Hugh de Morville."

Gareth had no choice but to take the king at his word. "Thank you, my lord, for explaining. I'm sure you're right."

The opening of the door had brought a rush of air into the church, and such was Douglas's forceful haste that he hadn't pulled it properly closed behind him. The door swung open again and banged against the wall. With the breeze came the scent of grass and clean earth, as opposed to the musty smell that had filled the church because of the body. Dai took it upon himself to stride after Douglas in order to catch the door before it banged again. He found a stone on the porch by which to prop it open. All of them began to breathe more easily.

King David's expression now became one of amusement. "I don't know whether to be pleased or appalled at having such an accomplished diplomat in our midst. I will have to examine everything you say to me for similar treatment. I can see why your king sent you and will leave this investigation in your capable hands."

He reached out to turn Prince Henry around in order to follow after the others, but Henry shook his head. "We are not quite done here, Uncle." And then he murmured something low enough that Gareth couldn't overhear.

"Ah." The king glanced back at Gareth, a speculative look on his face. "As a veteran of several encounters with you over the years, my nephew tells me that a more formal designation of authority, beyond what I told Douglas and James just now, might be necessary, in case others are initially unwilling to cooperate." He put up both hands as if making an announcement, though only the few of them remained in the church. "I hereby designate Lord Gareth ap Rhys as chief investigator charged with determining the circumstances around the death and appearance of this man here. Lord Gareth has my full confidence and countenance." He dropped his hands. "I will return to the hall and repeat it."

"I will endeavor to make myself useful, my lord." At a minimum, Prince Hywel and King Owain would be pleased that, within moments of Gareth's arrival at Carlisle, he had proved indispensable. Gareth's abilities and loyalty only added to their standing.

"That should do it." Prince Henry grinned but still didn't move.

The king eyed his great-nephew. "I am quite sure that Sir Gareth intended you to return to the hall with me."

"Of that I am well aware, Uncle. But we still have one more piece of business. What of Hamelin and Llelo? I promised them a knighthood, and I am loath to go back on my word."

"That would be neither wise nor fair." King David looked at the two young men with something of a jaundiced eye, as if he'd forgotten about them up until this moment, which perhaps he had. "Well ... they can't stay here, and it is too late in the evening to send them to the cathedral." He nodded sharply, as if he'd made a decision someone else had put forth after a discussion, instead of having that conversation take place in his own head. "They may remove themselves to my private chapel in the keep. Perhaps I should have sent them there in the first place."

"Then Margaret would have stood screaming on the porch," Henry said softly. "I'm thinking all is as God intended."

"It always is." The king made a *come on* gesture in the young men's direction.

Hamelin's expression had become one of relief, and he took a few steps forward, but Llelo stayed where he was. "As much as I desire to be knighted, my duty to my father and my apprenticeship must come first."

"In Wales you do raise men to have their own minds, don't you?" Before Gareth could reply, not that he had any idea how he could possibly reply to that comment, King David said to Llelo, "So it must, and I honor you for choosing to serve your father. However, I must insist."

Gareth grasped his son by the shoulders. "I honor your sacrifice as well, but I can do without you for one night—a matter of hours, really. I have enough help until then. You can pick up the investigation tomorrow morning as a full-fledged knight."

"He has me, for starters," Dai said.

Gareth turned to his other son. "You will go with your brother, as you did before. This service is not one you want to miss either."

But Gareth's words had done nothing to relieve Llelo's tension. "Father—"

"That's an order, son."

Llelo still looked pensive, his determination to sacrifice what he wanted for what he still believed was required of him in no way diminished. Gareth didn't even see a war within him on the subject.

"This is important too, son," Gareth said gently. "There will always be another investigation. All will be well."

"You are certain, Father?" Llelo asked in Welsh. "Do you mean it?"

"I have never meant anything more. I honor your commitment and that you were willing to sacrifice what you hoped for most in this world for what you thought was right. That tells me all the more that you deserve the honor the prince is offering."

Gareth smiled to see the hope in Llelo's eyes and released him. "Go." He gave him a little shove. "Put the investigation out of your mind for now."

"Excellent." The king gave a sharp nod. "It is decided. The ceremony will take place tomorrow morning before we break our fast."

The renewed prospect of knighthood had put a smile on Llelo's face that he couldn't suppress, and there was even a spring in Dai's step that hadn't been present when he'd left the great hall after his brother the first time. By the time he reached the door again, Dai was grinning from ear to ear, and he gestured with a flourish for the others to exit in front of him. It was one of the things Gareth had always been able to count on with this found son of his: he was irrepressible, even in the face of dead bodies and—far worse—personal disappointment.

As the two soon-to-be-knights reached the door, Prince Henry came up between them, one arm around each of their shoulders, though he was shorter than both. He was a prince *and* a knight, however, and the possibilities of life were spread before him like the food at an elaborate feast. "You made the right choice, Llelo. Aelred, if that's his name, is past caring about your future. I am not."

8

Day One

Godfrid

Godfrid and Conall had initially held back, posting themselves on opposite corners of the hall to converse with some of David's nobles. The two of them had spent the initial portion of their friendship pretending they hated each other, so this was like pulling on a pair of old boots that had been discarded because the leather was stretched and no longer fit as comfortably as it once did, for all that the garb was familiar and easy on the feet. Like the boots, this guise couldn't be worn too long.

For now, their pretense was primarily that everything was well and that they weren't interested in whatever had taken the king and prince from the hall. But with the return of the king, each man separately paid their respects, made noises about retiring for the evening after their long journey, and hastened directly to the church.

As they'd discussed in the ship on the way to Carlisle, they thought it best if King David remained in the dark as to the closeness of their relationship with one another and Gareth. It was less that they were wary of letting him see into their hearts than outright fear that their attachment could be used against them later. This was a foreign castle, for all that each of them had been invited. So far, Gwynedd was the only country to which anything had been pledged or from which anything was expected.

"This isn't what I envisioned when Dai said *body*." Godfrid came up behind Gareth, who was crouched before the corpse.

Gareth's mouth twitched. "The king said exactly the same."

Conall moved around the eastern edge of the dais, not getting too close just yet. "You seem to have a predilection for finding dead bodies in churches."

"It was Llelo who found this one, not me."

"He's been dead longer than the last one," Godfrid said.

After a bark of a laugh, Gareth proceeded to tell them what he knew so far, which even Godfrid, with far fewer investigations under his belt, could see wasn't enough.

Still, the only way Godfrid could have been more pleased about how the day had turned out was if the three of them had been sitting together in a tavern instead of standing over a corpse. Over the last few years, he'd had too few moments when he'd been able to associate with these two men who'd become his closest friends, for all that each of them had a different native kingdom and tongue.

"So what's next?" Godfrid rubbed his hands together. "Tell me what to do, and I'll do it."

Conall laughed. "You are far too cheerful, my friend."

"I was just thinking to myself that Dai has the right of it. He manages to find joy in any event, even when his brother is being readied for knighthood, and he is not!"

"And you didn't even see him just now. He bowed his brother out the door like a French courtier." Gareth's head had come up at the mention of his sons. "I'm as proud of Dai as of Llelo. You remind me that I should tell him so."

"I suppose you're right, Godfrid, that things could be worse," Conall said. "Up until we arrived in the hall, I was quite gloomy, afraid the week we spent here would be uneventful and far too full of diplomacy and polite talk."

"I, on the other hand, would have been perfectly content to be a diplomat for a while," Gareth's voice was gloomy, though Godfrid was quite sure it was tinged with amusement too, "but as Conall noted, dead bodies seem to appear wherever I go."

Conall acknowledged Gareth's words with a sardonic smile and took it upon himself to light a few more candles. After a glance at him, Gareth pulled out his book of investigations and a pencil and set to work.

Godfrid eyed the book. "Was bringing that to the feast foresight ... or prescience?"

"It isn't prescience if I'm never without it. It's small enough to fit into my breast pocket, next to this treaty King David didn't even want to look at. I make notes when I've nothing better to do." Gareth looked up from the sketch of the scene he was drawing. "Besides, weren't you just commenting on the way things go when I travel?"

"If I were a superstitious man, I might say bringing the book ensured something like this would happen."

"Then it is good you're not." Conall nudged Godfrid to move so he could look over Gareth's shoulder too. "I've never seen you sketch anything but faces before. You rendered the whole scene in a few strokes!"

"It's something I've been working on. I did one the other day of the ship." Gareth flipped to a prior page in his book to show Conall and Godfrid the image. It was a good rendering, as Godfrid might expect, and he itched to keep it for himself. Perhaps later he would ask if he could have it. They were close enough friends that he didn't think Gareth would mind the imposition.

"I sent Llelo away, but drawing what I see will allow him or anyone else to relive the scene." Gareth flipped back to his current drawing. "It occurred to me that with the body so decayed, we may have less to learn from it than from what surrounds it. That's the only part of what is happening here that's recent."

"Very recent." Godfrid's eyes were assessing. "Maybe we can't know exactly when he died as yet, but we do know the window of opportunity for placing the body here."

"After evening mass and before Margaret arrived." Conall bobbed a nod. "Most residents of the castle will be able to account for their whereabouts during that time. Most were at the ceremony."

"Maybe." Gareth was still focused on his drawing. "You can be sure that the majority of the residents of this castle will not have been in the same place for the entire period, even if many say they were and produce witnesses to prove it. Who remembers if a man was gone for half an hour at some point over a three hour period? And if he was gone, it proves nothing, since he could have been in the latrine or clearing his head on the battlement."

On that decidedly pessimistic note, Godfrid crouched before the body, his eyes moving up, down, and over the decayed remains. From the attitude of the others, only he himself appeared bothered by the smell. He hadn't ever thought of his nose as particularly sensitive, but he was missing the lavender sachet Gareth had given him in the past when forced to examine a body.

And then, as if prompted by the thought Godfrid hadn't actually voiced, Gareth reached into his purse, which was more of a small satchel with a strap worn across his body. "I'm not bothered right now, but does anyone want—"

Godfrid had his hand up to catch the sachet before Gareth finished speaking. "Thanks."

"You're not with child too, are you?" Conall spoke in the same amused tone as before.

"If you were a true friend, you wouldn't make light of my sensitive nose," Godfrid said loftily. "Nor my wife's. Watch me tell Cait you mocked her suffering."

"If you did, she would only mock me back." Conall laughed. "As she should. She also knows you would never tease her about it. I am as happy as both of you that you will soon be parents. We all feared it would never happen." He tipped his head. "Though I have to say I am surprised by how much the smell is bothering me too." And then Conall caught another sachet Gareth chose that moment to throw at him, holding it to his nose and breathing deeply.

"To me, the body smells more of dirt and general decay, like the musty floor of a forest, than of mortified flesh," Gareth said.

"You have smelled too many dead bodies, my friend," Conall replied. "You've become inured to it."

"Wouldn't that be nice."

"Or not, given what it implies." Godfrid gestured a hand to bring them back to the specifics of their situation. "Did you notice that his face is clear of dirt, unlike the rest of him?"

Gareth, who'd gone back to drawing, spoke absently, "It's obvious the body was placed with care. It feels like a message."

"If so, what exactly *is* the message?" Conall said. "Why put him in the priest's chair instead of before the altar—or on it, as we saw in Dublin? Doesn't it defeat the purpose of the message if we don't understand it?"

"It would, but only if the message was meant for us," Gareth said.

"Are you thinking it was for Margaret?" Conall said. "She definitely responded with fear and hysterics."

"Or the priest, or the king, or Prince Henry," Gareth said. "Though I was watching the faces of the latter two when they saw the body, and neither responded in a way I found unusual."

"From what you describe, nor did Margaret, truth be told," Conall said.

Gareth grunted. "It was highly unlikely that either the prince or king would have been the one to find the body, but whoever put the dead man here would know that they would have to view it. King

David is too involved in the administration of Carlisle Castle to leave the observation of something this momentous to others."

"My money is on the priest," Godfrid said.

"That was quick," Conall said. "What do you have against Carlisle's priest?"

"Nothing. I'm just saying that there are few people who would know this church as well as the man who runs it. As I'm sure you recall from the last time, the message was for the Church and left by a monk."

"Your mind works in strange ways if leaving a body in a church indicates to you that the priest did it," Conall said dryly.

"He left it in his own chair." Godfrid had made the suggestion initially to spark a reaction, but now he was warming to the idea. "While, at first thought, to do so implies irreverence, it's *his* chair. He might have felt it was the only place he could leave it."

"Meaning he *wants* to be caught? Then why not just confess?"

"You two are impossible," Gareth said from behind them. "Need I remind you that we have a long way to go before we have gathered enough information to draw any conclusions?"

Godfrid and Conall hung their heads, feigning contrition for Gareth's benefit (and amusement). Though, the more Godfrid considered the matter, the more he thought his idea, initially said in jest, might be a good one. It wasn't as if any of them needed to be reminded of what had transpired last year, which now that Godfrid thought about it, may have adversely affected his attitude towards death, investigations, and churches in general. The way the body in Dublin had been displayed had definitely been meant as a message, and its discovery had led them down some winding paths. Determining the culprit had taken some doing, and ultimately involved the identification of traitors, the putting down of an insurrection, and the ascension of Godfrid's own brother to the throne of Dublin.

"Look at this!" Conall plucked something from amidst the soiled clothing and then held out his hand for the others to see. A dried flower petal that once might have been purple lay in his palm.

Gareth leaned in. "Crocus?"

Godfrid came closer too, having grabbed a candle from a side table so he could see better. "That would be right for February, if that really was when Aelred was last seen, and if this is really Aelred."

Conall made a fist to prevent the petal from escaping. "What do I do with it? Is it worth keeping?"

"At this point, everything is worth keeping." Putting aside his sketching, Gareth hastened into the vestry and returned with a shallow wooden bowl. Conall gently placed the petal into it.

Godfrid then began to move around the body in a widening circle, his eyes searching for any sign of the man who'd desecrated the church. "Aelred didn't put himself in this chair, but I see nothing of use, not even a clump of dirt that might tell us the identity of the one who did."

"The floor was swept clean after the body was left." Gareth was now standing in front of the dead man, his arms folded across his chest and his finger to his lips.

Godfrid himself had no thought to get closer again but said, "Implying yet again that this entire scene is a mummer's play for someone's benefit."

"It *is* a mummer's play," Gareth said, "down to the dramatic death at the end. A man died, his body was buried, and today dug up and deposited here. But until we know for what reason, we'll be hard-pressed to discover who did it."

"Unless someone saw him doing it." Conall had also given up on the body and began to move deeper into the church.

Godfrid followed. "Wouldn't that be nice."

"Though if someone witnessed the digging up of a body and the transport of it into the church, one might wonder why he hasn't come forward already." Conall reached the entrance to the vestry a step ahead of Godfrid, who said, "If you're going outside, I'll come with you."

Behind them, Gareth made a noise of dismissal. "I'll be along as soon as the king's men remove the body."

"We'll make sure to step on everything important." Godfrid looked back to make sure Gareth saw his departing smirk.

Conall grinned too. "We can count ourselves fortunate that the body wasn't left in the cathedral. We'd have more men sticking their noses where they don't belong there than we will here."

Godfrid grumbled. "At a minimum, it would have sent a different message."

"I didn't mean for that reason." Conall shoved his shoulder. "The cathedral is the seat of the bishop. I'm thinking Bishop Æthelwold would have been more put out by the appearance of a dead and decaying body left in his chair than King David appears to be."

"Of course, it wasn't left in *his* chair." Godfrid's bantering reply was almost obligatory, for all that it meant he and Conall were thinking along similar lines. "Imagine if poor Aelred was left on the king's throne."

"Now *that* would have been a disturbing message."

"And this isn't?"

Conall laughed.

Godfrid shook his head. "It's you, my friend, who is far too cheerful!"

Although St. Mary's wasn't a cathedral, the church was large enough to have two entrances. When they'd arrived initially, they'd come through the front door that brought parishioners first into the porch, then the narthex, which was an entryway just inside the door, partitioned off from the rest of the building, and then the nave. Now they were making their way through the vestry where there was a side door that allowed the clergy to enter and exit unseen by their parishioners. The vestry was also where vestments, candles, and accoutrements for worship were kept. What child in Christendom hadn't taken refuge at one time or another amongst the priestly robes and put off for an hour his punishment for an ill deed?

From the glance Conall shot at the collection of assorted robes on hooks on the wall, he was among such miscreants too. And then he said, as if reading Godfrid's mind, "I wasn't always a good student."

"I'm shocked, Conall, shocked I tell you." Godfrid smiled again at his friend and pushed open the door that would take them outside. "I'm sure you'll be surprised to know that I wasn't either."

Once through the doorway, however, Godfrid immediately pulled up short, causing Conall to run into his back.

"At last, something to see." In an attempt not to put his feet where they shouldn't go, Godfrid jumped off the side of the steps to the ground without touching the stairway. "I knew we would eventually find dirt somewhere."

They both gazed with satisfaction at the clumps of dirt and grass on the steps leading down from the vestry.

"And boot prints." Conall indicated the footprints visible in the moist earth leading away from the stairs. "Well done not touching those either."

Godfrid accepted the accolade with a nod. "Using this doorway makes the culprit all the more likely to be the priest." And then he grinned at Conall's exaggerated sigh of exasperation. "I don't mean to be difficult. I just want us to consider all the options."

"So far, that the priest did it is your only option." Then Conall gave a low grunt that might have indicated a tiny bit of agreement. "It is a little surprising that we haven't seen him yet. Most parish priests of my acquaintance would have been shadowing our heels by now if something like this happened in their church."

"Maybe he made himself scarce until we found the body."

"I do admit a priest is more likely than some to have cleaned up after himself inside the church." Conall bent low to the ground. "And I do think we are right about the body coming in this way. Even with jumping down from the top step, and how big you are, your boot prints are barely as deep as these. So unless the priest is very fat, I'm more inclined to think these could belong to a normal man carrying a dead body."

"I knew you'd eventually agree with me!"

Conall's subsequent eyeroll pleased Godfrid enormously. "This many months into decay, I wouldn't make a bet on how heavy the body actually is. Gareth can determine that when they move it to the laying-out room."

Godfrid shook his head in mock dismay. "Even if it wasn't the priest, and I'm only suggesting it to avoid a fight, he *didn't* clean up after himself here. Why not?"

Conall frowned. "It was dark, and he didn't notice? He ran out of time?"

"He cared enough to clean the man's face." Godfrid bit his lip, turning serious for a moment. "He cared enough to clean the church."

"But he didn't care about propriety enough to leave him where he was buried." Conall was focused now too.

"Could he have thought digging him up and leaving him in the church *was* honoring him?" Godfrid said.

"How could that be?"

"Because ... he knew he'd been murdered."

Conall broke the intensity with a laugh. "What are you saying? After all this time he could no longer stand the guilt?"

"Or ... the man who left the body in the church, St. Mary's priest, let's say, isn't the killer."

9

Day One

Conall

"If the one who killed and buried the dead man and the one who left the body in the church are two different people," Conall said, "we've just hugely complicated the investigation. Gareth won't be thanking us for that."

"But still, you can see how it could have happened, even without my mad idea about the priest."

Conall gave him a rueful smile. "The priest idea is actually growing on me."

"Really? I was jesting for most of it."

"I think what you were getting at just now, whether you knew it or not, is that the killer could have confessed his sin to the priest, who of course is forbidden to act on what he knows, given the sanctity of the confessional. The priest, then, might have felt he had no choice but to unearth the body, since it would be the only way to tell the world what he knows."

Godfrid let out a thoughtful *humph*. "And, as I said earlier, that could explain why he chose to leave it in his own chair."

"If it weren't for your imagination, he could have remained anonymous, sure the act would never get back to him." Conall then made a slashing motion in Godfrid's direction. "Listen to us! If Gareth were here, he would reiterate that it's too early to make assumptions about who might have done what when or their motives for doing it."

"Agreed." Godfrid grinned, not taking offense. "Thus, we need to focus on what we can determine, such as *when* the clods of dirt were left here."

"How can we possibly know that?"

Godfrid sniffed the air. "If I'm remembering correctly, it wasn't raining when we arrived at Carlisle's dock." They'd come up the River Eden and docked at the wharf to the north of the city, just past the confluence of the Caldew and the Eden. "But it had begun to rain hard by the time we reached the priory."

"And had stopped again for our walk to the castle and hasn't rained again since." Conall pursed his lips. "Scotland is hardly different from Ireland or Wales. Likely it rained on and off all day, so was it raining when the person moved the body?"

"I think we can conclude it was not. These clods of dirt aren't soaking wet. Nor is the dead man."

Before they could speculate further, Gareth appeared in the vestry doorway. He held a lantern in each hand, one of which he passed to Conall, whose candle had almost burned out.

"Men are moving the body to the laying-out room, and I've finished the rest of the preliminary work." Gareth made a motion with his head. "What have you found?"

"Dirt," Godfrid pointed, "and tracks leading that way."

"Into the graveyard." Holding his lantern high, Conall directed their attention to the footprints that disappeared into the darkness at the rear of the church.

Grass grew right up to the foundations, but it was patchy. Thus, with the recent rains, the footprints were distinct. Some sixty yards distant, the palisade doubled as the churchyard wall, and was much higher, obviously, than the rest, which a grown man could easily see over. The churchyard wall was designed to keep out animals, not people. The entire space between the church and the wall was scattered with graves.

"Dead bodies do generally come from graves." Gareth's tone was dry, but he was also serious. And correct.

Although Conall was no tracker, having spent (as he'd implied to Godfrid earlier) far more time with books as a youth than outdoors, he had no trouble following the prints. Gareth strolled along next to him, implying he had all the time in the world.

"You seem less concerned about this mystery than some," Conall said.

"I suppose you're not wrong. The body isn't recent. Until a fresh body turns up, I'm hoping to maintain my equilibrium. And really, investigating death—and maybe murder—is easier when I don't know anyone involved."

"King David didn't seem overly concerned either," Godfrid said from behind them. "I wonder why?"

Gareth glanced over his shoulder. "King David is in a place in life where he is very clear about what he needs to worry about and what he doesn't."

"The war with England, you mean," Godfrid said, not really as a question, just asking for confirmation that he'd understood Gareth correctly.

"That is important, of course. But from what he said to us in the hall, he knows he has a limited amount of time left on this earth and a great deal to do before he dies. Prince Henry is only sixteen and not quite ready to lead. David takes his responsibilities towards the boy seriously. That's why he knighted him."

King David's own son (confusingly, also named Henry) had no claim to the English crown. Putting his great-nephew on the throne would go a long way to securing his own son's rule of Scotland and Northumbria after David died.

Unfortunately, David's son suffered from an unnamed illness that had threatened his life more than once. It was another reason, knowing the real possibility that his son might not survive him, and his heir would be his grandson Malcolm, that David was looking for all the allies he could get.

"And because Prince Henry's father wouldn't." As he spoke, Conall acknowledged a touch of bitterness. He'd had a difficult relationship with his own father, who hadn't knighted Conall either, leaving the job to a great-uncle, just as Prince Henry's father had.

"I don't get the sense his father thinks very much of our young prince," Gareth said.

Conall tsked. "Geoffrey of Anjou thinks little of anyone but himself, even his heir."

"Though really," Godfrid put in, "he may see Henry as his wife's heir before his own. In Geoffrey's eyes, being the Count of Anjou is equivalent to being the King of England—but only in Geoffrey's eyes."

"Which is why Henry is here, with David, rather than being supported in his claim to the English throne by his own father." Gareth shook his head. "Geoffrey is probably right that achieving the throne by his own hand and merits means Henry will deserve it, but it's hard to understand why he won't lend *some* support."

"Maybe he has," Godfrid said. "Maybe there's much we don't know."

"That is undoubtedly true," Gareth said, "and not just about Prince Henry!"

Conall stopped for a moment at a grave marked by an upright stone. The writing was so weathered it was unreadable beyond a few letters. "This graveyard is old."

"For hundreds of years, my people ruled from this palace—the one that existed before the current keep. This church has been a sacred place since before Rome fell." Gareth slowed as the tracks weaved among several similarly old stones and then curved behind an ancient oak. "It reminds me very much of King Owain's palace at Caernarfon and St. Peblig's Church next to it. I don't know if St. Peblig's was built over a Roman temple the way the palace at Caernarfon was built over the ruins of a Roman fort, but the graveyard is older than the church. It's still possible to read the Latin inscriptions on some of the oldest stones. One grave is that of a *centurion.*"

"I don't know that word," Godfrid said.

"A centurion commanded a company of men." Conall shot Godfrid a grin over his shoulder. "Now ask me how I know that."

Godfrid laughed. "Do tell."

"I had to learn Latin, just as you did, and my teacher had a fondness for the writings of Livy." And he quoted at length from a passage before stopping abruptly, too embarrassed to continue.

Gareth slapped his thigh. "Bravo. I came to reading late, and my lessons did not include Roman chroniclers!"

"I came to reading reluctant," Godfrid said. "That was me hiding behind the priests' robes while others recited Latin. I wasn't one to appreciate learning when I was younger. I do now."

Conall knew his friends were trying to make him feel better for expounding on what he knew, and he loved them for it.

And then Gareth added, "While we're talking about everything other than the dead man in the church, I might as well finish my part of the story and tell you that this palace was the seat of the Welsh Kingdom of Rheged, which was lost to King William Rufus only sixty years ago."

"You never cease to amaze me, my friend," Godfrid said. "I expect such pearls of wisdom from Conall, but where did you learn all that?"

"My father-in-law is a bard. He has forgotten as many songs as he maintains today in his repertoire. *The splendid prince of the*

North; The choicest of princes." Though Gareth's voice couldn't rival either Meilyr's or Gwalchmai's, it was perfectly passable, and he sang with the same casual *by-the-way* attitude as he'd spoken.

In fact, since they'd left the vestry door, Gareth had remained content to let Conall lead. It was one of the things Conall admired most about the Welshman: he had no need to take charge or assert his authority. In Conall's experience, few men knew themselves that well.

At last, Conall skirted a large raised stone grave, implying it housed the remains of an important man—and then stopped abruptly, his toes on the edge of a gaping hole in the ground.

The others crowded close to the edge as well, Gareth holding up his lantern, as Conall was doing, and peering into the depths.

By now, they were near the edge of the graveyard and within a few yards of the palisade.

Conall swung the lantern back and forth to illuminate the vegetation and graves nearby. Just within the ring of his light, a wilder growth began, as if the workers who maintained the graveyard had decided that those beyond had been dead so long nobody cared to remember them. In truth, if Conall had needed to hide the body of a man he'd killed, he would have buried him there. Really, one wouldn't even have needed to dig a grave at all. He could simply have left him in a thicket.

"I think we can safely say that whoever removed the body had no interest in hiding where he got it." Godfrid crouched lower to the ground, his great boots compressing the dirt of one of the mounds created when the body had been excavated.

"And why would he?" Gareth said. "It isn't as if we weren't going to notice the body he left in the church. It wouldn't have taken much, really, to dump some of the dirt back into the grave, or even scatter a few downed branches and leaves to cover the hole."

"He did care about stealth, though," Conall said, "to the extent that he didn't want to get caught."

Gareth began to sweep at the dirt around the grave, first with his feet, and then, once he set the lantern on the ground, with his hands.

"What are you looking for?" Conall made to join him, but Gareth pointed him to a pile of dirt on the opposite side of the open grave.

"I'm looking for a grave marker. I want to know if this hole was dug specifically to bury our dead man, or if he was piggy backing on another and there's a second body down there."

It was a gruesome thought, but just as Gareth finished speaking, Conall's hand hit something solid. He brushed away more dirt and pulled out a flat, square stone, one foot on a side.

Gareth nodded to see it. "Like that."

Many of the graves in the near vicinity were marked by a similar stone. Some, like the one Conall had found, featured a dove, which usually indicated it was a woman's grave. A few farther on were larger, real stone slabs meant to cover the full body as it lay in the earth. The bigger the stone, the more wealthy the individual buried beneath it. The very wealthy would be interred in the church itself—if they didn't choose instead a giant stone sarcophagus like they'd passed earlier.

Godfrid made a rueful face. "I'm having a hard time reconciling our Aelred with a dove."

"We need the priest in order to know who is supposed to be buried here," Gareth said. "But since he isn't here, we'll have to dig a little deeper."

"When a killer buries his victim in the grave of someone recently dead, the earth is easy to turn and nobody remarks on the fresh scar in the grass." Godfrid spoke without emphasis, as if remarking on the weather. "We've seen it before."

"We have." Gareth matched his tone. "It isn't all that easy to get rid of a body, you know."

"We've noticed." Conall kept his tone dry.

Gareth spun slowly on one heel, surveying the area. "This is a good spot for some illicit gravedigging too. Secluded—or as secluded as any place can be in a castle as busy as this one."

"Where exactly did this happen before?" Conall asked him.

"It was before Rhun died," Godfrid said heavily. "I was there."

"If the garrison captain is right that the body in the church belongs to this soldier, Aelred," Conall spoke slowly as he thought it out, "the only way he could have ended up in a grave with a second body, without anyone knowing and without the proper rites, is if he died an untimely death."

"So are we or are we not hoping there's another body down there?" Godfrid was now on his knees, reaching into the hole. After discovering even his long arms were insufficient to the task, he swung his legs into the grave so he was briefly sitting on the edge, and then jumped in.

Up until now, their mutual irreverence had been confined to a verbal back and forth, but Conall flinched when Godfrid landed heavily on what could be another body, hidden beneath a shallow layer of dirt. Then again, Godfrid, as a Dane, had no fear of death at all, never mind that his peoples' pagan ways had ended two centuries earlier.

They'd been talking the way they had, not because they didn't respect the dead, but as a way to accustom themselves to their task. By this point, even Conall would have been just as happy to return to the hall for a nice cup of mulled wine and diplomatic conversation.

Both Conall and Gareth would have investigated the grave if Godfrid hadn't decided to take on the task himself first. Scuffing about in the dirt much as Conall and Gareth had been doing with their hands above him, Godfrid came up with a shovel. After gazing at it for a moment, he let out an unamused laugh and then set the shovel on the edge of the grave. "Whoever dug up our Aelred really was in a hurry, wasn't he?"

"We can't know if the shovel was left behind today or three months ago." Gareth tucked his toe under the handle, tossed the shovel into the air and caught it. "It could have been left by the one who buried him."

"In that case, we would have found it on the surface, not at the bottom of the hole." Conall inspected the blade. "I see rust and dirt, but if it was a murder weapon, I can't tell now."

Gareth had handed off his lantern to Godfrid, who lowered it to the bottom of the grave, discovering in the process a length of soiled, linen cloth. With a sigh, he passed it up to Conall, who shook it out. After Gareth took the other end, they stretched it between them. It proved to be roughly ten feet in length.

Neither of them felt the need to say that it was long enough to wrap a body in.

Instead, Conall said, "Perhaps this isn't a murder. Someone just moved a body."

"The man in the church still isn't a woman." Godfrid was crouched down now, scraping at the earth gently with both hands, not wanting to risk an injudicious prodding with the toe of his boot.

"Please tell me she's there, and I won't be finding her body left somewhere else." Gareth gestured to the opposite end of the grave. "Her head would be to the east, Godfrid, if she's here at all."

"I know; I'm looking." If possible, his motions became even more gentle, but instead of a skull, he handed up his next find: a man's purse, simpler than the one Conall wore at his waist, but still a leather sack tied with a string.

Gareth's fingers were working to unknot the tie, when Godfrid's boot made a crunching sound. He swore. "Just what I was trying to avoid."

"No one is blaming you, Godfrid," Gareth said. "It could be either of us in there."

Working quickly now that he'd found what he'd been looking for, Godfrid scraped away dirt to reveal the outline of a body. Unlike poor Aelred, this body was still wrapped in its shroud. Godfrid hesitated in the act of pulling back the covering over the face. "How important is it that we look?"

During the pause where they each considered the consequences of *not* looking, Conall felt a drop of rain on the back of his head.

"I suggested we look for her in the first place because I was concerned about rain getting her wet." Gareth gestured to Godfrid. "Do it quickly."

Conall crouched on the edge of the grave, holding his own lantern so Godfrid could see better. It would be best if this part happened once and only once. By now, they were all filthy, something Conall hadn't been for a long time. He was always dressed well, the better to represent Leinster. Suddenly, it didn't seem to matter.

Godfrid carefully pulled the piece of linen aside. The face revealed was nearly indistinguishable from that of Aelred in the church: skin turned brown by decay and time, lips pulled back and teeth exposed. The dead person's hair, however, was still present and braided in a long plait—and when Godfrid pulled the linen shroud down further, the person was revealed to be wearing a dress with a high collar.

Gareth sighed. "Now we really do need the priest. That nobleman, James Carr, either forgot to send him to me or was unable to accomplish the task." He looked at Conall. "While Godfrid and I cover her again, can you find him for me, please? Tell him that more than one of his parishioners is in need."

10

Day One

Godfrid

"What do you make of all this, Gareth?" Godfrid was moving quickly at Gareth's side, both taking long strides to get out of the rain, which was coming down hard now.

Fortunately, a folded hemp tarp had been readily available in the shed that housed the tools for the maintenance of the church grounds. Both Godfrid and Gareth had gone to enough funerals to have expected to find it there. Usually gravediggers mounded the dirt taken out of a grave on a tarp so the soil could be easily deposited over the body after the funeral, and the surrounding graves were not inadvertently covered over with excess dirt.

"I'm trying very hard to make nothing of it as yet." Gareth hunched his shoulders against the rain.

Godfrid had no such qualms about speculation. "Someone killed a man and, to cover it up, buried him in a grave already belonging to someone else. Then either that man or another man—"

"Or woman," Gareth interjected. "Best not to rule anyone out this early."

"I don't see a woman doing this," Godfrid said. "Few women would have the strength to bury Aelred, much less unbury him."

"I would not have said *unbury* was a word, but if it isn't, it definitely should be." Gareth reached the church porch a stride before Godfrid and pushed back his hood, the water from it dripping onto the stones at his feet.

"We will keep it for our own private use." Godfrid joined him, grateful to be out of the wet.

"Hopefully, we won't have to use it very often after this."

"Regardless, someone dug up the body—"

"Unburied it," Gareth corrected.

"—hauled it into the church, and propped it up in the priest's chair." Godfrid finished his sentence as if Gareth hadn't spoken.

"That does seem to describe the facts as we currently know them. It is possible, if you are feeling we must dismiss the idea of a woman doing the heavy lifting, that it would be a different matter if she had help."

"You do not comfort me." Godfrid laughed. "And you don't have to tell me what's possible. My own wife, were she not pregnant, would be perfectly capable of digging a hole and dumping a body into it if she had to." He loved his wife to distraction, and part of the reason he had found her so attractive was because she was very practical. If Cait saw something that needed doing, she did it. And if she'd felt threatened by Aelred, she would have done what *she had to*, up to and including killing him, to protect herself. He couldn't pretend he wasn't proud of that fact.

"That's the crucial issue, isn't it?" Gareth said. "*If she had to.*"

"Thus, before the hauling about, burying, and unburying, there was an initial murder—"

"Let's just say *initial death*," Gareth put in.

Godfrid nodded, neither of them in any way fussed by the back and forth between them. Rather, that they could speak to each other this way made the pursuit of this investigation more palatable. If Conall had been with them, rather than off to find the priest, he would have joined in with enthusiasm.

"Initial death, then. Burying the body in a convenient spot smacks of desperation, not premeditation. Whether an accident or on purpose, the death was not planned, and the burial of it was not planned either."

"Which is why I can't rule out the possibility that a woman did this."

Godfrid grunted. "Agreed. I will hold my speculation in abeyance for now."

"I'm not ruling out robbery either, but ..." Gareth untied the leather thong that held Aelred's purse closed and spilled the contents into his palm.

Out came tinder and flint, for lighting a fire, and a smooth stone, one that could have been picked up from any creek bed. These items could be found in any man's purse. Really, Aelred was just so ordinary, it was hard to imagine why he'd died, been buried over the top of another body, and then unburied. If he'd had money, which seemed unlikely given the quality of the purse, the person who'd buried him had taken it with them.

"Is it time to examine the body?" Godfrid suddenly wished Gareth had asked him to find the priest instead of Conall.

"Long past time, but there's something I want to show you inside the church first."

Shaking out their wet cloaks, they stood for a moment in the entryway. The church was unchanged from when Godfrid had last seen it, except for Aelred's absence, which was a relief. The smell seemed a little better too, though still musty and lip curling the closer they got to where the body had been.

Gareth led Godfrid past the priest's chair to the chancel, the area reserved for churchmen. "What do you see?"

"Choir stalls." Godfrid's eyes narrowed as he looked them up, down, and around and could find nothing amiss. "What are you seeing that I'm not?"

"They're new—or at least newish." Gareth put his nose to the front rail and sniffed, after which he gestured for Godfrid to do the same. "You can still smell the oil used on them. It wasn't done this week, but it was done in the past few months." He paused. "Maybe even, one could guess, three months ago. You couldn't smell it before from over there because it's faded with time and, of course, the scent of Aelred was overwhelming."

Godfrid sniffed as he was bid. Linseed oil permeated the wood and thus his nostrils. "All right. I smell it. Why is it important?"

"Now step away and put your nose to this." From underneath his cloak where he'd tucked it, Gareth pulled out the length of linen likely used to wrap Aelred. He didn't bother unfolding it for Godfrid's momentary sniff.

Given that a dead man had been wrapped in the cloth for the last three months, Godfrid was reluctant in the extreme to put his nose to it, but Gareth kept holding it out, and Godfrid accepted that his friend was trying to make a point. He sniffed, and then took an involuntary step back. "It smells the same. Linseed oil."

"So I thought."

Godfrid tipped his head towards the door. "Let me clear my senses, and then I can try again."

Gareth obligingly walked out the door and back into the porch. The squall that had driven them from the graveyard was coming to an end, and the air was fresh with the smell of wet grass and earth.

This time, Godfrid was willing to keep his nose in the cloth for a few heartbeats longer. It was still appalling to be smelling the cloth used to wrap a dead man, but he no longer feared the scent of decay.

"Oil," he said definitively.

"Even after three months in the ground," Gareth agreed, "which means that this cloth came from the church and had potentially been used to protect the floor, let's say, during the oiling of the new choir stalls."

"Now we know where he died!" Godfrid looked at Gareth over the cloth. "This could also tell us when."

"Maybe. At the very least, we can place the person who buried Aelred inside the church when he died."

11

Day One

Gareth

"What's this? What's this? What did I hear happened?" A priest bustled through the church gate and up the walk to the porch where Gareth waited.

Gareth had been about to enter the church one more time, following after Godfrid, who'd taken the linen cloth with him, with the idea to try to match it to another in the vestry.

Although Gareth was impatient either to go after Godfrid or to start work on the body in the laying-out room, speaking to the priest was a top priority, and he met him at the entrance to the porch.

Over the years, because of the natural connection between death and the Church, Gareth had met many priests. He'd also been a guest in many religious houses, and a community of nuns had taught him to read. First impressions of this priest were dominated by his six-inch long gray beard, waggling in his dismay, and concerned brown eyes. He was in his fifties, with rounded shoulders and a comfortable belly. Perhaps it was just as well the priest hadn't found them when they were sniffing the cloth—or worse in the laying-out room—since, on first impression, his temperament appeared ill-suited to easy acceptance of decayed bodies.

But he was the one they had to deal with, so when the priest stopped in the porch, a step from where rain continued to drip off the roof, Gareth bent his head respectfully. "Father."

Conall made the introductions: "This is Father Dunstan, Gareth. Father, Lord Gareth is ambassador from Gwynedd to King David's court. He is also an investigator."

Conall actually used the Danish word, *sleuth*, which Gareth had first heard from Godfrid.

Dunstan didn't question the term. "What-what-what has happened? Lord Conall here insisted you be the one to say." He stood on his tiptoes, trying to look past Gareth through the open door behind him. "He says you found a body in the church!"

Gareth had a great many questions for the priest, but the man's evident agitation had him wondering if he should get him a reviving cup of wine first. So instead of launching into a description of Aelred, Gareth put out a soothing hand. In the same moment, his eyes went to Conall, who'd followed in the priest's wake, still holding the lantern he'd been carrying since Gareth had given it to him. Conall made a slight moue with his lips and rolled his eyes, giving Gareth a clear indication that he'd tried to calm the priest during the walk from wherever he'd found him, and he was sorry he'd failed utterly.

"Is there some place we could talk privately?"

"In the church, of course." Dunstan made a move to push past Gareth, who didn't stop him, since the body wasn't there anymore anyway.

Within two paces of the entrance, however, Dunstan pulled up short. Godfrid had come around the corner from the vestry, still holding the cloth, and was striding back down the nave. It took him until he was a few more paces along to notice the priest, and the moment he did, he came to an abrupt halt too. The pair looked at each other for a count of three, and then they both laughed.

"Godfrid! Praise be, Godfrid! Is that really you?" Dunstan, who was a foot shorter than Godfrid and dark where Godfrid was blond, opened his arms wide. "I had no idea you were here. Truly, I never thought to see you again!"

"Hello, Father! I'm so happy to see you too, though this is the last place I would have looked for you!" Godfrid came the rest of the way forward and leaned down to wrap his own thick arms around the small priest.

Gareth and Conall remained in the doorway, amused but not perplexed. Godfrid had a tendency to make friends—and to find them—wherever he went.

"How is it that you two are acquainted?" Conall asked.

Godfrid patted Dunstan's shoulder, more gently perhaps than he would have Conall's or Gareth's. "He's a Dane, though he pretends not to be."

Dunstan looked apologetically at Gareth, though as far as Gareth knew he had done nothing so far to apologize for. "My father was Danish, and I lived in Dublin for many years. I was Prince Godfrid's confessor a time or two when he was an errant youth." The implication was that whatever Godfrid had done had been forgiven with a minimum of penance.

"He was very strict." Godfrid grinned as he indicated the exact opposite. "These days, even Archbishop Gregory takes a light hand with me. Your punishments were far more inventive and to the point."

"You did get into mischief, my son. Though, to your credit, you never lied about it afterwards."

Godfrid made a face. "Brodar always told on me anyway."

"An elder brother's prerogative."

"I missed you!" Godfrid wrapped an arm around the priest's shoulders one more time and shook him. Gareth had been on the receiving end of Godfrid's hugs plenty of times and been shaken until his teeth rattled.

The priest took the affection in stride. "Scotland called to me, my lord."

"But Carlisle? Last I heard you were headed to the Hebrides." Godfrid looked at the others and added, by way of explanation, "As you may know, portions of the north are settled by Danes and Scots together, but still, priests of either nationality remain few and far between."

Dunstan nodded. "I found a home there for a time, but once the priest at Carlisle Castle died, and King David was reconciled with

Bishop Æthelwold, the bishop himself asked that I come. I did so, believing that I was needed." He waggled his head as if to imply *it's a long story*. That was certainly true about the parts he'd left out that Gareth knew about. Æthelwold was a former confessor to King Henry I of England and had been the Bishop of Carlisle for more than fifteen years. "He felt my varied background would serve well the residents of the castle and the townspeople who worship here. King David agreed."

Godfrid made a motion with his hand, not so much dismissing what Dunstan had said as to say *it's time to put this aside*. At least that's what Gareth thought he was saying. The two of them obviously knew each other so well, even after all this time, that they could communicate with signals and motions as much as with words. "Were you not in the hall for Henry's knighting? The body was discovered immediately thereafter."

"I would have enjoyed seeing the young prince knighted, but one of my parishioners died tonight, and I sat at her bedside until the end—until Lord Conall here came and got me." Dunstan's expression turned rueful. "He tells me the body is that of one Aelred, a soldier."

"So Lord Douglas suggested," Gareth said. "We don't know yet for certain."

"Was he a member of this garrison? I'm surprised nobody missed him before now."

"We were too, actually," Gareth said. "But according to Lord Douglas, he was meant to march south three months ago and never joined his company, which was why nobody here knew of his disappearance."

"Three months?" Dunstan made a face, understandably so if he was thinking of the condition of the body. "Grim. Who found him?"

"Lady Carr." It was a little amusing to have Dunstan asking the questions, but Gareth answered easily anyway.

"She does usually enter the church in the middle evening when she is here at Carlisle."

"When were you last in the church, Father?" Gareth decided he ought to at least make an attempt to be in charge.

Dunstan's lips pursed as he thought. "This evening, I said mass as I always do, for those who choose to come here. With mass being said in the cathedral in preparation for Prince Henry's knighting, the worshippers here were few." He made another motion with his head. "Sometimes that's just as sweet as a full house."

"And after that?"

Dunstan's eyes didn't quite narrow, but he did look hard at Gareth for a moment. This was a very different man from the bumbling priest he'd appeared to be on first acquaintance. "Do you think I had something to do with Aelred's death?"

Godfrid stepped in and said, seemingly without irony, "Of course not, Father. We are simply trying to establish when someone could have entered the church with the body."

"I see." Dunstan grunted his understanding. "Do you know where he came from? He didn't spend the last three months in the church."

Again, his calm demeanor was a far cry from the way he'd fussed his way to the porch and made Gareth worry about his competence. Perhaps the bumbling priest was a mask he put on for strangers so as to be less intimidating and to hide the intelligence now evident in his eyes. Gareth wondered at what point he would have shown this version of himself if Godfrid hadn't been with them. It was an important reminder that everyone, even priests, had many faces, not all of which were obvious on first, second, or even third acquaintance.

And since Dunstan was clearly a man of intelligence and also knew the terrain, Gareth decided he would use him. "The issue before us, Father, is twofold: this man died, somewhere, somehow, and was buried in your churchyard in a grave that already contained another body, that of a woman, who appears to have died in the same time frame and whom we could not help but disturb. Our working assumption is that the killer took advantage of the newly turned grave and buried this man, Aelred, over the top of her."

Dunstan's face took on an expression of horror. "Whose grave?"

"A woman, buried in the far back, almost to the palisade wall. A dove was carved on her grave marker."

Dunstan hastily crossed himself and was already moving out of the church before Gareth could stop him. "I must see for myself!"

The others followed, and he led them unerringly through the graveyard to the site in question. He sped up as he came around the large stone sarcophagus, and by the time the others arrived he was crouched on the edge of the grave, lifting the tarp to look underneath. The rain was more of a mist now, so Gareth didn't stop him from pulling it back.

"My apologies, Father," Godfrid said, "but we had to make sure someone really was there."

"You looked at her?"

They all nodded. Gareth couldn't help thinking that they looked like very large, contrite schoolboys, lined up as they were on the other side of the grave from the priest.

"A long gray braid, blue dress with a high collar?"

"Yes," Gareth said.

"That's Mary, wife of Roger." Dunstan threw off the tarp with a flick of his wrist. A moment later, he had pulled a vial from his own small satchel, one very much like Gareth's. Unplugging its cork, he sprinkled a few drops in the grave, recited a prayer in Latin, and then, before Gareth could stop him, picked up the shovel and began filling the grave with dirt.

Godfrid hastened to his side and took the shovel from him. "Let me. You'll do yourself an injury."

"Thank you, my boy." Dunstan took a step back before looking at Gareth. "Unless you have a reason to keep the grave open?"

"We think we found everything of interest," and he explained about the discovery of the purse and the cloth. "Father, when were the choir stalls built?"

Dunstan frowned. "About ... three months ago. Why?"

Godfrid produced the cloth and offered it for Dunstan to smell, which he did, as tentatively as Godfrid himself had done the first time around.

Conall drifted close and sniffed too. "Linseed oil?"

"We've been in the church, so we know that oil was used to treat the choir stalls," Gareth said.

"Yes." Dunstan looked from the cloth to the grave. "Do you … do you think this man died inside the church?"

"We don't know, but this cloth spent time in the church—unless there was some reason for Aelred himself to be covered in linseed oil."

"Not that I know." Dunstan reached out a hand to Godfrid's shoulder. The big Dane had almost finished the job of refilling the grave, but the priest took the shovel back for the last bit of effort.

"Did you know Aelred?" Gareth asked.

"I suppose I know the name, but these soldiers come and go, hundreds of them. He didn't come here for services, or not often enough for me to note him. Nonetheless, he was of my flock." Dunstan threw a last few shovelfuls of dirt on the grave.

All things being equal, Gareth would have liked to come back in the morning and make sure they hadn't missed anything, but from the thickness of the cloud cover, more rain was in the offing. Even more, morning would bring onlookers and gawkers. Better for everyone concerned to let Mary, if not Aelred just yet, rest in peace.

Gwen had come up silently behind her husband to find him deep in conversation with his friends and someone she didn't know, but whom she guessed to be the church's priest, judging by his attire and his lack of tonsure. Godfrid was resting a shovel on his shoulder, and Conall carried a lantern in one hand. Both were listening intently to Gareth and the priest, who said, "I should look at the body now."

12

Day One

Gwen

None of the other men responded immediately, prompting the churchman to *tsk* in exasperation. "I am well used to death. You don't need to protect me from something unpleasant as if I were Lady Carr." He shook his head. "She must be quite distraught. I should speak to her when we are done here."

"I was just with her," Gwen said softly, prompting the men to notice her. "She has returned to the hall."

Gareth put out an arm to bring Gwen into their circle. "This is my wife, Gwen. Gwen, this is Father Dunstan, one of Godfrid's old confessors, as it turns out."

"And friend," Godfrid said.

Gwen acknowledged the introduction with a smile, but Dunstan still looked worried. "Where exactly is the body?"

"We arranged for it to be taken to the laying-out room," Gareth said.

The priest spun on his heel and set off for the church gate. Godfrid went after him, followed by Gareth, though he touched hands with Gwen on his way by, letting her know that he was glad of her presence, but that his tasks for the night were not finished.

Gwen let them go, deciding she had no need to keep up.

Conall must have decided the same, because he fell into step beside her. "It's been an eventful evening."

And then, without any prompting on her part, he related what they'd discovered since she'd left the church with Lady Margaret: the man's possible name, when he was last seen, where he'd been buried, and the circumstances at the church three months ago.

"You've learned a great deal in a short amount of time." Gwen made a rueful face. "I don't know that I managed to learn much of anything, other than that Margaret has a notable capacity for wine." But she nonetheless told him the little she'd gleaned from her conversation with Lady Carr.

Somewhat to Gwen's regret, over the years she'd become well-versed in laying-out rooms. Carlisle Castle's was larger than most, to accommodate numerous dead at the same time in the case of an attack or siege, and built right over the top of a water channel, which she could hear flowing beneath her feet. It was also located next to the laundry, as laying-out rooms often were to facilitate cleanliness. Unlike last year at King Owain Gwynedd's palace at Denbigh, which was built on a plateau, nobody needed to haul water from a well to wash a body.

In addition to diverting a river, in this case the Caldew, to send water into a surrounding moat to protect the castle, further channels had been dug to allow water to flow freely through the baileys. Fresh water was also available from a well over which the keep itself had been built, the better to provide a last refuge in case the castle walls were breached.

When they reached the laying-out room, the door was already open, to mitigate the smell that threatened to be overwhelming. Gwen hung back, seeing no reason to enter the room, which, with the four men, was already plenty crowded.

Father Dunstan made it a pace inside the doorway before halting at the sight of the uncovered body on the table. "Oh."

"The smell isn't that bad after a while." Gareth spoke in a placid tone Gwen recognized as one he used when he was trying to make everyone feel comfortable with a situation that wasn't entirely normal. "What's most obvious is a moist and musty odor, indicating he was buried in soil. Once he's undressed and cleaned, we won't be left with anything more terrifying than moldy clothing and bones."

Gareth was trying to put into perspective for Dunstan what he was seeing, and Dunstan responded by straightening his shoulders and entering the room more fully.

This time, he got as far as the foot of the table before stopping. "Thank you, Lord Gareth, for explaining. You are correct that the body is much decayed, but not as terrible as all that." The priest met Gareth's eyes. "I hadn't thought to ask before, but is part of the concern here, beyond the fact that he was left in the church, that he was murdered?"

"I don't want to say. I agree that it seems unlikely that he could have ended up in someone else's grave otherwise. *Someone* buried and then *unburied* him." Gareth shot an unreadable look in Godfrid's direction. "We do fear it, yes, but we cannot say one way or another until we have examined him more closely. This is my first real look at the body too."

"I believe the word you're looking for is *unearthed*, though I admit *unburied* says exactly what you mean." Gwen kept her eyes on the priest rather than the corpse. "You said you didn't know him before. Do you know him now?"

"I'm sorry. I wish I could tell you more." Dunstan passed a hand over his face. "Even if I knew him to look at when he was alive, he could be anyone now."

Gareth bent his head. "Thank you for your help."

Dunstan still hesitated, hovering at the end of the table. "He will need to be buried again."

"Yes, Father," Godfrid put a gentle hand on Dunstan's arm, "but it cannot be tonight. Perhaps a restoring drink in the hall wouldn't go amiss?"

Dunstan allowed himself to be turned away, and Gwen stepped out of the doorway to let him pass.

"*Diolch*, Godfrid," Gareth said as they left. That was *thank you* in Welsh, for Godfrid's ears alone.

Godfrid didn't acknowledge that he'd heard Gareth, but Gwen was sure he had by the slight straightening of his shoulders.

"He's wrong, though, isn't he?" Gwen said softly. "It couldn't be *anyone*."

"No. Carlisle is a city, but a small one at that. Douglas said one soldier was missing as they departed, and one soldier we have here."

"It isn't impossible that this man could be merely dressing in a soldier's clothing," Conall said. "We've seen that before too."

"True. And that's why we try to limit our assumptions until we have a preponderance of information." Gareth set Aelred's purse on the table next to the wall where the cloth tainted with linseed oil already lay.

"According to Conall, you've made considerable progress," Gwen said.

"Well, we have a body, and we found the grave." Gareth gave a little laugh as he began to walk around the table, his eyes moving up and down as he examined the corpse. "We are still in the first hours. There's much more to know that we currently don't."

"Gareth, it is very late, and the body isn't going anywhere," Gwen said. "Could this examination wait until morning?"

"I would prefer to get it over with and not leave it until the morning. You know me, *cariad*."

"I do, but I had to ask."

"I am also worried that too long out of the grave will speed up the rate of decay. What we see here now might not be visible tomorrow."

"Why would that be?" Perhaps despite himself, Conall moved closer.

"I have observed in the past how quickly a formerly buried body can decay when it is exposed to air." Gareth unhooked three aprons from the wall—the first time in Gwen's experience that a lay-ing-out room came with aprons—and tossed her one.

Conall tied his on. "He looks pretty decomposed to me."

Gwen looked at her apron for a moment, deliberating, and then tied hers on too. Up until now, she hadn't fully entered the room, but now she moved to the side table, rather than to the body itself. She still wasn't quite ready for that.

"Will we be able to tell what killed him?" Conall asked.

"The skin has dried, but there is still more here than if it had been years, as we saw with Hywel's cousin. This was moist ground he was lying in, not a dry space behind a wall."

What Gareth was explaining to Conall had become almost second nature to Gwen after all this time. Although Gwen herself hadn't been involved in the dissecting of dead animals with Gareth and Llelo, she retained what they told her about the process as they'd learned it, both from their own investigations and in consultation with others. Decomposition followed a natural progression for all no-longer-living things, occurring at a predictable rate, even with differences in temperature and location.

Thus, within moments of the cessation of breathing, a body's blood—whether man or animal—stopped flowing and began pooling in the lower parts of the body. Even in a body that had been dead for some time, the resulting discolored skin was one way to tell if the body had been moved. The way the blood flowed or didn't flow and pooled or didn't pool also affected bruising and open wounds. Obvi-ously, if a wound was the cause of death, it would bleed until death, but if a body had been cut after death, blood wouldn't truly flow from it.

The ancients had known, and any investigator worth his salt concurred, that one of the best ways to determine immediate time of death was how cold and stiff the body had become. The process of stiffening began within the first hours of death and gradually eased off over the course of the second day. A body was warm and not stiff, then warm and stiff or stiffening, then cold and stiff, and then cold and not stiff.

This process was complete by the third day, when the body really began to decay (and smell) in earnest, some parts turning almost liquid. By the fifth day, the body had bloated and turned greenish. By ten days, a body became reddish in color, and the belly bloated even more. By three weeks after death, nails and teeth might fall out—though that wasn't always the case, and didn't appear to be the case with Aelred. After a month, most of the soft tissues could be gone, depending upon the amount of water in the soil and the presence of bugs, worms, and other creatures that lived in the ground. Eventually, unless the corpse became dried out completely, all that would remain were the bones.

Conall and Gareth had worked quickly and efficiently, so it hadn't taken long to strip the body of its garments. Gwen inspected one boot and then the other. They'd come off easily because Aelred's muscle and tissue had shrunk to the extent that they no longer held the boots on his feet. With the aprons, Gwen couldn't help thinking the three of them resembled somewhat ghoulish cooks.

Next, she unfolded the cloth. It was dirty and smelly, as she'd expected. Further examination also revealed a swath of dark staining on one end. She brought it over to the table and held it up to the light. "Could this be blood?"

"It could. It's hard to tell in the dark, but the back of the coat might be stained with blood too, as if he lay for a time in a pool of it." Gareth gestured back to the table where he'd piled the clothing he and Conall had taken off the body. Gwen narrowed her eyes as she inspected the coat. Maybe that was blood, but it was so soiled it was hard to tell.

Gareth was still talking: "If it is blood, it goes a long way towards explaining what I see before me." He drew her attention back to the body. "Someone, or something, hit Aelred very hard on the head."

"So it *was* murder!" Conall said.

Gwen didn't even have to lean closer to see what Gareth meant. "He still could have died by accident. It's still too early to assume he was murdered. We've done that before and been wrong before."

"You are right about that, Gwen." Gareth's voice had a grimness to it that hadn't been there before. "But this amount of blood has me worried. We can't forget that Aelred was buried unshriven. The line between murder and accident is starting to blur."

13

Day One

Godfrid

As they left the laying-out room, Dunstan laid a gentle hand on Godfrid's arm. "May I invite you to my home instead of the great hall, Godfrid?"

"Certainly, Father, but the hall is just there." Godfrid was still damp from the earlier rainstorm and a cup of mulled wine and a warm fire beckoned.

"I don't know that I am in the right frame of mind to succor my flock."

Godfrid's step faltered. "My apologies, Father, I didn't think."

Dunstan lifted a hand. "To you, the hall is a source of fellowship and warmth, which of course it is to me as well. But while being a priest is a calling, there are times I need to not be on duty."

"Of course."

Dunstan led the way to a line of houses that clustered on the northern side of the outer bailey. While many of the castle workers lived in the town, others had homes within the walls, and the priest was one of them. The bailey was so large, really, that it could have fit an entire village inside it. In a way it did. The priest's house was a typical wattle and daub structure with a thatched roof. It wasn't large, but it was certainly large enough for the needs of the priest, who lived alone.

A fire burned low in the central hearth, and Dunstan stirred it to life. When next he spoke, it was to the fire rather than to Godfrid, for whom the words were obviously meant. "Are you going to tell me what is troubling you, or do I have to drag it out of you?"

"I'm sure I don't know what you mean."

"I'm sure you do." Dunstan reached up to a shelf and pulled down two cups, which he filled by ladle from a pot hanging over the fire. Godfrid was getting mulled wine after all. "I may not have seen you since you were a youth, but I know you, Godfrid. You can't lie to me—or at least not successfully. We are both troubled by the discovery of the body, but your concern goes deeper than mine. Tell me."

With a sigh, Godfrid accepted the cup and then settled on a stool before the fire. He took a sip before he spoke, letting the wine warm him and knowing the priest was willing to wait. "I did not mean to lie to you. I'm sorry if I attempted to hide what was in my heart."

"That is the second time you've apologized to me since we left the laying-out room. I am not fragile, my friend. You don't have to soothe me."

"But maybe you have to soothe me." Godfrid rested his chin in his hand. He'd felt like he'd been looming over the priest, and the change in elevation put them on more equal footing. "Honestly, I'm almost embarrassed to tell you."

Dunstan sat opposite Godfrid on another stool and sipped his wine, his eyes dark and the firelight dancing over his face.

Finally, Godfrid couldn't let the silence drag out any longer. "Back at the church, before you arrived, I spent a considerable amount of time postulating all the ways the church's priest could have been responsible for the unburying of the body."

Dunstan smiled into his cup. "Should I be offended or relieved you didn't suppose I'd murdered him?"

"It seemed unlikely, but with the world the way it is, nothing is impossible."

"And you need me to say that I didn't do it?" Dunstan nodded in answer to his own question. "I didn't kill poor Aelred, if that's really who is dead. I didn't bury him or unbury him."

Godfrid let out a tremulous breath. "Thank you."

"I wouldn't lie to you either, my son. Truly, I wish I had done it, if only to relieve the concern I see in all of you." Now he shook his head. "I see death and grief on a daily basis, but investigating death is not something I have ever encountered before."

"Surely men have died by unnatural causes in your parishes? I know it happened weekly growing up in Dublin."

"Of course it did, but the one responsible was always obvious and thus quickly dealt with." Dunstan made a rueful face. "That would be even more true in Dublin. How many Danes of your acquaintance are likely to commit murder in the dark? We raid, yes.

We love the element of surprise. But when we attack, you have to admit we tend to be loud about it."

"That was what King David said about Scots too, and I suppose that was always my experience before encountering Gareth. Since meeting him, I have discovered that sometimes the culprit isn't the first man who comes forward, even if he's Danish."

"And in the case of Aelred, the culprit isn't obvious at all. Is that what you're saying? Is that why I've become someone you suspect?"

Godfrid tsked under his breath. "I don't suspect you."

"But you did before you realized you knew me. Tell me why." It was a command, certainly, but not an unwelcome one.

And still, even though he trusted Dunstan, Godfrid wasn't quite ready to give up all his secrets so easily, even to his old friend. As he sat before the fire, in the back of his mind he couldn't help thinking that he'd been lied to in the past and done his fair share of lying himself. Danes weren't quite so open and predictable as Dunstan was saying. "Why are you asking?"

"Because maybe I can help. You obviously suspected the priest for a reason. Maybe someone else in the castle or the city of Carlisle is like me but you don't know him yet because you haven't asked." And then he smiled. "And maybe you'll decide you still suspect me."

Godfrid took a drink of the wine, rolling the liquid around in his mouth while he thought. He had to admit that by now the priest knew most of what he himself knew. It seemed petty to hide the rest. "You had access to the graveyard and church more than anyone. You knew what grave would be easy to dig into when Aelred died three months ago, so you would have known where he was buried to un-bury him today. You would know when the church was empty and when it wasn't, and you are such a familiar sight around the place that even if someone saw you, they wouldn't think you were lurking."

"The church is within the castle walls," Dunstan said gently. "It has a hundred visitors a day. In the dark, anyone could move about unseen."

"Not anyone. Not really. King David can't."

"His steward could, however."

Godfrid hadn't considered that possibility. Really, he didn't know anyone at Carlisle well enough to guess how easily they could have wandered the graveyard for a period of time before Margaret Carr went to the church.

"I'm not sure the steward's heart would survive the digging." Godfrid felt a little better about being so open with Dunstan.

"Nor mine?" The old priest prodded the fire with a tong. "If I could do it, he could do it."

Godfrid bobbed his head. "Then there's the way the body was left in the church. The person who left him in the priest's chair—your chair—not only brushed the dirt off his face but cleaned the floor af-terwards."

"Why would I have done this?"

"Out of respect for the holy place and the dead."

Dunstan looked down, pressing his lips together, and Godfrid could see the objections forming.

"Just say what you're thinking."

"If I killed this poor fellow, wouldn't I simply leave him in the ground?"

"You would."

"Then I don't understand."

Godfrid made a motion with his cup. "The idea was that either you killed him or you left him in the chair, but not both, for exactly the reason you're saying. One idea put forth was that the killer confessed to you that he'd killed Aelred, and leaving the body in the church was the only way to expose this killer without breaking the sanctity of your office. Since speaking to you, every theory has fallen apart, since you were with a dying woman all evening, I can't see how you would have had time between the end of mass and your duties to dig up the body, never mind leave it in the church and clean up after yourself."

"I can bolster my alibi further by telling you that the son of the woman who died came to mass and stayed with me while I put away my vestments. We walked together to his mother's house." Dunstan's head was up. "But I am curious now! While it could not have been me, you are suggesting that someone left poor Aelred in my chair as a warning or a message to the killer that God sees him, and he can't get away with murder?"

"Yes. That was the general idea."

"Why wait three months to do this?"

Godfrid sighed, returning his chin to his hand. "I don't know. It's a good thing Gareth is the main investigator, because none of this makes any sense to me."

"Thinking like a murderer is unnatural to you. If you were to kill a man, you would own the deed, whether or not you intended it to happen. This fellow—" Dunstan shook his head, "—both the murderer and the one who unearthed the body, if they are not one and the same—lurks about in the dark. If I had to guess, as a lifelong student of men, something changed recently, or even today, that made this a secret someone no longer felt he could keep."

14

Day One

Gwen

wen finally moved closer to the body, interested despite the way the sight of the desiccated remains turned her stomach. It wasn't even the smell at issue any longer. "Dare I ask if you can tell the type of object that hit him—or he hit?"

"I have a pretty good idea, actually, again somewhat surprisingly after all this time. In a way, with the condition of the body, it's easier to see." As Gwen and Conall gathered close, Gareth was able to show them what he was talking about. "The object in question wasn't round, because that would have created a circular pattern in the bone. From the indentation in his skull, the item definitely had an edge, maybe even a point. It cut through the skin, which in the process of drying has pulled back, and you can see the cracks in the bone underneath."

"Could it have been a pick?"

"Possibly, though I checked the tools in the church shed earlier when we retrieved the tarp. As with the shovel, after all this time, it's impossible to know if one of them was the weapon."

"What if he hit his head on the corner of a table—or a sarcophagus like that large one in the graveyard?"

"Whether or not he was pushed?" Gareth asked dryly.

"Could that wound have happened in the course of moving him after he died?" Conall asked. "Please don't think I'm questioning your expertise. I want to learn."

"One learns by asking questions. Never fear you could offend me. It is actually helpful for you to bring up questions about what I'm proposing that might occur to others as well, King David among them. He, at least, will need a lengthy report, and I should have my facts clear before I speak to him." Gareth gestured to the wound. "For starters, if the injury happened after death, the edges of the wound would be dry and brittle and wander a bit. As with every wound a man experiences, those that occur before death or at the time of death—"

"Or are the cause of death," Conall put in.

"—look different."

Conall bent to within inches of the skull to get a better look, and then, as he straightened, Gareth glanced at Gwen. "Do you want to see more closely?"

"I hope you don't think less of me for taking your word for it."

That prompted a genuine grin. "I am pleased, overall. I hadn't expected to learn much of anything from the body after all this time." He turned the corpse's head from side to side. "Even without the break in the skin, you can see from looking that his skull is misshapen in that location."

There was no help for it: Gwen was interested now, even if she didn't enjoy looking at the body directly. She wasn't sure when she'd become so squeamish. "The wound also explains the blood on the cloth. That portion might have been wrapped around his head." She stepped to the doorway and took in a cleansing breath. The rain had begun falling again, softly this time. "I think it's time I returned to the priory."

"Gwen." Gareth said her name softly, but with intent. She turned to see her husband giving her a hard look. "I don't want you walking home through the town by yourself, not at any time but especially not at this hour. We are strangers here, and we can't forget it." He indicated the body one more time. "A man died, and you are involved in investigating the death. If there's a chance Margaret is in danger for seeing him, you are too for knowing too much."

"You don't have to explain it to me, my love. I hear you; I will check the hall to see if Godfrid is available, and if not, I can get Dai to escort me." As Gwen set off towards the inner gatehouse, she was happy to be putting the inspection of the body behind her. These days, most of the time, Gareth had so many helpers he didn't need her assistance anymore with that aspect of an investigation.

And thank goodness for that!

Earlier in her marriage, she might have resented the camaraderie among these men. Not anymore. She'd learned, five years and four children later, that no couple was sufficient unto themselves, no matter how much love they had for each other. She counted herself fortunate that she was able to share Gareth's work with him, and that they were rarely separated and never wanted to be.

Back in the inner ward, the castle was settling down for the night, but the great hall still had a few residents present. However, Godfrid and Dunstan were not among them. King David and Prince Henry, on the other hand, were still sitting at the high table on the dais. Prince Henry rose from his seat in a slight bow as she approached. Such deference was in no way her right, given their differing ranks. But she was older, and a lady, and the wife of someone he admired.

"How are things?" the prince asked.

In truth, she had a soft spot for Prince Henry. Maybe it was safe to say that she had a soft spot for young men. While she couldn't say she understood everything about them, she seemed to be surrounded by them, between her own sons, Gwalchmai, whom she'd raised from infancy upon the death of their mother, and now Henry. She wished very much that the future she saw for him didn't hold so much war and betrayal. Like her own son, who even now was preparing for his knighthood, Henry saw only the power and glory of his birthright, not what it was going to take to attain it—and worse, to keep it.

Such conflict, above all, was what had prevented King Owain from sending Prince Hywel—or coming himself—to Carlisle. Owain feared giving his enemies a royal hostage, his heir, for example, by which they could then control him.

The other participants claimed to understand his concerns, as well they might, given the back and forth of hostages that had gone on over these last years in the conflict between Empress Maud and King Stephen for the control of England. Earl Ranulf himself had been imprisoned by Stephen for several months. And although he had not yet arrived in Carlisle, his own loyalty had been, in a sense, bought by King David. With this treaty, Scotland had given up pursuit of the southern portion of Lancaster between the Rivers Ribble and Mersey in exchange for Ranulf resigning his claim to Carlisle. The inclusion of Owain in their alliance was perhaps also a way to appease Ranulf, who preferred not to fight a war on two fronts if he didn't have to.

For his part, Owain was also emphasizing, in case anyone misunderstood, that, just like David, he was a king in his own right. His standing was far higher, in fact, than either that of Henry or Ranulf. Henry so far had achieved no actual conquest in England for himself and was merely the son of the pretender to the throne. Ranulf, in turn, ruled only the Earldom of Chester, never mind that it was called a palatine and near in size to Gwynedd. King Owain bowed to no man, only to God.

Thus, as she thought about how to reply to the prince, she made herself remember that Gareth, and by extension, she herself, was standing in for Owain in this moment. It had her squaring her shoulders and telling herself not to be lulled into some sense of security just because she liked Henry as a person.

So she bobbed a curtsey in return, and replied with a platitude. "All is well, my lord, or as well as could be expected." If they'd been alone, she would have spoken more freely, even without what she'd just reminded herself. But they were in the presence of a number of other Scottish nobles, who'd been circling around the margins of the dais since her arrival.

One of them, an auburn-haired woman in her thirties, smiled sweetly up at the king. "My lord, you must introduce us to our distinguished guest."

King David, ever gracious, proceeded to reel off a list of names, some Norman, some Scottish. The woman herself, by the name of Edith, stood with a proprietary air as close as she could to the king without appearing unseemly. Several others looked at Gwen with an air that she couldn't help thinking was somewhat jaundiced. She was from *Wales*, which to these people was the backwater of civilization. The irony was that many English people thought the same thing about Carlisle and the Scots.

Gwen had not taken a seat, and she stayed where she was on the other side of the table from the prince and king. King David finally seemed to realize that she was hesitating, and he made a dismissive gesture to those he'd just introduced. "If you will excuse us."

They obeyed, though not without reluctance and a few piercing glances at Gwen.

Then the king shifted his attention to Gwen's face, tapping a finger on the table as he studied her. He was a powerful man, with a piercing gaze, and every time he looked at her she felt like he was seeing right into her heart. Gesturing her to a chair next to him, he said, "Is there something we can do for you?"

Gwen sat in the chair he'd indicated, one vacated a moment before by Prince Henry so she could sit between them. "I wasn't looking for anything from you, my lord, except perhaps to say that my husband should be along soon. If you are still awake then, he might have something to tell you of what he has learned so far."

"We should be awake. We are waiting for Ranulf, who should be moments away from the castle." The king looked intently at her. "It is very late, however. I would hope you would be prepared now to retire, even if your husband cannot."

"I was going to borrow Dai to escort me."

Prince Henry was on his feet in an instant. "No need for that. I would be happy to do the honors."

"Henry." King David's tone carried a warning not unlike what Gwen had heard in her husband's voice a few moments earlier.

Henry was wide-eyed innocence. "I'll just be walking her to the priory, Uncle. Someone has to, and Dai is busy with Llelo and Hamelin."

King David's eyes remained narrowed. "You are not an investigator."

"If I am to be king, then I will have investigators not unlike Lord Gareth. Why not learn as much as I can when the opportunity presents itself?"

Gwen looked past Henry to the king. "I will take good care of him, my lord."

That prompted a laugh from David, as Gwen meant it to. "See that you do, madam! See that you do."

15

Day One

Dai

When his father had suggested that Dai take a leave of absence from his duties with the Dragons to sail to Carlisle with his family, Dai had been torn. He'd wanted to go. Of course he'd wanted to go, but the very fact that he wanted to go made him think that he shouldn't. If he was going to become a Dragon and a true adult, he needed to think about more than just what he wanted. Staying behind would have been a way to prove himself and punish himself at the same time. He didn't need Abbot Rhys to tell him that.

Now, as Dai stood outside the chapel door, with his brother prostrated before the altar within, it occurred to him that it had been that same feeling of guilt at getting what he wanted that had prompted Llelo to suggest that he help their father with the investigation rather than accept the chance for knighthood.

For the first time in a long time, Dai felt as if, maybe, he and Llelo weren't all that different. Llelo had always been the responsible older brother, while Dai was the one who was always making jokes and diving headfirst into trouble, whether or not he meant to. And since his captivity in Ireland last summer, things had only gotten worse. For some time, he'd had a hard time remembering tasks or doing as he was told for any length of time. All winter long, he'd find himself daydreaming at inopportune moments: practicing with his sword in the yard, struggling over Latin, or even being part of a conversation at dinner. He knew his mother worried about him. Dai had been a bit worried about himself.

Things had been markedly better lately, however, and he was happy that at least the part of his brain that could learn languages was still working. It had taken him all of an hour to pick up Scottish Gaelic, since it was really Irish Gaelic in disguise.

Though his mother hadn't intervened before the decision was made as to whether or not he should come on their journey, afterwards she had asked Dai one of those sharp and pointed questions of hers: *Why wouldn't you decide on your own to come? Do you think you shouldn't get what you want? Do you think you don't deserve it?*

As usual, she was able to touch the heart of his fears: that he wasn't worthy; that he was the dead weight in this family; that he didn't deserve what he had. Just as with Llelo and his knighthood, it hadn't been Dai himself who'd ultimately made the decision about coming to Carlisle. Prince Hywel had told Dai that not only did Prince Henry want him to come, but he would be representing the Dragons. Thus, the choice to go or not go had been made for him.

Even the relief at having the decision taken out of his hands prompted guilt and shame.

It occurred to him only now that Llelo might feel the same way.

Tomorrow, Llelo would receive his knighthood, which both burned Dai with envy and swelled him with pride. Given that fact, he had to consider his acceptance into the Dragons in a new light as well. Llelo *did* deserve to be a knight. Did that mean Dai one day would too?

All of a sudden, he was no longer jealous of his brother. If Dai had been knighted tomorrow morning—if he'd had the honor of being asked and included—he would have carried a twisting in his stomach for the rest of his life that once again he'd been lucky by merely being in the right place at the right time, just like when he and Llelo happened to be in that monastery in Newcastle-under-Lyme where Gareth found them. Dai wanted to earn his knighthood by his own deeds.

The thought straightened his spine a little and made him feel better for Llelo and for himself too. Abbot Rhys, were he here, would have told him that it was God, not luck, that had put him and his brother in Gareth's path. He had to trust that Rhys was right—trust in God and his parents. His mother would be hurt, though maybe not surprised, that he found that hard to do so sometimes.

The chapel was one of many rooms accessed off a central open space in the keep that contained chairs and tables. A low fire burned in the fireplace set against one wall and Dai was still standing against the wall a short while later when one of the serving girls approached with a tray. She was red-headed, as many in the castle seemed to be, with a freckled nose and hazel eyes. She was also very short, perhaps not even five feet tall. At first, her small stature made him think she was a little girl, but then she looked him full in the face, and he realized she might be the same age he was.

"I thought you might be hungry." She pulled off the cloth covering the tray to reveal a loaf of bread, a few cooked onions and carrots, a piece of cheese, a carafe, and two cups. The scent of fresh bread, onions, and ale wafted towards him. His stomach growled.

"Thank you." And yet, even as he thanked the girl, he hesitated again, reflexively doing a canter around his conscience to determine whether the prohibition against eating that applied to Llelo and Hamelin also applied to him. He concluded that it did not, was struck by an immediate attack of guilt for coming to that conclusion, since he wanted to eat, and then rationalized accepting the tray because it would afford him an opportunity to talk to the girl—about the investigation, of course.

He also noted that she'd brought *two* cups with that carafe. Having set down the tray on a side table, she poured a cup for him and brought it over.

He took it and said, "Pour one for yourself, if you have a moment."

"Thank you."

She was speaking to him in English—or what people here in the north called *English*. While it was true that the words they were saying had identical counterparts in what he knew as English, the heavy Gaelic accent practically rendered it a different language. He understood her perfectly well, however, and thought he'd try out some Gaelic while he was at it. As if he'd grown up in Scotland, he said, "I'm Dai. What's your name?"

Her eyes widened. "You speak my language!"

"Only a little."

"But I understand you so well!" She smiled sweetly. "I'm Jonet."

"You are Scottish, then?"

"Through and through. I was born and raised in a village northwest of Carlisle. When my father died eight years ago, my mother sent me to work here."

It was a common story, and not too dissimilar from his own. "My father died when I was ten."

"I don't understand." She frowned. "Your father is dead?"

"Sorry." He made an apologetic motion with his cup. "My birth father died."

Jonet put a hand to her heart. "While I can't be glad to hear it, it does explain how it is your parents are so young but yet have such mature sons."

"My birth father was a wool trader, who died while we were on the road. We were left in a priory. Lord Gareth and Lady Gwen happened to be in the same place at the same time and adopted my brother and me shortly after they found us."

"What about your birth mother?"

Dai pressed his lips together, almost not wanting to say. He had been thinking about her often in the past year too, after refusing to think about her at all for years before that. "I don't know what became of her. She ran off when I was a baby. I never knew her. Llelo might be able to say more, but he never talks about her either."

Instead of sympathizing, Jonet looked at him with something that appeared to be admiration. "You're so lucky!"

Again, her words struck a chord within him, though they weren't necessarily what he wanted to hear, given his earlier thoughts about what he did and did not deserve. He knew she meant to be complimentary, but the sentiment made Dai feel even more like a fraud than he had before.

Jonet, however, had no such doubts. "Not that I would say you were lucky to lose your mother and father so young. It must have been a very difficult time. And yet, look how far you've come since then! Your father is a lord, and your brother is about to become a knight. I heard in the kitchen that you're here representing the Dragons!" Her eyes widened. "I have never known a man to have come so far from so little, even with the aid of adoptive parents."

She was only saying what his own parents (whose opinions, quite frankly, counted for little in this matter) and Abbot Rhys (whose words meant more) had told Dai many times before. Even if his emotions were under constant assault, his rational mind knew that Jonet wasn't wrong about how far he'd come and that some of it—maybe even a good portion of it—was truly on his own merits.

So he smiled and answered in the only way he could so as not to offend her. "We do what we can with what we are given. I am lucky to have had the chance to start over and prove myself."

"I have heard stories about the Dragons. You must be very brave to have survived so much!"

As that was true too, Dai nodded and managed to admit, even to himself, that when faced with adverse circumstances he had comported himself well—even if he had struggled with the memory of it afterwards.

"I heard you were there when they found the dead man in the chapel?" Jonet actually fluttered her eyelashes at him.

Dai managed not to blush at her admiring look and was glad Llelo was in the chapel rather than beside him. He would have teased Dai unmercifully to see a pretty girl paying attention to him. But since Dai was on his own, and the girl had brought up the investigation without Dai having to, he nodded again. "Yes."

Then, to cover his embarrassment, he took a big bite of bread and cheese.

Jonet dimmed slightly when so little information was forthcoming. This was a technique of questioning that Dai was working on developing: to let the person being questioned come to him rather than Dai himself having to draw every word out of him—or her, as in Jonet's case. And, pleasingly, she tried again. "They say it is Aelred, who was meant to have marched to Worcester three months ago."

That she knew the name was a little disconcerting. "That is what Lord Douglas suggested. Did you know Aelred?"

"Of course I knew him. We all did." Then she hesitated.

Dai pounced. "But?"

"Why does there have to be a *but*?"

"Because you hesitated."

She didn't answer right away, her eyes flicking towards the fire and not returning. Finally, she said, "Aelred was sweet. All the girls liked him." She stopped again.

Dai took a guess: "All except you?"

She hummed a little under her breath, still deliberating. "I hate to speak ill of the dead."

"My father is in charge of the investigation, and he says that all information is of value, even if it leads nowhere. We won't know what's important until we gather as much as we can, and we need to learn as much as possible about Aelred as quickly as possible if we are to discover how and why he died."

"I will tell you what I know, but you mustn't say you heard it from me." Then, to Dai's relief, she capitulated. "Aelred did as little work as he could get away with. I know everyone thought he was simple; it looked more to me like he was lazy. Lord Douglas censured him more than once for not doing his work in a timely fashion."

Dai's eyes narrowed, a sign of concern Jonet interpreted correctly. "He didn't tell you?" She tossed her head. "I don't know why he wouldn't. Maybe he didn't want to speak ill of the dead either. All I know is, even when faced with his weaknesses, Bronwen wouldn't hear a word against him."

"Who is Bronwen?"

"A girl from the kitchen." A little 'v' formed between Jonet's eyebrows. "She's so lovely. She could have any man in the castle, but for some reason she wanted *him*. They were betrothed—or so *she* thought." The moment she spoke, Jonet put a hand to her mouth. "Listen to me going on! I shouldn't have said anything."

"Why not?"

"They were keeping their love a secret until after Aelred returned from Worcester. He was betrothed to someone else, you see, someone from his village. Mariota is her name. He had to break it off with her before he could marry Bronwen."

Jonet paused again, and this time when she spoke, her voice was soft. "I wonder if Bronwen already heard the news too? Should I tell her he's dead?"

On the whole, Dai knew that his parents would have liked to be the ones to tell Bronwen, to watch her face when she got the news. But if Jonet already knew about the possible identification of the body, Bronwen would hear of it long before any of them could get to her. "I couldn't say one way or the other, but the news will eventually reach her. It might be a kindness for her to hear it first from a friend."

16

Day One

Gwen

"I must thank you again for coming to Carlisle, my lady." Prince Henry spoke casually as he and Gwen strolled the three hundred yards from the castle gate to the entrance to the cathedral grounds.

The evening wasn't particularly warm, but they were both well wrapped, and it wasn't raining. Though Prince Henry was significantly taller than when she'd last seen him, he was still stocky and a bit bow-legged, as sometimes occurred in young men who were constantly on horseback. His red curls were somewhat disheveled, not surprising given the number of times he'd run his hands through them just during their walk from the great hall.

"I am not fond of water journeys, my lord, but otherwise it was our pleasure. We are not averse to travel, especially when it is in a rare time of peace rather than war."

"We are not at peace," he said flatly. "The war is just beginning."

Even with his somewhat intense comment, Henry seemed more relaxed in this moment than he had been in the hall, perhaps simply because he was now outside the castle and alone with Gwen—albeit trailed at thirty paces by two members of his guard. Henry might one day be King of England, and thus, for the entirety of his life he had never been—and would never be—able to wander freely, no matter how safe Carlisle appeared. Gareth, were he aware of who was escorting her home, would have been pleased at how well protected she was.

"As you say." She bent her head slightly in acknowledgment of his statement. "But not today."

He glanced over at her. "You can't think we lack resolve!"

"Of course not. Not in the least. Clearly, you are here again *because* you are determined to gain the crown. With the loss of your Uncle Robert, however, and with you returned to France, some in England dared to hope that the conflict between Stephen and your mother could be resolved peacefully."

"We cannot have true peace as long as Stephen sits on the throne of England, a throne that rightfully belongs to my mother." Henry spoke as if by rote.

Gwen had no doubt he'd said the same words so many times they came without thought. They'd been so ingrained in him since he was a child that he couldn't believe or think otherwise, even for a moment. "I am not arguing with you on that score, only speaking on behalf of the people of England, who have been caught between Stephen and your mother—and now you—all these years."

Henry eyed her again. "Do you speak also for the throne of Gwynedd?"

Gwen laughed. "In this, I do not. My opinions are my own."

"Uncle David has been preparing to attack King Stephen's holdings for months."

"The castles at Newcastle and Bamburgh aren't enough?" She spoke lightly, though the topic wasn't light at all. "He has dominion over all of northern England as far south as the River Tees and the Pennines. What more does he want?"

"York."

That was news indeed. Up until now, none of them had known the target. It could be a slip of the tongue, but more likely their intent was clear enough to those paying attention, not Gwen apparently, and the attack was imminent enough that it didn't matter anymore who Henry told.

"I see," she said, and she thought she did. "York will give King David true control of the north and any approach to Scotland, not to mention he would have a say in who was appointed the Archbishop of York."

"My uncle is a devout man." Henry's tone was matter-of-fact.

Abbot Rhys had counseled them at length about King David's conflict with the English Church, which claimed dominion over all of Scotland, under the jurisdiction of the Archbishop of York. David refuted these claims and would continue to do so as long as the Pope had not yet ruled on the matter. And maybe after. But it meant nobody could be surprised that York was David's newest target. Gwen wondered if Stephen knew it too, and what he was thinking to do about it if he did.

The same objections were being made all over Wales regarding the interference of the English church in Wales' own ecclesiastical tradition. King David wanted Carlisle elevated to an archbishopric in the same way many Welshmen wanted that status for St. David's.

It wasn't any wonder, then, that David supported Empress Maud's claim to the English crown and had worked out this treaty with Henry and Ranulf of Chester to split England among the three of them if they were able to depose King Stephen. David had long wanted uncontested control of Northumbria, and the ascension of either Maud or Henry to the English throne would ensure it.

Gwen didn't dare ask if Henry shared King David's opinion of the best place to attack or if the first target of their new alliance was a compromise on his part to ensure King David's full and wholehearted participation. The fact that David had sent men to Worcester gave some indication that he was serious about following this campaign through to the end. Still, once David gained control of the part of England he wanted, he might have trouble committing quite as fully to gaining the rest of the country for Henry.

So Gwen paused, deliberating what she could say next and whether her husband would want her to say anything at all. "Sending Prince Cadwaladr to us was like putting a cat among the pigeons."

Henry looked down at his feet as he stumped along beside her. "I am not unaware of what Cadwaladr has done. But I have to tell you that, in this war, I will use every tool in my arsenal, even those that are unsavory."

Gwen heard a note of apology in his voice. She accepted it as all they were likely to get. Even if Henry was so inclined, kings were notorious for not apologizing.

It was a good reminder too that Henry had done what he'd done with intent; he'd known that Cadwaladr would disrupt Gwynedd's court and sent him anyway. She'd be wise to remember that, with Robert of Gloucester gone, Henry did nothing without the approval of King David, and it could be David's hand, more than Henry's own, behind this treaty. They would also be wise not to forget Ranulf's influence. While he was far less close to Henry than David was now or Robert had been, they all knew by now—the entire world knew by now—that Ranulf cared only about himself and his own power, no matter which side he was on. In that, he and Cadwaladr were cut from the same cloth, even if Ranulf was more intelligent, devious, and clever than Cadwaladr and had been born to a more powerful station.

Rather than say any of that to the prince beside her, Gwen threw caution to the winds and added, "It is the age-old problem of when the end justifies the means."

Unexpectedly, Henry grinned. "You're here, though, aren't you, Cadwaladr notwithstanding? And the alliance is in the making! We will move the moment we are done here."

"So soon?"

"Why wait?"

Gwen was thinking that the point of the treaty had been for King Owain to send men to assist, but she didn't say that either. Henry was sure of himself and what he was doing. She would share her thoughts with her husband now, and Prince Hywel when they returned home, but not with this Norman prince.

They passed through the front gate of the priory grounds and reached the entrance to the guesthouse to find that, even though it was nearing midnight, the front door was open and raised voices were coming from the common room.

With a glance of concern at Gwen, Prince Henry stepped inside first, perhaps thinking to protect her, but then Gwen recognized the lower, soothing tones of Caitriona, Godfrid's wife, and realized that the person to whom she was speaking was also a woman.

"It can't be him. I tell you it can't be!" The woman had her back to Gwen, but with her dark hair and accent, Gwen recognized her as Bronwen from the castle kitchen.

Much to the relief of Cait, whose eyes were wide with questions and curiosity, Gwen glided forward in order to put her arm around the younger woman as she sobbed into her hands. "How is it you are here, Bronwen, and in this state?"

"When we spoke earlier, you said to come to you if I learned anything about the man found dead in the church. Just now I heard from my friend that they're saying it's Aelred, but it can't be!"

Gwen met Cait's eyes over the top of Bronwen's head, prompting Cait to turn to a table near the fire where a carafe of wine and several cups were waiting. She poured Bronwen a cup and brought it over, at the same time urging the younger woman to sit on a nearby bench.

As Bronwen took her first sip, Gwen tipped her head to Prince Henry, whose eyes were also wide and curious, and mouthed *thank you*.

He pressed his lips together, understanding that she was asking him to leave, even if he didn't want to. As a prince, he didn't have to do as she said. Nonetheless, he put his heels together, bent his head, and accepted the dismissal without complaint. "Please do not hesitate to ask anything of me at any time. I am always happy to be of service."

"Thank you, my lord. I will see you in the morning for Llelo's knighting."

Henry's mouth opened. "I almost forgot! Yes, I will see you then, God willing!" He left.

God willing was a common sentiment, thrown about casually in conversation. In this case, Gwen really hoped that He *was* willing. Llelo was always going to be knighted one day by someone, but for him to receive the honor so young and from the hand of Prince Henry meant something not only to them but to all Wales.

Meanwhile Bronwen continued to weep softly, in between sips of wine.

Cait said in Danish, for Gwen's ears alone, "We have a murder?"

"A body, anyway, left in the church." Gwen's Danish didn't really extend much beyond those few words, but it was all the information Cait needed to know in this moment. Then Gwen sat beside

Bronwen on the bench and put an arm around her shoulders. "If you can, please explain about Aelred."

Bronwen took in a gulping breath. "He is ... my betrothed." The heaving sobs were lessening as she drank more. Gwen felt a little bad that, in one night, she was going to be responsible for two weeping women overdrinking over Aelred.

"Why do you say the dead man can't be Aelred?"

"Because he went to Worcester! I know he did."

"Lord Douglas reports that he was supposed to join his company, but never did."

"That—that—that's impossible. Of course, he did."

Gwen rubbed Bronwen's back and asked the question that Bronwen so far had not answered. "Why is it impossible?"

"Because I received a token from him this very evening when Lord Douglas returned to Carlisle!" Bronwen pulled a stone from her pocket and held it out. It was smoothed by water and time and, more remarkably, green in color. "Aelred knows how much I love green, and this stone matches one we found on a walk the day he asked me to marry him."

"Lord Douglas brought you a token from Aelred?" Gwen was truly astonished to hear it.

The young woman shook her head. "Of course not. It came with one of his men who rode with him."

Gwen took in that bit of information, chewed it over for a moment while Bronwen took another sip of wine, and then asked, as carefully as she could, "Are you certain the token was from Aelred?"

"Of course, I am! Why would Brian lie? He brought many tokens and even letters, for the few who can read, to the families of the men in Worcester."

Gwen or Gareth would be speaking to this Brian, whoever he was, first thing tomorrow, if he himself didn't come forward to explain.

"When did you last hear from Aelred before that?" Gwen asked.

"A month ago, Brian brought me a green ribbon for my hair." She turned her head to show Gwen where it resided at the back of her head. Then she started weeping again. "Aelred said he loved me, and we would be married when he returned."

"Was it announced that the two of you were betrothed?" From Lord Douglas, Gwen knew already that it could not have been, since Aelred was supposedly betrothed to a woman in his own village, but she wanted to hear it from Bronwen.

Bronwen's weeping continued, but she managed to say, "No."

Cait had initially given Gwen a puzzled look at the question, but now she asked, "Why would that be?"

"Because nobody could know about it! No soldier can marry without the approval of his commander, and Aelred knew he wouldn't get it. He hoped that he would distinguish himself in Worcester and change Lord Douglas's mind."

That was a great deal more interaction between Douglas and Aelred than Douglas had let on in the church. Lord Douglas had been sure of the man's identity, and now Gwen understood why. What she didn't understand was why Douglas hadn't just said so.

"When did you last see Aelred in person, Bronwen?" Cait was catching on now, at least in part, to the story Bronwen was telling.

"It was a few days before he left for Worcester. He told me he would send me trinkets when he could, which is why I *know* they're from him! Besides, Brian knows him. He wouldn't lie."

"What did you love about him, Bronwen?" Gwen said.

Bronwen's face crumpled, but she had stopped overtly weeping, instead looking sad and dejected. "I know he wasn't the cleverest man. And the men didn't think he was a hard worker. But he was always kind to me. He had such big plans for us! I knew they'd never come to pass, but I loved that he dreamt them." She shook her head. "He can't be dead. He can't be that body in the church!"

The body wasn't in the church anymore, but Gwen saw no reason to tell her so. She was also reluctant to outright deny what the girl was saying and even more to mention the girl from the village. It was perfectly possible that Douglas was wrong about both the betrothal and the body's identity. It wouldn't be the first time an initial identification proved mistaken.

And again, none of that did she say. "Lord Douglas was quite certain, Bronwen."

"I don't know why he would lie, but he is lying!" Now she straightened. "I must see this body immediately!"

Gwen put out a hand. "That is not a good idea."

"But I must!" Bronwen couldn't have been more adamant, and she rose to her feet, looking as if she intended to set off right at that moment.

"The morning will be soon enough, if Gareth agrees." Cait moved to divert her. "Perhaps another cup of wine, and then we'll see about finding someone to escort you home."

Gwen bit her lower lip. She hadn't been present in the church to hear the story from Douglas himself, but Gareth wouldn't have relayed the details incorrectly. Either Lord Douglas was mistaken, and Aelred had marched south after all, or Bronwen was getting trinkets from a ghost.

17

Day One

Gareth

Conall closed the door of the laying-out room behind them. "You are off to see the king?"

"I am. Briefly." Gareth yawned. "It's been a long day."

"How much does the king know already?"

"He left the church shortly before you arrived. He knows the name of the man, if Douglas is right about that, but little else." Gareth's shoulders fell. "It's discouraging that we can't know for certain if Aelred was murdered, or if this is even Aelred! But someone buried the body, and someone unearthed him. That's enough mischief to be going on with. The king should know what we know, and I will tell him as much as I can."

"Don't give him my best."

"Oh, I won't. I know the plan."

Conall had been very serious, but then he grinned as Gareth rolled his eyes. "I know how hard it is for you to deceive, but I still think it's important that he not know what close friends we are. Our cart was moving easily along our chosen path, and this body is like a wheel has come off."

"I will be circumspect," Gareth said.

They went their separate ways, to further disguise the fact that they'd just spent all this time together in the laying-out room. So far, nobody had seen Gareth with Godfrid or Conall except for Father Dunstan. In his current guise, he didn't seem one to speak out of turn.

Gareth arrived in the hall to find Prince Henry replaced by Ranulf, who was deep in conversation with the king. They broke off at his approach, and he quickened his steps so as not to keep them waiting.

The first time Gareth had ever seen Ranulf, he'd appeared somewhat unkempt, with his cloak awry around his shoulders, stained trousers, and mud on his boots. Today, his boots were dirty, not surprising since he'd just arrived in Carlisle, but none of his clothes were actually stained or frayed. He did have a rumpled look to him that seemed part and parcel of who he was. Even so, his eyes glinted with intelligence—something Gareth would be unwise ever to forget.

What was more unusual was his attempt as Gareth approached the dais to greet him with a smile, followed by an accompanying, "Welcome, Lord Gareth. It has been too long."

"It is good to see you again, my lord, and under better circumstances." Since the last time they'd seen each other had been the day Prince Rhun had died, it would be hard to find worse. "How was your journey?"

"The weather was not too unpleasant, thankfully."

Bowing to Ranulf was irksome, but Gareth did it anyway and kept his private thoughts private.

For over ten years, Ranulf himself had been at odds with David rather than allied with him. In 1136 King David had invaded England as far as Durham as part of his perpetual quest to expand Scotland's borders. Rather than fight a war on two fronts, Stephen had negotiated a truce that had given lands owned by Ranulf, Stephen's ally at the time, to Scotland.

In the aftermath, Ranulf had allied himself with Stephen's enemy, Empress Maud—and, as a result and inadvertently, with David. It had been a very strange result no matter how one looked at it.

Ranulf's anger had been directed at Stephen, however, not at David, whom he saw as merely pursuing his own interests to the same extent that Ranulf routinely pursued his. To that end, he attacked and took Lincoln Castle in 1141. When King Stephen retook the castle shortly thereafter, Ranulf enlisted the help of Robert of Gloucester, Maud's brother and Ranulf's brother-in-law, to fight back. The forces of Cadwaladr ap Gruffydd of Gwynedd had also taken part that day, on Ranulf's side, and marked the beginning of Cadwaladr's on-again, off-again alliance with Chester. Their success had resulted in Cadwaladr's marriage to Ranulf's niece, Alice.

While this battle had also resulted in King Stephen's capture and imprisonment, Stephen's wife, Matilda, had subsequently defeated Ranulf's forces at Winchester. The resulting treaty had bought Stephen his freedom and allowed him to resume the throne. Ranulf, typically, remained dissatisfied, since he still had lost all those lands to Scotland.

So he switched sides yet again, back to Stephen. Things didn't go well there either, however, since such blatant self-interest engendered suspicion even among the men who were now his allies, namely Stephen's advisers. They didn't trust him and convinced the king to reject the alliance and imprison Ranulf. Although Ranulf managed eventually to negotiate his freedom, once loose, he immediately rebelled, taking his nephew, Gilbert Fitz Clare, with him.

The Clares had since returned to Stephen's side, but not Ranulf, who had reconciled with King David instead.

Ranulf knew that Gareth knew all this. Perhaps that was the reason for the outsized smile.

"Do you have news for us?" King David seemed to have no interest in going to bed, despite the fact that it was very late, nor in keeping what was happening from Ranulf. Gareth decided he didn't need to be worried about it if King David wasn't.

"Thank you for arranging for the body to be moved to the laying-out room. I have examined it, and I can say with certainty, that Aelred, if Lord Douglas is correct about his identity, had a fractured skull."

If Prince Henry had been present, his eyes would have brightened. As it was, King David merely tapped a finger to his lips. "So it's murder?"

Ranulf leaned forward. "We have a murder at Carlisle?"

"Possibly, my lords." And then Gareth related much of what they had discovered, including finding the open grave and the woman's body still within it. He did not mention the presence of Conall and Godfrid.

King David grimaced. "More sacrilege." He shook his head. "This is all extremely disturbing."

Earl Ranulf was less moved by the tragedy than David, more focused on the mystery rather than the repercussions. Of course, he wasn't lord of Carlisle Castle either so had less investment in the matter. "So we have the body of a man with a head injury buried illicitly in the graveyard months ago and unearthed today."

"Yes, that seems to be an accurate summary."

"Do we have any suspects?"

Gareth just managed not to laugh at Ranulf's *we*. "It is very early in the investigation as yet, my lord. Lord Douglas is speaking to the men of the garrison as to whether they saw anything or anyone in the graveyard tonight—or three months ago, for that matter—though if nobody came forward then, it seems unlikely they'd come forward now. We will need to inquire similarly of all the residents of the castle. At the moment, all we have to go on is the name of the man, again if Lord Douglas is correct about his identity, which means we also have a possible date of death."

"Which isn't nothing," Ranulf said. "Your inquiries can begin tomorrow as to this Aelred person's last days."

King David gave his ally a side-eyed look, undoubtedly wondering at his interest. At another time and place, Gareth might have been curious about that too, but he didn't seem to have the wherewithal for it now. Ranulf had no connection to this death as far as Gareth knew, and inquiring into it was Gareth's task. Ranulf was a great lord. He could do and say what he liked.

"Do you have enough men to assist you?" King David said. "With your sons otherwise occupied, I fear you are left short-handed."

"It is for a few more hours only," Gareth said.

"You have two fine sons there."

The king had overtly changed the subject, but since Gareth had nothing more to tell him, he didn't object: "Thank you. My boys are a gift from God."

"As are all children, but adopted sons perhaps even more so."

Gareth couldn't help thinking he was referring to Prince Henry.

"You have found your rooms sufficient?"

To go from discussing murder to inquiring about Gareth's accommodations seemed a strange jump, but again, Gareth answered politely. "They are. Thank you for arranging for them."

"And ... you are content in the company of Prince Godfrid and Lord Conall? I hope it wasn't too much of an inconvenience to share the journey from Aber, but since Lord Conall was already in Gwynedd's court, and Prince Godfrid was coming that way, it seemed reasonable to request that he bring you."

Now Gareth understood what was happening: the king wanted to know what relations were like among them. It could be mere politeness, but Gareth was wary nonetheless, especially given what they themselves had discussed. "I cannot complain."

King David gazed at him intently, but Ranulf barked a laugh. Gareth had made sure to keep his tone completely even and thus imply the direct opposite of what he was actually saying.

King David bent his head very slightly. "I apologize for overstepping. I'd forgotten that Dublin had allied with Prince Cadwaladr in that unfortunate incident several years ago. I should have considered that relations between Gwynedd and Dublin's new king and prince, whom I believe participated, might not be perfectly cordial."

In one sentence, King David had revealed more than he intended—or maybe it had been exactly what he intended. It was hard to tell. Nevertheless, Gareth knew now that he was entirely aware of Cadwaladr's exploits over the years. Gareth also didn't believe for a single heartbeat that he had somehow forgotten Dublin's role in them. Too bad for David that his spies hadn't learned that Dublin, Leinster, and Gwynedd had more than reconciled.

"All is well, my lords. Do not trouble yourselves on my account." Gareth made a slightly deeper bow.

"Always the diplomat. You do your king a great service." King David canted his head graciously. "I look forward to speaking again in the morning."

18

Day Two

Llelo

Llelo hadn't meant to sleep. He knew he wasn't supposed to, and thus he was relieved, after waking with a start, to see Hamelin also with his eyes closed, breathing deeply and almost snoring. Though perhaps it wasn't honorable or kind, Llelo was glad to know that if he was going to lose his chance at knighthood because he'd failed to stay awake, Hamelin was too.

They were both lying on their stomachs in the shape of a cross before the altar. The floor of the chapel was just wide enough for them to lie side-by-side, with Llelo's fingers touching one side wall, Hamelin's touching the other. Their other hands were a few inches apart in the middle.

During however many hours had passed since they'd taken up this position, Hamelin hadn't stirred once—or, at least, if he had, Llelo had been asleep for it. Regardless, he could see well enough by the moonlight coming through the narrow window above the altar that his companion was in the exact same position he'd been in the last time Llelo had looked.

Fortunately, nobody else was about at the moment to notice, and Llelo breathed a sigh of relief into the wooden planks of the floor. In addition, it was very dark in the chapel, as the altar candles had gone out. It had been Llelo's understanding that it was Dai's job to refresh them, but he had not done so.

Before Llelo could start dozing again—or praying for that matter—the door to the chapel opened, casting a faint light from the corridor on the far wall, though a portion of the doorway was blocked by a human shape. Llelo stayed where he was, prone on the floor, assuming that it was merely Dai coming to check on them. And renew the candles.

Except, just then, before the door closed, a second shadow appeared, crowding inside the chapel after the first person. Llelo felt, more than heard, a skitter of footsteps, which were followed by whispering voices. The steps hadn't sounded like they came from Dai, who was wearing boots and wasn't known for his soft footfalls. Llelo began listening harder.

More whispers emanated from the back where Llelo remembered seeing a small alcove in the wall. And then the sounds grew stranger—and more than a little horrifying once Llelo realized what he was listening to. Then a woman moaned with pleasure, loud enough to be unmistakable and almost bring Llelo off the floor.

He didn't know that he'd ever been more embarrassed in his life. He could neither say something nor lie on the floor a moment longer, and he was deliberating what to do and how angry to be at

Dai for letting these people into the chapel—until he had a moment's fear that one of the participants *was* Dai.

He immediately dismissed the thought. Dai would be under no illusions that the chapel was empty. He made friends wherever he went, but even he would be hard-pressed to have found a lover while standing guard outside the chapel.

Then Hamelin reached out a hand and touched Llelo's arm, almost causing him to jump out of his skin for a second time. When Llelo looked at him, he put a finger to his lips, telling him to stay lying down and that they shouldn't speak. They stared at each other in the moonlight. It was some comfort that even Hamelin didn't know what to do.

The sounds didn't last long, thankfully, and then the intruders were back to whispering. For the first time, Llelo could make out what they were saying.

"We should go," the higher voice said. "My husband will miss me."

Llelo had been uncomfortable before, but now he bit down on his own wrist to keep himself from exclaiming. He knew one woman in this entire castle; he'd held her in his arms a few hours ago, and thus couldn't mistake her voice. It was Lady Margaret.

A low voice grumbled back, "He sleeps like the dead, and you know it."

"I daren't risk it!"

"When will I see you again?" Something about the man's voice was familiar too, but Llelo couldn't place it like he could hers. He'd heard many male voices in the quarter of an hour before they'd left the great hall. And really, her lover could be anyone, from someone at Aelred's level all the way up to the king—though Llelo was quite certain the voice was not that of King David.

It was certainly better to wrack his brains for a clue as to who was speaking than to think about *why* he was speaking.

"I can't say," Margaret said. Then there was a pause which even Llelo could tell was potent. "Maybe never."

Then the door opened, spraying light again on the wall, but only long enough for the form of the woman to slip through it. For a moment, the man remained behind, but then he gave a low curse and followed.

Llelo was still on the floor, cursing to himself, when the door opened yet again, and Dai called into the chapel. "Llelo? Lord Hamelin? Are the two of you all right?"

"We're fine, Dai." Llelo turned his head to look at his brother. "Did you see who just left the chapel?"

"No ..." Dai's voice was wary. "Someone was here?"

Hamelin rolled his eyes at Llelo before settling back into the shape of a cross. "Yes."

"Who?"

Since Hamelin refused to elaborate, Llelo felt he had to: "Two people just came into the chapel, stayed for a short while, and then left."

Dai took another step through the doorway. "I'm sorry I wasn't here. I didn't think I was gone that long."

"Long enough to have missed it," Hamelin said dryly into the floorboards.

Dai disappeared and then returned a moment later with a lit candle in one hand and fistful of new ones in the other. He stepped over Llelo's outstretched arm and began replacing the old, burned out candles on the altar. If they hadn't gone out, likely the couple would have seen Hamelin and Llelo on the floor.

"What were they doing in the chapel?"

Llelo wanted to answer like the mature adult he was, even to make a joke, but he didn't feel like joking.

Hamelin snorted. "Take a guess! Afterwards, they argued, and then they left."

Dai was aghast. "Why do it in here?"

"Because the woman has a husband, that's why," Hamelin said. "There isn't any place else for them to go."

With Hamelin answering so matter-of-factly, Llelo decided he no longer needed to be embarrassed. It was the couple who had disgraced themselves in the chapel, not him.

"I shouldn't have left!" Dai was contrite. "If I'd been here, they wouldn't have come in."

"Where were you?" Hamelin had given up any pretense of praying or reverence and had been following Dai's progress around the chapel.

"I went to the latrine." Dai lit two more candles. "I waited as long as I could, but I couldn't wait any longer."

"Did you see anyone about as you returned?" Llelo asked.

"Only Lady Margaret. As I passed her, she was standing in an open doorway wearing her dressing gown. She stopped me to ask if I knew anything more about the body."

Llelo thought about that for a moment, still struggling to picture Margaret as the woman in the chapel, appalled to even be thinking it, but knowing in his heart it was true. It didn't matter that he'd heard her voice earlier tonight only when it was full of tears. He wasn't quite ready to tell the others what he knew yet, however. "What was she doing?"

"I couldn't say." Dai's brow furrowed. "I assumed at the time she was just coming out of her room and was on the way to the latrine, like I'd been."

Llelo closed his mouth over recriminations. And truly, who was in the chapel was only of interest because Llelo and Hamelin had been forced to listen to their tryst. Still, Llelo wasn't quite ready to let it go and looked at Hamelin, "You've been here for a while. Do you know who the man was?"

Hamelin laughed. "I do not, and I assure you, I do not want to know. Better that we forget all about it." He settled himself more fully back down on the floor, his arms spread out as before. "It is none of our business. If you'd grown up in Anjou, as I did, you would have forgotten it already."

Llelo wasn't sure how that could be possible. Was Hamelin implying that men and women of the court were so prone to late night illicit rendezvous that they were commonplace and unremarked upon? It seemed an incredible notion—especially because gossip was a way of life for any court. Even he knew that. Perhaps Hamelin was just trying to show his sophistication, though he hadn't displayed a tendency to lord over Llelo before now.

Having lit ten candles, Dai made for the door. "Is there anything else you need?"

"No." Llelo lay back down too. He was growing quite used to the floor by now, and he was feeling very sleepy. "Don't leave your post again."

"I won't! I promise!" Dai opened the door and now looked left and right. "Soon it won't matter anyway. Dawn is approaching. You have only an hour or two more."

Dai slipped through the chapel door and closed it behind him. As the darkness settled around them once again, Hamelin said, "I have longed for this day for as long as I can remember. As a bastard son, I assumed I could achieve knighthood only in battle. That isn't why I have accompanied my brother to England every time he has come, but I knew that if my father had no thought to knight Henry, he would never knight me."

"Things are no better between you and your father than when we last spoke?"

"They are not." From the floor, Hamelin shrugged. "Then again, they could hardly be worse."

"Growing up, I knew better than to long for something I could never have. My father was a wool merchant, and I had every expectation that I would become one too."

"You, a wool merchant?" Hamelin laughed into the floor. "I have never heard anything more absurd."

"My birth father would have beaten me if I'd voiced a desire for a position above my station."

"My father didn't care enough about me to beat me."

Hearing Hamelin talk, Llelo was thinking now that the two of them weren't so different, never mind their differing births. Meeting Hamelin a year and a half ago had opened new vistas to Llelo as to the lives of those born to a higher station than he. It had never occurred to him, even with his adoption by Gareth and Gwen, that a nobleman such as Hamelin might deserve sympathy or have led a life of more deprivation than Llelo. He'd come to see, through his new family, that being raised without love could be a far worse fate than being poor. A parent's love could give a man the strength to weather any hardship.

Llelo's initial comment had been said without thought as to its impact on Hamelin, an unwanted bastard son, and he deserved a little more consideration. "I don't know that *care* is the appropriate word. My life has been so different with Gareth and Gwen that it almost isn't the same life."

"The son of a wool merchant and the bastard brother of a prince." Hamelin reached his hand a few more inches so he could touch the tips of Llelo's fingers, just for a heartbeat, in a kind of solidarity. "I have spent my life feeling as if I am unworthy and lesser than other men. You would have been born thinking it. After today, we will be equals, my friend, and I, for one, can't think of a man I'd rather be standing beside when we receive this honor than you."

19

Day Two

Gareth

To have two knighting ceremonies within twelve hours of one another was an unusual enough occurrence that the great hall was packed with people once again, seemingly all diving into the morning meal with hearty appetites. It might even be that more residents of the castle were present than had been in the hall the previous evening, though Gareth would never say such a thing to Prince Henry.

The residents' interest wouldn't derive from a lack of respect for the prince himself anyway. It was rather that the knighting of Llelo and Hamelin represented an entirely different prospect. There was never a moment's concern that Prince Henry would not one day become a knight. The fate of these two young men, on the other hand, both of whom had been disadvantaged by their births, was a bard's tale come true.

Although he'd found his bed after midnight, Gareth had made sure to rise when the monks said their morning prayers so that he could be standing outside the keep's chapel when the priest arrived to say mass and give the young men communion.

It hadn't been any hardship to wait: this level of the keep was composed of sleeping chambers, the chapel, and a small central room with a fireplace, before which he'd sat on a stool and dozed until it was time for the ceremony.

Gareth had been under the impression that Father Dunstan would be officiating today, but the Bishop of Carlisle himself had appeared out of the stairwell, coming up from the lower level.

"Your Grace," Gareth had bowed. "I had no idea you would be here this morning, or I would have provided an escort from the church."

Though of Saxon origins, obvious because of his name, Æthelwold was educated, as he would be, and spoke perfect French, which was the language Gareth had been speaking. "I had no need of an escort, my son, not with God as my protector."

It was a platitude Gareth had come to expect from churchmen. Still, it was a little disappointing to hear something so trite from the mouth of a bishop. But then, as Æthelwold continued to look gravely at Gareth, he realized that the bishop was completely serious and meant what he said.

Gareth bent his head. "Of course."

As Æthelwold turned towards the chapel doorway, beside which Dai remained at attention, Dunstan came huffing up the steps. "My apologies, Your Grace, if I kept you waiting. I overslept."

"I heard this morning from several of my flock that you had a late night, Father Dunstan. You have nothing for which to apologize."

And then King David arrived too, having simply stepped out of his chamber, which took up most of the north side of this floor of the keep. His appearance should not have been unexpected, since it must have been he who asked for the bishop, but it was still an honor. It also showed his attention to detail regarding the goings-on in his castle, and for these young men in his charge.

"Well, then, if everyone is here." The bishop gestured to Dai, who opened the door to the chapel and ushered everyone through it, with something of a lesser flourish compared to his behavior with Llelo and Hamelin the evening before.

The chapel had been awash with light, less from the candles Dai had kept lit on the altar, than from the sunlight flooding the room. This time of year, the sky was light sixteen hours a day, so the sun had risen some two hours earlier. Both young men had remained prone on the floor in the shape of a cross, as they supposedly had been all night, though Gareth himself knew the truth from his earlier hasty, and whispered, conversation with Dai.

"In the name of the Father, the Son, and the Holy Spirit." Bishop Æthelwold made the sign of the cross. "Rise, my sons, for today you enter the brotherhood of knights."

The young men hadn't stirred when the chapel door had opened, but now they popped to their feet side-by-side, making Gareth suppress a laugh.

"We are ready, your grace," Hamelin said.

The bishop progressed to the altar and then, assisted by Father Dunstan and with King David, Gareth, Dai, and Prince Henry (who arrived a moment later, somewhat breathless) looking on, said mass and administered communion to the young men. Then, once they were cleansed, he led the way out the door and down to the hall where the knighting ceremony would take place.

This time, instead of King David, it was Henry doing the honors. He wore robes worthy of the king he one day hoped to be, and said the words of knighthood, using the sword he'd given Llelo and backhanding him across the face with real ferocity. He'd clearly wanted to do the job right. At no point did Llelo's eyes dim, even as he rocked back at the force of the blow.

Both young men broke their fast next to Henry at the high table. Once the meal ended, however, they hastened to where Llelo's family waited for them, accepting along the way the congratulations of the other diners, who reached out hands to them as they passed.

Llelo presented himself first to his mother for inspection, and once she'd hugged him sufficiently, he turned to Gareth. "We are ready to begin work."

"We?" Gareth raised his eyebrows and looked past his son to Hamelin, who was nodding vigorously. "No resting on your laurels for the two of you?"

Hamelin stepped closer. "I have leave from my brother to aid the investigation in any way I can. Llelo and I worked well together last time, so we thought ..." He left the sentence hanging.

Gareth was charmed by their enthusiasm and saw no reason to dissuade them of something they'd clearly worked out together.

"Of course." He looked his son up and down, wanting to give him a task worthy of his new station and to indicate his respect. "According to Lord Douglas, Aelred's mother and his betrothed live in a village outside of Carlisle. What do you say to riding there together, the two of you as well as Dai, to speak to them? They will have to be informed of his death."

Gareth could see that he'd chosen exactly right. The duty was grave and important and not one Llelo perhaps would have chosen for himself. But he was Sir Llelo now, and no task, even one as terrifying as this, was too great.

"What's more," Gwen put in, "we would like you to bring them back to Carlisle. The village is five miles away. Hopefully, you will be able to return before sunset when Father Dunstan wants to bury Aelred again. We can't bury him until they see the body. The sun sets late here, so you should have time."

Llelo was aghast. "You're going to show it to them?"

"We have to." Gwen sighed. "Last night Dai learned from one of the serving girls that Aelred was betrothed to a kitchen worker here, Bronwen. I have since spoken to her at length, and she insists the body cannot be his. She will have to see it too."

Hamelin leaned closer. "Did I just hear you say that Aelred was betrothed to two separate women?"

Gareth was about to answer in the affirmative, when he felt a hand on his shoulder and looked up to see Conall above him, shaking his head. "Not two, my friend. Three." He gestured to a tall, auburn-haired woman who'd come with him. She was approximately thirty, with porcelain skin and gray eyes rimmed with red from crying. "Joanna here was betrothed to him too."

20

Day Two

Cait

It was Gwen and Caitriona—again—who found themselves comforting a sobbing woman. It wasn't Cait's first choice of available tasks in a murder investigation, and she was quite certain it wasn't Gwen's either. Then again, neither Cait nor Gwen wanted their husbands putting their arms around a suddenly bereft betrothed either. It wasn't that there was any concern about fidelity, but that their husbands, by their stricken looks, would be even less adept at the role than their wives.

It wasn't even the tears. Of late, Cait had cried plenty in Godfrid's arms. Somewhat to her dismay, she found herself weeping easily since she'd become pregnant. And Gwen had no qualms about showing her emotions. But as Gwen told it, this was her third woman to cry over Aelred in a matter of hours, and Cait's second. Overall, Cait found herself really starting to dislike the man, if only for having the discourtesy to leave so many weeping women in his wake.

Conall's arrival had delayed the departure of Llelo and Hamelin, though Dai had already been halfway across the floor when Conall had arrived. The newly dubbed knights hovered in the aisle, uncertain as to whether they should go or stay.

Gareth made a motion of dismissal. "In any investigation, one can always learn more. Today, your task is of the utmost importance." He lowered his voice. "You might think about letting Dai take the lead in the questioning, since he is the only one who speaks Gaelic."

"Yes, Father, I understand." Llelo tapped a finger to the side of his nose, Hamelin bobbed his head in a nod, and the two young men followed Dai out the door.

"It can't be Aelred! It can't be!" When Joanna had arrived, she'd been weeping somewhat delicately, but this new storm of tears had made her face red and blotchy. She was also repeating almost word-for-word what Bronwen had said the night before, though Joanna spoke in English-accented French.

With the crying, the woman's beauty was diminished, but even with the tears and the blotchy face, her hair remained an enviable rich auburn shot through with colors from blonde to red. She wore it loose down her back, as was the right of an unmarried woman. Bronwen had potentially been quite lovely too, with her dark Welsh curls and pert nose. Though Cait hadn't yet met the third woman in Aelred's life, judging by the first two, she wouldn't be surprised if his village betrothed proved to be attractive as well. Whatever Aelred may have been, he'd had an ability to draw lovely women to him.

"Where did you find her?" Gareth asked Conall.

"She was inside the laying-out room, looking at Aelred's body."

This information prompted a renewed round of sobbing from the woman. "What am I going to do?"

"She saw the body?" Gwen looked up at Conall for confirmation.

He nodded, looking rueful.

Then, being the gentle soul that she was, Gwen put an arm around Joanna's shoulders and guided her to a seat on a bench, where she sat her down facing outward before sitting beside her. "I know it's hard, but it's really important that we ask you why you don't think the body is Aelred's?"

Gwen was being gentle, but not gentle enough. Joanna began to sob all the more.

Cait appreciated the difficulty in seeing the body of the man one loved. When Godfrid had gone to war before their marriage, Cait had paced Dublin's wall-walk, desperate for news, every heartbeat fearing the worst. Maybe if Godfrid had died, God forbid, she would have been equally annoying to anyone wanting to discover what had happened.

Even so, the short while that Joanna had been in the hall was far too long to be crying as hard as she still was. If anything, the sobs were increasing, and they were starting to draw the attention of nearby diners. It was a distressing comedown from the jubilation when the two young men had been knighted. What's more, it was unseemly.

Cait glanced towards the front of the hall, where the high table was still filled with noblemen and women. King David was speaking earnestly to Ranulf of Chester, who'd arrived late the previous night. James Carr, one of his higher-ranking noblemen, was looking down his long nose towards where they were clustered two-thirds of the way along the hall. When they'd arrived for the ceremony, Gwen had pointed out to Cait both him and his wife, Margaret, who had been the one to find the body.

Cait turned back to the wailing woman, who still wasn't stopping. Everyone else was standing around looking helplessly at Joanna, at a loss at what to do, so Cait went to a cup of water on the table, dipped her fingers in it, and flicked drops into the crying woman's face.

Joanna jerked, her wailing stopping abruptly. In fact, she went from hysterical to lucid in the blink of an eye. "What was that for?" Wiping at her cheeks with her fingers, she looked up at Cait.

"I could have thrown the whole cup at you, and I would have done if you hadn't stopped. Your tears are not helping us discover anything about this death. I am sorry you are grieving. I am sorry you fear you have lost your beloved. But this is neither the place nor the time for sobbing."

Joanna continued to stare up at Cait and, for a moment, Cait felt bad about her harsh words. But then when Joanna's lip renewed its trembling, Cait's resolve returned too, and she made a threatening motion with the cup.

Gwen, bless her heart, took the opportunity to intervene, not with soft words but by handing Joanna a full cup of wine and essentially forcing her to drink it. Three swallows later and several further gulps of air, Joanna had control over herself at long last.

"Now," Cait pulled close the bench from an adjacent table and sat across from Joanna so their knees were almost touching, "we would be grateful if you could tell us why you think the body on that table in the laying-out room is or is not Aelred's."

Joanna took a long trembling breath through her nose, prompting Cait to fear she was about to collapse into tears again, but then she began to speak: "He is dressed as Aelred always was. Though I know you could say that about anyone in King David's colors, I went through his things. It's all his gear. I would know it blindfolded. Not only does the gear belong to Aelred, he looks like Aelred."

That spoke of an intimacy heretofore unmentioned by anyone else.

"And yet you implied earlier that the body couldn't be his." Cait's voice was gentle now too.

"I don't want it to be. The features are strange and distorted." Her voice firmed. "I still can't believe it's him. I won't believe it." Then in almost the same breath, she added, "How could he be dead? How did he die?"

"We don't know the circumstances." Gareth spoke for the first time. "That is what we are trying to discover, and we are grateful that you are here today to speak to us. If you hadn't come forward, we would not have known about you."

Gareth's potentially impolitic words could have reduced Joanna to tears again, but she took another sip of wine instead.

"Anything you can tell us about Aelred, particularly about the last time you saw or heard from him, would be helpful," Cait said.

The no-nonsense approach finally seemed to be working. Joanna's grip tightened around her cup, but she was able to ask, "What exactly do you need to know?"

Cait patted her knee, willing to relent her severe attitude now that Joanna was more coherent. "First of all, where are you from, Joanna?"

"From here in Carlisle." Joanna wiped a few last tears from her cheeks. "I live with my father. He makes and sells candles."

"How did you meet Aelred?"

"He came into our shop looking for candles. We started talking, and one thing led to another." Joanna smiled, and Cait saw that she was right about the woman's beauty. "I can't imagine that anyone could know Aelred and not love him."

"You as well, I gather." Cait was afraid she'd spoken too dryly, but Joanna didn't appear to read anything untoward in Cait's tone.

"Yes! I did love him! He was so smart, clever even. He could discuss any subject at any time. He knew everything about everything. It didn't take long for us to realize we were meant to be together. We were betrothed, you see."

"What were your plans for marriage?"

"We were to marry when he got back from Worcester."

This was exactly what he'd told Bronwen.

Gwen then stepped in to ask what needed to be asked. "Are you aware that he was betrothed to two other women?"

This might have sent her into fresh gales of tears, but Joanna answered calmly enough. "Not until I heard people talking in the street this morning about how he was dead and that his body had been found in the church. They said King David was going to send to Aelred's village for his betrothed and that he had another woman here at the castle." Her lower lip jutted out. "That's why I had to come. There were no other women. Aelred didn't love anyone else. He loved *me*."

She was certain she was right. It might even be true, but it was equally true that Aelred had spent enough time with his other women to convince them of the same. He wouldn't be the first man who didn't want to confine himself to one woman and chose to lead his women on rather than being brave enough to make a decision and speak the truth.

"Did he allow you to publicize your engagement?" Again, this was from Gwen. Sadly, the question needed to be asked. For all that she was sweet, Gwen's mind skipped along some devious paths. Perhaps that was why she and Cait got along so well, even for being so different.

Joanna glanced at Gwen, hesitating, and for a moment Cait feared the tears were going to start again, but then the woman sighed. "No. He asked that I tell no one about him; I wasn't ever to inquire at the castle for him either. He preferred I never come here at all."

"Where did you meet with him, then?" Gwen said.

"Always at my house after I'd settled my father for the night."

Gwen and Cait exchanged a meaningful look. A man who didn't want to show his woman around was a man hiding something.

"Why was that?" Cait said.

"He said that he hadn't been given permission to marry and didn't want any rumor to get out that he and I were betrothed."

"You didn't mind that he didn't want anyone knowing about your engagement?" It was a potentially perilous question, but Cait thought it worth risking.

Joanna was more angry now than weepy. "Of course I minded, but I understood. I was willing to wait."

"So your father did not know about him either?" Gwen still spoke in that gentle tone of hers to lessen the sting of the question.

"No."

"How did you keep him a secret?" Gwen continued.

Joanna paused, and for the first time, a look of real maturity entered her eyes. "My father is not well. I take care of him and, in truth, do most of the work in the shop."

By *most of the work*, Cait took her to mean *all of it*. It wasn't an uncommon situation to maintain the guise of an older male running a business, but really to have a daughter or wife doing most of the work once the father or husband grew too old or infirm to do it himself. It was the work that was important, as any merchant knew, not who was doing it.

Joanna tossed her head. "Even if he knew about us, which I'm quite certain he didn't, he wouldn't remember the next morning." Then, all of a sudden she slumped forward, her face in her hands. "Have I been a fool?"

Cait thought, but didn't say, *most definitely.*

"When did you last see Aelred?" This came from Gareth, a question he was clearly trying not to ask urgently.

Joanna managed to straighten again and meet Gareth's eyes. "Two nights before he left."

"Is part of the reason you didn't think he was dead because you'd heard from him since he left for Worcester?" This was Gareth again. It was an absurd question on the surface, but they knew by now to ask it.

"Once, about a month ago, one of the other soldiers was sent back as a messenger to King David. He stopped by my father's shop and gave me Aelred's greetings. Aelred could read and write, you know, and he'd written a letter. That's also why I didn't believe he was the man in the church. He couldn't have died months ago and still sent this to me." She fumbled in her scrip. "I have it here. I keep it with me always."

"Aelred could read and write?" Cait was more than a little surprised at this news.

Nobody else had known either, and they gathered around as Joanna brought out the letter. Cait hadn't been present last night during the discussions over Aelred's body in the church or the laying-out room, but she was really beginning to wonder if the body wasn't Aelred's. It was hard to disbelieve a commander and lord like Lord Douglas, but greater people had been wrong before. Then again, even Joanna had said she thought the body was his.

"Yes. He taught himself. He said he wrote letters for everyone in his village when they asked him."

"Am I to understand, then, that you can read too?" Cait said.

"And write. How else to keep accounts for my father?"

For all that a candlemaker would never be short of customers, candle making itself had never struck Cait as a particularly lucrative profession, nor one that would lead a candlemaker's daughter to learning to read and write. Cait herself was literate, however, and was impressed that the woman had learned, given her more disadvantaged background.

By now Joanna had brought out the letter and held it up for Cait to read. It was less a letter, per se, than a scrap of paper, but the writing was legible, written in English, and spoke of Aelred's journey to Worcester, his wish for better food, and his desire to see her the moment he returned to Carlisle. It was signed *with love, Aelred.*

"This messenger who delivered the letter," Gwen said, "did he return to Worcester?"

"I assume so, though he's back now, of course, since where Lord Douglas goes, he goes. If he hadn't come to find me first I was going to seek him out today to see if he had any more word from him, even if Aelred had told me not to." And then, as if summoned, Joanna pointed towards the door where a man had just walked in at Lord Douglas's side. "There he is! Brian MacGregor's his name."

"I will handle this." Gareth moved so quickly the words were thrown over his shoulder on his way by. Speaking to Brian, as well as Douglas, had been at the top of Gareth's list of things to do today anyway.

Cait personally found it curious that Lord Douglas, as one of King David's trusted men, hadn't attended the knighting ceremony, either last night or this morning, but perhaps he'd attended so many he no longer saw them as important. Regardless, he was here now, and she knew that Gareth would elicit whatever information he could from both Douglas and his aide.

Joanna had been looking a little brighter as she'd talked about her memories with Aelred, but now she frowned. "I don't know why these other women told you they were betrothed to Aelred." She puckered her lips as if she was about to spit but then thought better of it, seeing as how she was in King David's hall. "Aelred would never have lied to me!"

"And you believed that, after Worcester, everything was going to change?" Cait said, trying to match Gwen's light tone of earlier.

"Aelred was going to force the issue with his captain." Joanna had been looking towards the door, where Gareth was now talking to Douglas and his companion. "There's one of them now!"

Before Cait could ask *one of whom?* Joanna was on her feet, glaring at Bronwen, who'd just arrived and had spied Joanna at almost the exact same moment Joanna had pointed at her. Bronwen changed direction from wherever she'd been going, charging across the hall towards them. Gwen rose to intercept her and reached her within a dozen paces, forcibly spinning her around and marching her the other way.

"They spoke of her in the street," Joanna said before Cait could ask how she knew of Bronwen. "I knew who they meant from the few times she'd come into the shop. She's a beautiful girl. It would be hard not to know her."

"She never said anything to you about Aelred?"

Joanna shook her head, her eyes still tracking Bronwen.

"How old are you, Joanna?" Cait tried to attract her attention again.

"Twenty-nine."

Bronwen was a mere girl, besotted with the wrong man. Joanna, on the other hand, ran a shop on her own and could read and write. She'd said that Aelred—all other testimony to the contrary—was the cleverest man she knew, making her attraction to him a little more understandable. At twenty-nine, she was well past the usual age of marriage.

While Cait had married young initially, she'd then refused a second marriage until she found the right man. Namely, Godfrid. Unfortunately for Joanna, if the *right man* had been what she'd been waiting for too, she had clearly made a mistake with Aelred.

<h1 style="text-align:center">21</h1>

Day Two

Gareth

"Lord Douglas." Rather than calling him by only his given name, Gareth chose to accord him his title, just to ensure his continued cooperation. Gareth's promotion to Hywel's steward, combined with the land he held now in Anglesey, had made him a *lord* of the same stature as Douglas, who essentially had risen to his station in precisely the same fashion as Gareth. "I was hoping to speak to you and your confederate here."

Douglas's brow furrowed. "I am quite busy now, Lord Gareth." To his credit, he didn't pause between his initial thought and saying Gareth's name, unoffended by Gareth's formality and returning it.

"It is regarding the body in the church."

Douglas blinked. "Of course. It was on my duty list this morning to report to the king on the matter and then to come find you." He looked past Gareth to where the king was deep in conversation with Earl Ranulf and Prince Henry. "The truth is, I did not find any men who had seen or heard anything amiss in the church's vicinity last night. Even pressing them hard brought no change in their stories. Frankly, I saw no point in continuing. One can't squeeze water from a stone."

"One cannot. Thank you for trying." Gareth hadn't expected anything different, given that nobody had come forward before then, and by Douglas's own admission, he had little experience with investigations. Gareth had other questions as well, namely about how well acquainted Douglas actually was with Aelred, but they could wait until after he'd spoken to Brian. "If I need to return to the matter with any of them, I hope I can say I have your consent."

"You may." Douglas jerked his head to his companion and took a step, implying that he should come with him and that the conversation was over.

Gareth, however, put out a hand. "If I may speak to—" He let the sentence hang, since Douglas hadn't bothered to introduce him. Gareth himself had held a position similar to Brian's for many years too and knew it wasn't unusual to stand silently by while one's betters talked.

"Brian MacGregor." Douglas flapped a hand in his underling's direction. "I use him as a messenger. He travels with me sometimes. Brian, this is Lord Gareth from Gwynedd."

"My lord." Brian bent in a bow.

"Thank you," Gareth said to Douglas, not acknowledging Brian's greeting just yet. "I won't keep him long."

A speculative look entered Douglas's eyes, interested and wondering what possible reason Gareth could have for speaking to Brian. But he was too polite—and maybe too preoccupied—to ask.

Once Douglas had departed, Gareth tipped his head to indicate an empty table in the back of the hall. Nearby were a serving pitcher and two cups, and he poured out ale for both of them. Since his arrival, as with Douglas, Gareth had been more than usually aware of the status of everyone in King David's hall, and while he didn't want to undermine his own station, he wanted Brian at his ease for what he was about to ask him. Gareth gestured him to a seat at the end of the table and sat opposite, each now with a cup.

As Gareth took a sip of his ale, Brian did as well, despite being obviously hesitant about why Gareth wanted to speak to him. After swallowing, he cleared his throat. "How may I assist you, my lord?"

Gareth had been deliberating internally as to the proper approach, and he decided he would first try to go roundabout in his questions to get the answers he needed. "It is my understanding that you carry messages from Lord Douglas to King David and back again, and have done so for the last three months."

"That is true, my lord." Brian's face was open and guileless. "And it's been far longer than three months. I have ridden from here to Edinburgh and Stirling, Dundee and Inverness, and many places in the south. I've been to Chester several times."

"I have heard that you also carry messages for others, perhaps soldiers who want to reassure their loved ones that they are well or from loved ones to soldiers in the field."

Brian wet his lips. "Yes. That is true. It makes no sense for a man to ride all that way and not carry many messages."

Gareth put up a hand. "I am not suggesting there is anything untoward in this task. I assume Lord Douglas knows you do this. It must be common knowledge among the general population, soldiers and loved ones, as well."

"Yes." Brian was more confident now. "Do you need a message carried? Is that why you pulled me aside?"

"I do."

"I am happy to oblige." Brian looked expectant.

Gareth would also have said he bore a tinge of superiority at the oddness of the nobility, and Gareth in particular, for making so much of such a small task.

"I would like to send a note to a soldier, one named Aelred, from whom I understand you have brought messages to Carlisle over the last three months—to at least two different women."

Brian sat frozen in his seat. "I-I-I don't know any Aelred and have never carried any messages for him."

"Haven't you?"

"No." This was said more firmly as Brian warmed to the lie, which was why Gareth had asked him a second time to confirm.

Denial was an interesting choice, given the other possible responses. Because of it, Gareth studied the other man carefully. Brian could merely have said, in a casual tone, that he knew the man and would be happy to carry any message to him. Gareth then would have asked if he'd heard that Lord Douglas had identified the body in the church as Aelred, which would have presented Brian with a whole different problem. The fact that Brian had not only denied carrying messages for Aelred but also denied that he knew him, revealed, more than anything, that all was not well with the messages he *had* carried. He also hadn't reacted to the name as if he knew about the identity of the body in the church.

Gareth kept his gaze fixed on Brian, who looked steadily back, giving nothing away. In this moment, his commitment to his lie was absolute. Gareth needed to change that. The question was how.

"You do know him. I have two witnesses that will attest to Lord Douglas, or to the king, if necessary, that you brought items from Aelred to each of them. One was a note written in his own hand."

In the face of the truth, Brian was unable to keep his eyes on Gareth's face and dropped them to his cup. It was both an instinctive response to being caught in a lie and a sure sign he was about to lie again. "I don't know what you're talking about, my lord. The young ladies must be mistaken."

Gareth let the pause following that comment lengthen before pointing out Brian's obvious mistake, which by now Brian himself must have recognized, as evidenced by his flushing skin and the sweat beading on his temple. It gave some comfort to Gareth that the messenger wasn't a natural liar. "How did you know they were young women?"

"It-it-it seemed obvious."

"It would have been more obvious that one was his mother." Rather than press further on this particular matter, which he'd conquered anyway, Gareth changed tack. "I assume you've heard about the body in the church."

Brian had no reply to that but a nod. At this point, he was afraid of saying anything at all out of fear of incriminating himself further. If Gareth was to get him to talk, he had to break through his reluctance as well as any new barrier Brian might be busily putting up. With his tensed shoulders and set jaw, he had the look of defending the fortress he'd constructed to his dying breath.

The unfortunate thing about hastily built fortresses, however, was that they could be rickety. Sometimes they had no foundation at all.

"Lord Douglas thinks the dead man is Aelred. If so, he died some three months ago, and it's a little difficult to see how he could have been sending tokens from Worcester to Carlisle."

While Brian was incapable of looking directly at Gareth now, he also knew better than to look down, away, or around the room. In his mind, everything he did would appear suspicious. So he hesitated. And hesitated again.

Men who are fundamentally honest have two choices when caught in a lie: to double down on the lie in hopes of weathering the storm, or to face the wind and rain. Brian had tried the initial strategy already. To Gareth's relief, and possibly Brian's as well, he chose the latter option now.

Leaning forward, he lowered his voice to barely a whisper. "I'll tell you, but I beg you not to tell Lord Douglas what I've done."

"If I don't need to tell him, I won't, provided you had nothing to do with Aelred's death."

"I didn't!" Brian's agitation was such that he almost shouted the word, prompting him to look hastily around for anyone who might have overheard.

It was well known to everyone by now that Gareth was leading the investigation into the body in the church. Some residents of the castle might be avoiding their table as a way to disassociate themselves from murder, as if the stain of it could rub off on them. Others, and perhaps most, longed to know what was happening.

Gareth reached for the carafe and poured more ale into both their cups, affecting as casual an attitude as he could manage, despite the beating of his own heart now that he had a real hope to hear something that would help move the investigation forward. "Then you have nothing to fear."

Brian closed his eyes briefly. "I didn't know Aelred was dead until the body appeared in the church. I was just doing as he asked me. You have to believe me."

Gareth did, but he didn't let Brian off the hook just yet. "What did he ask you?"

"To deliver the tokens to three women on my return journeys. I spaced them out so it would look like he was still in Worcester if anyone inquired."

"*Three* women?"

"Joanna, Bronwen, and Mariota, Aelred's betrothed."

Gareth bobbed a nod. Mariota was the only one they had left to speak to, and his sons and Hamelin even now were on their way to fetch her. "He paid you?"

"He did indeed! A goodly sum!" Brian waggled his head, and Gareth understood before he continued what the source of his guilt had been. "Lord Douglas knows that I carry messages for common folk. He encourages it, but he says I am paid for the journey by King David and should not be taking payment from anyone else."

Gareth eased back on the bench. "But you do anyway."

"Not often! But Aelred was insistent, and it was four whole pence! I couldn't say no to that. It was such a small thing too."

"When did he pay you this money?"

"It was the day before we left for Worcester—which, if what they are saying is true about the body, has to be close to when he died." His shoulders sagged as the tension caused by the secret he'd been carrying eased. "I knew Aelred wasn't in Worcester; I didn't know he was dead." His eyes were in his cup.

"I never met Aelred in life, so I can only guess as to his motives. What did you think he was doing?"

"It was obvious to me that he planned to desert," Brian shrugged, "and for some reason he didn't want any of his women to know. That's why I wasn't concerned that he didn't come to Worcester. I didn't even know he hadn't marched with us until some time after we arrived. I actually went looking for him before I left for my first journey back to Carlisle, and I was told he had deserted. Since I'd expected it, I simply did as he asked. He'd paid me, you see ...." His voice trailed off.

"You didn't think this was something you ought to mention to Lord Douglas?"

"What Aelred chose to do with his life was his business, not mine. I barely knew the man. In fact, before that day, I hadn't spoken more than two words to him in passing. We ran in different circles."

"How so?"

Brian's eyes narrowed. Now that the burden of deception was lifted, he was more talkative, but his mind was also beginning to work. "I am of higher rank, an officer. He was a soldier and nothing more. He would never be anything more."

"Why do you say that?"

"Hasn't anyone told you the truth about him yet? Perhaps not, since nobody likes to speak ill of the dead." Brian shrugged. "Well I'll say it even if nobody else will. He was the runt of the litter—not in size, don't get me wrong. He was built like any other man, and probably handsome at that, which is why women liked him so much, but he was never going to win any sheepherding contest. Nobody would ever be confused about how little was going on in Aelred's head."

"And yet, he conceived this plan to desert and had the foresight to arrange for tokens to be sent back to his women to hide that fact?"

Brian canted his head. "I wondered about that too. He *was* different that day. More confident. Less self-effacing. I remember thinking *if you took that attitude to your work, you'd make something of yourself.* But then he gave me the money and what he wanted me to bring to his ladies, and left."

"Where did this interaction take place?"

"In the church graveyard—" He broke off as a shocked look crossed his face. "Do you think—"

Gareth chose not to speculate with him. "Where did he get the money?"

"I didn't ask." The shrug this time was definitive.

After his initial lies, Brian had been open and as honest as his conscience allowed. He might not have wanted to know where Aelred acquired a week's wages to pay out for carrying messages, but Gareth surely did.

22

Day Two

Gwen

"I appreciate your doing this." Up until now, Gwen herself had avoided spending more than the minimum amount of time necessary over Aelred's body, but she could see the time for squeamishness had ended. If Gwen acted as if she was untroubled by the body, then Bronwen would be less likely to fall to pieces again. That was to be avoided—not quite at all costs, but certainly if Gwen could possibly help it.

So she pulled back the sheet and let Bronwen take a good long look at Aelred.

If that's even who this was. Gwen was having all sorts of doubts now. Joanna claimed that it was he, and Gwen fully believed that the clothing on the body and the gear that came with it were his. But if Joanna was right, there was a great deal more to Aelred than most people had thought.

For starters, the Aelred that Bronwen and Joanna described were practically two different people. To Bronwen, Aelred was sweet and gentle and none-too-bright. To Joanna, he'd been the cleverest man she knew. He could read and write! It was very hard to reconcile those two descriptions. It was almost to the point that Gwen was wondering if Aelred had an identical twin, and the two of them had systematically been deceiving all of Carlisle.

To follow the speculation further, one of them was the body in the church, and the other was out there somewhere, sending messages to his women and very much alive.

Bronwen stared at the corpse, her face expressionless. She was so still, she could have been a statue. The more she stared, the more convinced Gwen became that Lord Douglas—and Joanna—had it all wrong.

But then Bronwen stepped back, folding her arms tightly across her chest as she did so. "That's him. That's Aelred."

Gwen eased out a breath she hadn't realized she'd been holding. "You don't have to be so certain. I imagine he looks nothing like he did in life."

"He looks enough alike."

Gwen's twin theory grew more likely, to the point that she was going to have to broach it with Gareth, even if it was almost embarrassing to be thinking it. Rather than postulate about an unknown twin with Bronwen, Gwen gestured to the side table. "He was dressed in a uniform, and that's his purse beside his boots."

"His purse!" Bronwen leapt forward, her face lighting up for the first time since Gwen had spoken to her back in the kitchen, before she knew that her supposed fiancé was dead.

Gwen covered the body once again, so neither of them had to look at it if they didn't want to, before following Bronwen to the table. The girl had picked up the purse and then immediately put it down again. "It isn't here."

"What isn't here?"

Bronwen's face was pinched. "Nothing."

It was so obviously a lie Gwen had to work not to laugh. "Bronwen."

"A brooch." The girl gave herself a shake. "I wasn't going to take it back right now, I promise! I was just—" She gestured helplessly with one hand.

Gwen had to prompt her. "You were what?"

"I-I-I gave him my brooch the last time I saw him."

Gwen understood that this was a delicate moment. She wanted to get her tone exactly right to encourage Bronwen to answer truthfully. "May I ask why?"

"He had a venture." A tear leaked out of the corner of Bronwen's eye. "Always one for big plans, was Aelred, although of course none of them ever worked out. Pie in the sky, I suppose my granny would have called them. He loved talking about them, though, and he brought me along with him, even if only in our minds."

"What was the venture?"

"He was going into trade."

"As a trader, you mean?"

"With a wagon and everything. He said he would never be able to provide for me properly as a soldier. King David didn't pay enough." She snorted. "The king paid enough for many men to have wives, but not enough for Aelred. I suppose at the time I appreciated his ambition."

"So you invested in this plan?"

"Everything I had, which wasn't much, I know, but I had saved a few pennies, and my father had left me a brooch. I gave it to him so he could sell it and use the money to buy the wagon."

As Bronwen had been speaking, a cold feeling had been congealing in Gwen's stomach, and now she moved towards the girl in order to put an arm around her shoulders. It was time Bronwen faced that very difficult subject Gwen had been avoiding.

"Could this body belong not to Aelred but to someone else wearing Aelred's clothing and carrying his purse?"

Bronwen at first didn't comprehend the thrust of Gwen's question. "Why would someone else have Aelred's things? Why would you even think that?" She still didn't see that Aelred could have stolen the money and brooch from her, planning never to return.

He had three women, including the yet unmet betrothed in his native village. Gwen was willing to bet her father's latest ballad that Aelred had taken money from each of them too. "Because he wanted us to think he was dead."

"Why would he want that?"

She still wasn't understanding. Bluntness appeared to be called for. "So he could run off with the money."

Even then, it took a moment for Bronwen to truly grasp what Gwen was suggesting. "No! He would never do that."

"Bronwen, he was seeing three women at the same time, all of whom were convinced that he was going to marry them."

"He was going to marry me!"

Gwen looked at her sadly. "Did you know about Joanna?"

Bronwen bit her lip and looked down at the floor. "No."

"What about his betrothed in his village?" Gwen asked, more for certainty than because she thought she didn't know the answer.

"Mariota is her name. Everyone knew about her. It's hard to believe Joanna didn't."

"That was the real reason you were keeping your relationship a secret?"

Bronwen nodded.

"But you told your friend anyway?"

Another nod. "It was only Jonet. She wouldn't have said anything to anyone else."

Gwen didn't reply that Jonet had been free enough with the information to Dai. She didn't have to. It wasn't her job to convince Bronwen that the man she'd loved hadn't been deserving of that love. Instead, she gestured back to the body, which they thankfully couldn't see under its sheet. "Please tell me, if you can, why you are so sure this body is Aelred's."

Bronwen was still preoccupied with the previous questions, and it took a moment for her to focus on Gwen's face. Then she made a gesture with her hand, like the answer was insignificant. "He has a tattoo."

Gwen's mouth opened, but her surprise was such that no words came out.

Bronwen saw it. She was a smart girl, when she wasn't thinking of Aelred, and she gave Gwen a wry look. "He knew his commander wouldn't like that he had one, so he hid it from everyone but me."

Tattoos were an ancient practice, but for all that extremely uncommon in Britain. In fact, Gwen didn't know a single Welshman with one—or, at least, none had confessed to having one. Gwen had seen tattoos only on Danes in Dublin, revealed when men fought shirtless. Even then, tattoos were few and far between, since the Church frowned on them as marring God's perfect creation, the human body, made in His own image. Evidently men still chose to adorn themselves with them, else Aelred wouldn't have had one.

To visually illustrate her point, Bronwen pulled back a portion of the sheet to show Gwen a discolored patch on the corpse's upper left arm. As with the face, the arm was covered in a waxy substance Gwen found gruesome, and the skin underneath was like leather. It was no wonder Conall and Gareth, in the dim light of the lanterns last night, had missed it. Even having been to Dublin, they wouldn't have been looking for a tattoo. A disfiguring scar, perhaps, but even that, given the state of the body, might not be distinguishable from the wear and tear of three months in the grave.

But now that Bronwen had shown her where the tattoo was on Aelred's arm, Gwen was able to make out a circle with slashes across it, etched in black, or perhaps blue. She couldn't really tell what the symbol was supposed to be, even by the light of day and holding the lantern closer. But she could see it, now that she knew where to look.

"It's a Viking sigil, something to do with Valhalla. Aelred was Christian, of course, but he was drunk one night with some visitors from the north, Danes they were, and got himself talked into getting it. Even his mother didn't know about it." Bronwen shook her head indulgently. "It was just like him to leap before he looked."

Unfortunately, the memory brought a fresh storm of tears, prompting Gwen again to bring the girl into the circle of her arms. "I'm sorry."

"So am I." Bronwen clutched Gwen's waist. "I didn't know about Joanna. Everyone knew he was betrothed to Mariota, but he swore there was nothing between them, and he was going to tell her their engagement was over when the moment was right. He didn't want to hurt her, you see. I loved that about him."

Gwen had lived at Gwynedd's court most of her life. She had seen how, in such a small community, men and women were often thrown together more closely than was perhaps wise. More than one young woman had sworn that the man to whom she'd given herself was going to leave his current woman for her, and that if only she were to wait, he would break the news to his lover/woman/wife when the time was right. In Wales, unlike in England, divorce was possible, if rare, and available under certain circumstances. One of those was if a spouse was caught in an affair. Most of the time, however, the results were tears on the part of the mistress and a child out of wedlock.

Bronwen's forehead was in the hollow of Gwen's neck. "Now he's dead, and I can't even win him back."

"No, you can't." Again, Gwen wasn't speaking this way to be harsh, but rather because the truth was the only thing that would serve Bronwen now. "All you can do is help us discover how and why he ended up dead in the priest's chair."

23

Day Two

Dai

Hamelin, Llelo, and Dai had ridden faster to the village than maybe was strictly necessary. Dai's two companions were both still bouncing about after this morning's knighting, and their enthusiasm had infected their horses as well. Every now and then Llelo would laugh out loud for no reason. And every time Dai glanced at Hamelin, he was grinning.

Even the prospect of a negative reception to their news on the part of Aelred's mother and betrothed couldn't dim their good humor, though they did enter the village itself at a much more sedate pace than they'd ridden from Carlisle. Dai himself was happy to be out of the castle and had enjoyed the exuberant ride, so he too was still in a whistling mood as they dismounted on the village green.

"We need the headman first, right?" Hamelin tied his horse's reins to a hitching post.

"You're right that we should start with him as a matter of courtesy, since we are emissaries from the castle. Or rather, you are," Dai said, "but it's harvest, so he may not be here."

"You are as much an emissary as we are," Llelo said. "Yesterday if we'd come here, I wouldn't have been a knight, and we would have been doing this as much together as we are now. Besides, you have to do the talking anyway, since my Gaelic is nonexistent, and Hamelin here doesn't even speak English, much less whatever this language is that passes for English in Scotland."

"Aelred had an English father, so it's possible someone here does speak an English you might understand." Dai was trying to make his brother feel better about his ignorance. Normans were notorious for refusing to speak any language but their own, but the Welsh had learned long ago that to get along with everyone—or at least to pretend to—meant learning new languages when necessary. Admittedly, Dai's abilities were unusual, even for a Welsh person. "You tell me what we need to ask, and I'll ask it."

With the division of labor established, Dai approached a middle-aged woman, with two small children at her feet, who was pulling water from the well. "Excuse me, madam," he opted to speak in Gaelic, which he assumed was her native language, "we are looking for the village headman."

She appeared to understand him perfectly, and Dai was again grateful for their visit to Ireland last year.

"Lachlann is over there." Since the woman's hands were full, she pointed with her chin to a pen at the far end of the village where a ewe was standing with her head down, being examined by a man wearing a dirty shirt, breeches, and boots with muck up to mid-calf. "Bonnie there is sick."

Dai was a Welshman, so he knew she meant the sheep, not the man. He thanked her and motioned with his head that Llelo and Hamelin should follow him. Once at the pen, he rested his arms on the top rail. "God save you."

Lachlann, who proved to be quite a bit older than the woman, approaching sixty by Dai's guess, and mostly bald, had been studying his ewe's eyes. Now he glanced over. "You don't know anything about how to cure a ewe with rheumy eyes, do you?"

"I was raised to be a wool trader, but I confess I know little of the ways of sheep. Isn't there an ointment that might help?"

Lachlann grunted. "We've tried them all."

"I can ask my mother. She knows something about herbs."

Dai was worried that his lack of knowledge might be a mark against him, as if knowing about rheumy eyes was a test he'd failed, but the man just sighed resignedly before turning to look at him more fully. Then his eyes widened as he truly noticed not only Dai's sword but the two newly dubbed knights standing behind him. There was no way to tell just by looking that Llelo and Hamelin were knights, or that Dai wasn't, but even Dai could see how his brother and Hamelin were both standing a little straighter this morning.

"Excuse me, my lords. I didn't see you there. How may I help you?"

Dai glanced at his brother, who said, "Just ask him if he knows Aelred's mother."

Dai thought he could do a little better than that, but he was happy to start with what Llelo wanted. "Do you know the mother of a soldier named Aelred?"

"I do." The headman frowned. "Is something amiss?"

Dai didn't see why he should hide the truth. "Yes."

The man pulled out a cloth and wiped at his pate. "May I inquire as to who's asking?"

Dai gestured behind him. "Sir Hamelin, brother to Prince Henry, and Sir Llelo, whose father, Lord Gareth, has tasked him with speaking to Aelred's mother and his betrothed." He didn't mention that Llelo was Dai's own brother. His role was to translate; his identity was irrelevant.

Lachlann blinked, as well he might, at the station of the two men before him, and made a hasty, somewhat deep bow—as best as he could anyway while in the muck of the pen. "My lords. Many apologies for not greeting you properly from the start."

Even Llelo, whose Gaelic was extremely poor, understood the gist of what he said and made a dismissive motion with his hand. "Do you know Aelred?" He asked this in French, for Hamelin's sake perhaps, choosing it instead of English, or even Welsh, which might have been closer to what the headman was speaking.

Dai did his job, which was to translate, though the headman was already answering before he finished. "I knew him well, less so since he went off to be a soldier." He stopped.

It was, perhaps, an inevitable hesitation, given what they'd already learned about the man. Not that the headman would know it.

"But?" Dai prompted him like he had Jonet the night before, knowing there had to be a *but.*

Even then, Lachlann still hesitated. "I'm sure I don't know what you mean, my lord."

"I'm sure, actually, that you do. You hesitated. You are still hesitating. Please, we are interested in anything you might have to say about Aelred."

The moment he spoke, he kicked himself for thinking he could be a good investigator, rather than translating for Llelo and letting him do the questioning. Hastily, he translated the headman's words for Llelo and Hamelin, explained what he'd asked, and apologized for speaking out of turn.

Hamelin shrugged. "So far, I appear to be nothing more than an appendage."

First Llelo put out a hand to Hamelin. "Your name carries weight, which should help us here." Then he turned back to Dai. "And you did nothing wrong. Are you certain he knows more?"

"Pretty certain."

"I'll ask, you translate. That way he'll blame me, not you. You can be the beleaguered translator, while I'm the unreasonable lord." Llelo intended them to employ a technique of interrogation, one they'd learned from their father.

At Dai's assent, Llelo glowered, and Dai made sure to cower slightly, playing his part as Llelo intended. "Are you sure you are translating our words correctly? If I could do it myself, I would!"

Dai ducked his head and plucked at his forelock. "Yes, sir. I am, sir."

They were still speaking in French, but their motions were large enough that Dai thought the headman could have no doubt about what was happening.

Llelo scoffed his disdain, closely replicating the high-and-mighty attitude the two boys had witnessed when nobility interacted with those of lesser rank. Then Llelo went to the rail of the pen and said in French, even knowing the headman wouldn't understand, "Aelred is dead, friend, by unnatural means. If you know something about his death, or about his life that might pertain to his death, I require you to speak now."

Dai hastily translated, as if he too had been genuinely chastised, adding, "I really think it would be best if you tell him what he wants to know," with the implication that Llelo had the power to haul him back to the castle if he didn't speak. Truthfully, he did.

Lachlann swallowed hard, his eyes flicking from one brother to the other. His posture had him leaning away, desiring to get back to his ewe as quickly as possible, and trying to figure out the best and quickest way to do that. In the end, he decided it was by telling the truth.

"I don't believe I know anything that might help, my lord. His poor mother ..." His voice trailed off at Llelo's continued glare, augmented now by Hamelin's. The Frenchman had approached too, his hand on the hilt of his sword, as if at any second he hoped to unsheathe it and lop off Lachlann's head.

Dai felt sorry for the headman now and was uncomfortable with actually threatening him. The fear in the man's face made the whole scene feel less like a game, since one of the participants was unaware he was playing. He was about to murmur something along those lines in French to Hamelin and Llelo, when Llelo shoved his shoulder. "Do your job!"

Coming to life, Dai realized that his feelings of sympathy were actually part of the act. Because they were genuine, they would seem so to Lachlann. He bowed again, apologizing in French. Then, with much ducking and forelock tugging, he indicated that Llelo and Hamelin should move away again, so he could have a conversation with Lachlann without them looming over him.

They did so with obvious reluctance and a blatant sneer on Llelo's part. Hamelin sniffed and stalked back to his horse, still with his hand on the hilt of his sword.

After a furtive look back at them, Dai made a *come here* gesture to Lachlann.

Lachlann scuttled closer, getting right up to the rail of the pen upon which Dai was hanging.

Dai lowered his voice so it wouldn't carry, even knowing that Llelo and Hamelin wouldn't understand him anyway. He thought it went well with his overall subdued demeanor. "I don't want you to get in trouble with Lord Gareth, these knights, or the king himself, should he hear of it. The sooner you tell us your thoughts about Aelred, the sooner we will leave you in peace. I should warn you that Sir Llelo is his father's right-hand man. The next step for him will involve knocking on doors to ask the inhabitants of your village about Aelred. He would even knock down the doors if he had to. Better you tell us what we want to know first."

While Lachlann's reluctance to speak ill of the dead was impressive, and he hadn't become the headman of the village by being easily intimidated, he also hadn't reached his current station without being practical. "I see." He sighed, resigned to the duty even if he found it distasteful. "At one time, Aelred was one of the cleverest men you'd ever want to meet. Before the accident, he could read and write, even though nobody ever taught him. Even our priest claims he had nothing to do with it. One day Aelred simply picked up the Bible and started reading it. He was just that smart, was our Aelred. We were all so proud of him."

"What do you mean *before the accident*?" Dai latched on to the first thing Lachlann had said that didn't make sense.

"A year ago, he was helping to build the new village barn—well, not really *helping* since doing any actual work was beneath his magnificence. Supervising, more like—when a beam fell on his head. Knocked him out cold. We thought at first he was going to die, since he didn't wake for most of the day. Once he did wake, for a time it seemed like he was getting better, but after a few weeks it became clear that his mind would never recover."

Dai winced. "That must have been very hard." He had some idea what that had been like, since his uncle Gwalchmai, who was also one of Dai's closest friends, had experienced something similar last December.

"It was hard on everyone, but especially on his mother and his betrothed, Mariota. She refused to abandon him, even though we all could see that he would never amount to anything and could never properly provide for her."

"If Aelred was so clever, why was he building the village barn in the first place? I would have thought he could have applied at the castle to be a clerk, and they would have taken him on."

"We all thought so too! We told him so time and again, but he would never hear of it. While he became soft and sweet after the accident, I have to admit that before it—" here Lachlann shook his head, "—he was never *wise*, if you take my meaning."

"I'm not sure I understand ..." Dai made a motion with his hand, asking Lachlann to keep up the explanations.

He obliged. "Aelred hated being told what to do."

"And after?"

"You could tell him what to do, and he was amenable always, but that didn't mean what you wanted done would get done. He'd stand in front of you, smiling and nodding, repeating over and over again that he understood, and then go off to do your bidding. Two hours later you'd find him in the orchard, juggling apples. It was always such a shock to realize that there was no mind behind that handsome face."

"Handsome?" Dai canted his head. "Nobody has mentioned his looks up until now."

"Haven't they?" Lachlann blinked rapidly several times. "I am no expert, but if he'd been a woman, he would have been called beautiful. He'd been a pretty child, and as an adult, he drew every eye, man or woman. Believe me, nobody was more surprised than I when he became a soldier." Lachlann's lips pursed as he thought. "He hated getting his hands dirty and was always fastidious in his personal appearance. Not a hair out of place, not a spot on his clothes, even after the accident.”

None of that had been discussed by anyone at the castle. But then, they hadn’t known Aelred as a youth.

Lachlann continued: “It was a relief to have him gone, really. It was so hard to look at him most days.”

“Did he have a good heart?”

“Afterwards, I would say so. Before—” Lachlann hesitated again, less, Dai felt, because he didn’t want to speak but because he was thinking. “His heart was often in the right place. It was more that we lesser men were invisible to him. He didn’t *see* us, you understand? Too clever by half, and too attractive, was our Aelred. Of course, except for his looks, that was all gone this last year.”

“When did *you* last see him?”

“Months ago.” Then he frowned. “It was my understanding he was supposed to have gone with the king’s forces to Worcester.”

“Lord Douglas says the army marched through here three months ago on its way there. Was Aelred with them?”

“No, which was odd. We expected to see him.”

“Did anyone ask you about him at the time? Or did you ask anyone about him?”

The headman nodded. “His captain spoke to me, and I told him the truth: I hadn’t seen him.”

“Thank you for your cooperation.”

“He really is dead?”

“We think so.”

The headman’s eyes narrowed. “You *think* so?”

"We found a body that Lord Douglas says is Aelred's. We are here to collect his mother and betrothed in hopes they can identify him with more certainty. It is obviously important to be certain."

The headman took in a long breath through his nose. "I should come with you to break the news of his death to them. It's my job more than yours or those great lords." He gestured to Llelo and Hamelin, who were still looking haughty as they stood by their horses. "I'm sorry that man was cruel to you. Men like him don't understand men like us."

Dai wished Lachlann hadn't said that. Once the information had begun to flow, he had stopped feeling guilty about deceiving him. And then, he decided not to. "Sir Llelo is actually my brother."

"That explains a great deal. Older brother, is he?"

Dai nodded, prompting Lachlann to clap a hand on his shoulder. "Then I must wish you luck on the ride back. Brothers can be the worst."

It was long past time to change topics, though again, Dai was happy not to lie, even if he'd implied that he and Llelo were not, in fact, the best of friends as well as brothers. "I'm sorry to keep you from your ewe."

"She'll keep." He looked again at Dai, this time with hope in his eyes. "Your mother really knows something about ointments?"

"She does."

"Perhaps it would be sensible for me to come with you to Carlisle too. I can have a look at this body, and I can also talk to her."

24

Day Two

Godfrid

"Dublin will finally be able to throw off the yoke of Leinster." Ranulf of Chester was speaking in that way of his that managed somehow to be both smarmy and aloof. Only he, King David, and Godfrid were in the room. Although Prince Henry was the third in their triumvirate, Godfrid was guessing he would have balked at this conversation, which was why he hadn't been included.

"I will take your offer to my brother." Of course Godfrid would, if only to have a good laugh over it.

At least, he hoped Brodar would laugh.

Really, it wasn't funny. Not at all. Godfrid was trying to maintain as calm a demeanor as possible in the face of the treason they were offering him. That wasn't to say it wasn't potentially a good deal. Dublin was perpetually looking for a way to *throw off the yoke of Leinster* as Ranulf had so succinctly put it.

"What have you offered Lord Conall?" Godfrid made to speak as if he had nothing but disdain for Conall as well as Leinster, all the while speaking words that were an exact truth.

"We have not spoken to Conall." Ranulf said.

"What are you *going* to offer him? I am aware that he is here because he too was invited." Godfrid wasn't going to be put off by Ranulf's smooth words. "He is the ambassador to Gwynedd at the moment, but he will always be nephew to the King of Leinster. King Diarmait has more power and a wider reach at this time than my brother does."

"As Ranulf said, we have not made any offer to him as of yet because we do not know what he would view as appropriate," King David said smoothly, "and we would rather hesitate than put a foot wrong."

"Why does it matter what we offer Leinster?" A slight pinching around Ranulf's eyes gave the first sign that he wasn't quite as relaxed and casual about this conversation as his overt demeanor implied. Fifteen years younger than David, he appeared far less vibrant, even dressed as he was in a luxurious burgundy robe that was wrapped snugly around him. The castle wasn't cold, but he was prepared for winter. "Our relations with Leinster should have no bearing on Dublin."

Godfrid endeavored not to laugh outright that Ranulf could say those words with a straight face, knowing that Godfrid was married to Conall's sister and Dublin was subject to the authority of Leinster. By his marriage, Godfrid himself was now nephew to Diarmait too. Then again, for Ranulf to imply that Godfrid's relationship with Conall's family was irrelevant wasn't surprising, given that Ranulf's own loyalties were as variable as the wind, no matter his kinship or what he'd pledged to whom.

He didn't say any of this, of course. He couldn't afford to alienate either magnate, nor the King of Leinster for that matter, and he did very much want to hear exactly what was on Ranulf's mind. Suddenly, it had become urgent to know the full scope of what he was dealing with here in Carlisle. Ranulf and David had just offered Dublin the men and money to overthrow Leinster, in exchange for Dublin's assistance in the war against King Stephen.

Instead, Godfrid answered with an utter truth, if not the whole of it. "I care because Dublin *is* currently vassal to Leinster, and if you are allying yourself with Diarmait, you might find the bargain with him more profitable than with Dublin. I would need assurances that your deal with him would not interfere with your deal with us."

"In your opinion, what does the King of Leinster want?" Ranulf said, easily skirting the issue.

"For you not to interfere in Dublin, that's for certain." Godfrid laughed—with just enough lightness and irony to garner a smile from King David and a broader smirk from Ranulf. "If I had to guess, I would suggest that assistance against the High King of Ireland would be the most tempting offer. King Diarmait has searched long for allies in that fight."

"Such is what we supposed," King David said. "Thank you for confirming."

"I must point out that my brother will ask why Dublin would involve itself in a war in which we have no stake, even for the promise of men and resources to overcome Leinster. If you do not win here, you will have neither the men nor the resources to follow through with your promises. We will have sent men to you, but end up with nothing."

Ranulf didn't attempt to suppress his instinctive snort. "Your people have not come that far from your Viking past, any more than mine have. Even without our promise to assist you in overthrowing Leinster, participating in a war in England would bring your people wealth. I'm quite certain your brother is still interested in *that*, at the very least."

"You are not wrong. How many men are you asking for? Five hundred? A thousand?" Godfrid decided in that moment that his best option was to feign interest and keep them talking.

"Those details remain to be worked out with your brother," King David said.

Truthfully, his brother might well be interested. That Godfrid was married to the niece of the King of Leinster was a means to an end for him, in that tying the royal houses of Dublin and Leinster together made Diarmait more predictable. Certainly Ranulf, whose allegiances shifted with the wind and whose word counted for less than nothing, would not see Godfrid's friendship with Conall (if he knew of it, which they'd worked very hard to ensure he didn't) as a barrier to betraying him. It might even be that he wouldn't see this alliance as a betrayal at all.

And perhaps Godfrid shouldn't either—except that, because of Ranulf's history, Godfrid didn't trust the man as far as he could throw him. Even King David, who outwardly manifested such a kingly presence, had for decades behaved ruthlessly in his quest for more power and land for Scotland. *That* was his first concern, and Godfrid would be unwise to forget it. Helping Dublin, if in the end it was required, would be very low on his list of priorities.

"What of Gwynedd?" Godfrid said.

"What of Gwynedd?" King David frowned. "They are here because King Owain has aligned himself with us. Do you know something we don't?"

Godfrid put up both hands. "You cannot be unaware that King Owain's brother, Cadwaladr, called upon the men of Dublin when he sought to change his own fortunes and assassinated the King of Deheubarth." And then he caught his breath as an identical look that he could describe only as *avaricious* crossed the faces of both men.

For a moment, Godfrid sat stunned. "That's why I'm here."

"Yes," Ranulf said, without prevarication or apology.

"I see." Godfrid shifted on his seat. "You know that we were there. You know of what we are capable, and you would like to put those services to work for yourselves."

"We don't need a thousand Danes," Ranulf said. "We need forty."

"A small band," King David added. "That's all."

"To do what? Kill King Stephen?"

"No." Somewhat to Godfrid's surprise, it was King David who answered, though he wet his lips before he did so, the only indication that he had any qualms about what he was asking for. "No, of course not. It would be to capture his son, Eustace, who is much less well protected."

"You say *capture* him ... but you mean *kill* him." Godfrid wasn't asking a question. It seemed obvious. And it was very important to get to the truth.

Ranulf, however, waggled his head back and forth in a manner that didn't so much say *no* as was noncommittal. "His death is not required, but if he were to die in the fight, much like Anarawd, it would not be regretted on our part."

Godfrid gazed at the two men for several heartbeats, endeavoring to give nothing away with his expression. "I will, of course, bring your offer to my brother. By when would you like to hear his reply? What is your timeline for your next move—to York, is it?"

He knew from Gwen that Prince Henry had mentioned York as the goal. That wasn't something either man would know—he hoped, anyway—and he certainly didn't want them to know that he and Gwen were friends. So he spoke as if the destination was a guess, but a good one for any thinking man.

Confirming this target was, in fact, one of Godfrid's goals for this meeting, and he was very curious as to whether the pair would give him the same information Henry had given Gwen. Up until now, their target had been a closely guarded secret, one to be shared only with those they knew wouldn't betray them to Stephen. Henry had clearly felt that way about Gwen. As they'd already offered to enlist him in a plan to assassinate the son of the King of England, it hardly seemed a piece of information at which they would balk.

And they didn't. After a glance at King David, who gave a slight nod in response, Ranulf said smoothly, "We move within days. I have men marching from Chester as we speak. Others have left from Edinburgh."

"That soon!" Godfrid straightened in his chair. "Have you made Gwynedd aware of the immediacy of your attack?"

"No," King David said. "With this body in the church, and the two knighting ceremonies, we have not had a chance to meet formally. I would like to include you—and perhaps Lord Conall of Leinster, if he is willing—in our war council." He rubbed his hands together, a look of satisfaction on his face, and said, in mimicry of Prince Henry last night, whether or not he knew it. "After which, everything begins."

25

Day Two

Gwen

It took some time to calm Bronwen down and ensure she was fit to resume her duties. Unfortunately, the delay meant that they were just leaving the laying-out room as Caitriona and Joanna were coming towards it.

Instantly, Bronwen's demeanor changed (yet again) from resigned acceptance to anger, and she strode towards the other woman, yelling in Welsh along the lines of, "Who do you think you are, claiming that you were betrothed to Aelred? He loved *me,* and nobody else."

It was hardly the first time Gwen had encountered a normally reasonable woman who became crazed over a man, but it was one of the more extreme examples. For her part, Joanna shrunk back against Cait's side, almost cowering. Gwen was forced to stab out a hand and grab Bronwen's elbow, spinning her around with such force that both of them almost fell over. "That's enough, Bronwen! You are embarrassing yourself."

Bronwen's reply was a fresh storm of tears.

As Gwen held her, she was thinking that Bronwen's excessive response was *too* much, almost as if she were covering up her real emotions because they were even less acceptable: embarrassment at having loved the wrong man, perhaps, or anger at *him* rather than at Joanna or Mariota, who themselves were innocent of wrongdoing (as far as Gwen knew anyway). Gwen had felt the same when they'd questioned Joanna. If grief was really love in disguise, there was something else underneath what these women were displaying. It remained to be seen whether that something else was simple regret for what might have been, or a more sinister emotion.

Like shame. Or guilt?

They had converged near the church wall, where there was a bench, and Gwen forcibly sat Bronwen on it. "Stay there."

Then she turned to Joanna. "Bronwen tells me that Aelred had a tattoo on his upper arm. Did you ever see it?"

Joanna's eyes widened. "I did. Of course, I did." Then she looked down at Bronwen, this time with a sneer forming on *her* face. She opened her mouth to speak, possibly to say something cutting.

Gwen cut her off with a chopping motion before she could get out any words. "Don't say anything to her. It won't help even you."

Joanna subsided, not particularly resentfully. Gwen didn't think it was in the nature of either woman to be mean. Gwen had spent less time with Joanna, but the woman was running her own shop. She couldn't be as successful as she appeared to be and also shy and retiring. On the whole, Gwen would rather these women stand up for themselves—just not if that meant shouting at each other.

Being another strong woman, Cait saw it too, and she actually said what Gwen hadn't yet decided if it would be wise to say. "Aelred is dead; I'm sorry, but that is the truth. There is nothing to be gained by attacking each other. Bad enough that he led each of you on as if you were the only woman in his life. It is at him you should direct your ire, not each other."

"That's the problem, though, isn't it." Joanna spoke softly and clutched a handkerchief, with which she dabbed at the corners of her eyes. "What good does it do to be angry at a dead man?"

Cait's expression softened, and she put an arm around Joanna's shoulders. "I'm sorry. And I'm sorry to speak so bluntly."

"But no less than the truth." That was from Bronwen, who'd turned to face away from everyone, staring towards the laying-out room and beyond that to the wall of the castle. "Up until I saw the body, I told myself it wasn't Aelred; that he wasn't really dead. If that were true, then I could be angry at you for losing hope, never mind that he told you he loved you and that you were the only one. *I* knew I wasn't the only one. How could he do this to us?" She bent forward to sob into her hands.

Gwen patted Bronwen's shoulder. The girl's tears seemed less full of anger now as sadness, which to Gwen's mind was a positive progression. Acceptance of the truth wasn't so far away anymore.

Cait still had her arm around Joanna. "Conall found you this morning in the laying-out room, yes?"

Joanna nodded, though she was looking down at the ground.

"I take it that when you looked at the body, you saw Aelred?"

At the question, Bronwen's weeping quieted, indicating she was listening.

Joanna nodded again and said in a small voice, "Yes."

"You're sure?"

Again the barest of nods.

"What made you so sure?" This was from Gwen.

It took longer for Joanna to respond this time, but when she did, it was worth it. "I went through his clothing and his purse, which I recognized. His jacket had a three-corner tear that I mended."

"Bronwen also thought the gear belonged to Aelred," Gwen said to Cait before looking again to Joanna. "In your mind, is it possible that the body could be that of another man dressed as Aelred? Or rather, could it be that Aelred dressed another man in his own clothing and gave him his belongings?"

"And gave him the same tattoo too?" Joanna's head had come up at the question, and she looked positively astonished. "Of course not. Aelred would never do that."

"Wouldn't he?" Gwen could just barely believe either woman was as innocent as they were affecting.

Before Joanna could elaborate on her thoughts, Bronwen said in Welsh in a tone that was definitive, "The body is that of Aelred. We know—"

Gwen put out a hand to stop the girl from interrupting. "Let Joanna speak."

Joanna hemmed and hawed for even longer this time, prompting Cait to give her a nudge too. "Please tell us. The more we know, the greater the possibility of finding out why Aelred died. If there is any chance we should still be looking for him and another man died in his place, with his gear, and with a tattoo like his on his arm, we need to know now."

Joanna sighed. "I would love to hope that he's alive. Really, I would. Even now, even with Bronwen just there, I still don't want to believe Aelred deceived me. I see now why you could be thinking that he asked a friend to put on his gear and then killed him, so he could escape with none the wiser. Aelred would be dead to everyone but himself and have no more obligations to anyone."

That was exactly the scenario Gwen had postulated, though, in truth, with the added complication of the secret burial, it made no sense that Aelred himself would have buried and then unburied the body. There were far better ways to fake one's own death, as Gwen herself had seen in earlier investigations.

"But the body is that of Aelred. It isn't just the tattoo either. It's his feet."

That was definitely not the answer Gwen had been expecting. "What about his feet?"

"He had horrible bunions."

Cait made a face. "My mother has those. She's had them for as long as she can remember, even as a small child, and they have worsened with age. It was one of the reasons she let me go without shoes for much of my childhood, because she herself suffered when wearing them. Thankfully, I was spared the condition."

Gwen's feet hurt just thinking about the deformity. She herself knew people who suffered from them. But she hadn't noticed Aelred's feet.

"Aelred's had bothered him his whole life too." Joanna bent to her own foot and rubbed the instep. "Even with the dreadful state of the body you can't miss the bulges on the sides of his feet. Honestly, because of them, the idea that he didn't march to Worcester isn't horribly surprising. I still can't believe he's really dead—" She broke off, shaking her head.

She still wasn't crying. Nor, at last, was Bronwen. Gwen stood before them, looking from one to the other, thinking about all they'd said, separately and together.

She turned to Joanna. "How much money did you loan Aelred?"

Genuine shock appeared on Joanna's face, prompting her for once to answer without hesitation or apparent thought. "How did you know about that?"

"So you did. How much?"

The hemming and hawing was back, but another squeeze from Cait reminded her what was at stake. "Fifty silver pennies."

It was a fortune, and not even a small one.

"Fifty!" Bronwen was on her feet. "Why would you do that? Aelred was sweet, but he had no ability to manage that amount of money!"

Joanna's expression turned puzzled. "Aelred was the cleverest man I knew. Of course he could."

The two women gazed at each other, open-mouthed. Gwen was just glad they weren't attacking each other.

"What are you talking about?" Bronwen said. "Aelred was a fool. Everyone knew it."

Joanna raised and dropped her hands in a helpless gesture. "He was going into trade with another man. They would be supplying ale to the soldiers in Worcester, who would want more than they would get from the army's stores. One of the tavern keepers in the town had agreed to be his partner, but he needed money to increase his production."

Bronwen plopped herself back onto the bench. "He told me he was becoming a trader." She spoke in a hollow voice, shrunk into herself and visibly crushed. "He said he would come for me after he sold my brooch and bought the wagon, and we would leave Carlisle together."

"It seems that you and I ought to be friends rather than enemies." At long last, Joanna saw the truth and spoke it. "We were wronged by Aelred. We would only compound the error by continuing to wrong each other."

26

Day Two

Llelo

Llelo had seen Aelred's other women for only a few moments, but he'd noticed that both were good-looking, even Joanna, who was far too old for him. Given her beauty, he'd been surprised she hadn't married before now. Then he'd decided she could be a widow, which was why she'd fallen so hard for Aelred. By Llelo's estimation, Bronwen was the more lovely of the two, being younger and very Welsh, with skin so pale it was almost translucent and dark curly hair.

Mariota put both other women to shame. In fact, she was so stunning to look at, with blonde hair the color of sunshine down to her waist and the bluest eyes Llelo had ever seen, that he was finding it very hard to look away.

In an attempt to gain control of his thoughts, he narrowed his eyes and tried to look as severe as possible. "Did you know Aelred was seeing other women?"

"How could I have? He was in Carlisle, and I was here."

She was speaking in Gaelic, which he hadn't mastered in the last hour, so Dai continued to translate. He did find that he was paying special attention to tone, since he couldn't understand the words.

"I can't believe it of him." Aelred's mother, an aged, gray-haired woman named Agnes, shook her head. "If you weren't a knight and the other one the prince's brother, I wouldn't believe it."

When Hamelin, Dai, and Llelo had set out that morning, none of them had given any thought as to *how* they were to get Mariota and Agnes to Carlisle. Fortunately, the headman, Lachlann, had a cart and wanted to see the body too. He'd also piled the back with wool scraps. These were the dregs, since the wool season was over, but he had a friend who was in charge of stuffing mattresses at the castle. He was hoping to convince him to take the lot.

For the journey, the two women were sitting together on the seat beside Lachlann, who was driving, while Llelo, Dai, and Hamelin kept their horses to the cart's slow pace. The five miles were going to take at least an hour to travel, so Llelo thought to use the time productively.

"How long had you known Aelred?" Llelo asked Mariota.

(Dai dutifully translated.)

"My whole life. I loved him for most of it. After the accident, he changed, of course, but I wasn't going to abandon him just because he was no longer as clever as before."

"He was a good provider," Agnes said staunchly. "Always has been."

"Was he though?" Llelo asked Mariota gently. Lachlann's description of the changed Aelred squared with what Douglas had said about Aelred being *dumb as a post*, and that didn't sound at all like someone who could provide well for a wife.

"He became a soldier, even though it was the last thing he wanted to do," Mariota said. "It provided a steady wage, which was hard for him to achieve otherwise."

"I knew my son," Agnes said. "With his father gone, he was the man of the house and had the right to make his own decisions."

Llelo's next question should have been broached delicately, if at all, but with Dai translating between them, Llelo had to speak straight out and let Dai worry about how it sounded. He wasn't too proud to admit that his brother was doing a good job. He'd even told him so after their interview with Lachlann. Truly, as a newly dubbed knight, Llelo was finding it easy to be magnanimous and grateful.

"If you don't mind me saying, you could have married anyone."

"I am illegitimate." Mariota gave Llelo this news in a flat voice, as if daring Llelo to pass judgment on her. "My mother and father were not married, and my father died when I was small. My mother worked hard to care for me all my life, despite the hardships. I couldn't leave her." She shrugged. "She died last year."

"So you live alone?"

"I live with Agnes." Mariota reached out a hand to grasp Agnes's own.

On the surface that seemed reasonable, but Llelo had some experience in the world, and he knew better than to make assumptions so early into their conversation. "How was it that your betrothal came about in the first place? And why didn't you marry immediately?"

"I was fifteen when Aelred asked for my hand. My mother accepted, and we would have married right away, but Aelred was in need of a profession so he could support me as his wife. He was already supporting his mother. This was before the accident, of course."

"But why didn't you marry once your own mother died and you went to live with Agnes, since he was apparently supporting you both?"

"He wanted to wait until he was better placed, and even in his less-than-former state, he didn't want to see me saddled with a man who couldn't think. He knew what he'd lost, you see. He said that most of the time his mind was like mush, but there would be moments when he'd be able to push through it to speak and think as he once had. He lived for those moments. Unfortunately, they were few and far between."

Having translated Mariota's words, Dai added softly in Welsh, for Llelo's ears alone, "Gwalchmai would know exactly what he means."

Llelo looked over at his brother. "What—" But then stopped at Dai's rueful look. "His head is still bothering him?"

"Sometimes."

"Why hasn't he said anything?"

"A bard can't decide not to work just because he's feeling under the weather."

Llelo thought back to all of his interactions with Gwalchmai over the last five months, wondering in how many situations he had been suffering in silence, and Llelo had treated him callously.

"He's much better," Dai added. "He would be the first to tell you not to worry about him."

It was too late for that, and Llelo was going to talk to his mother the first chance he got. Though now that he considered the matter, perhaps she already knew.

Hamelin had been listening to all this with a frown, and he put in, "How old are you, Mariota?"

(Dai translated)

"Eighteen."

"How old was Aelred?"

"Twenty-three."

"So you've waited for him for three years?"

Mariota bobbed a nod.

None of this made real sense to Llelo—or rather, it made sense only if one or both of them weren't sincere in their wish to marry, and he couldn't help thinking that was Aelred. Clearly insincerity was a predominant trait in him, and it was hard to reconcile his lack of mental acumen with his courting of three women at the same time. "In Carlisle, you could have found a merchant husband who would have cared for you and your mother."

"I didn't want a merchant husband." Mariota's lips became a thin line. She appeared displeased for the first time about the questions and didn't answer easily. "I loved Aelred."

Even Hamelin understood those words, and he overrode Dai's translation. "But *why*?"

Mariota now looked directly at Hamelin, who was gazing at her. "Have you ever been in love?"

"Once."

"What happened to her?"

"She married another."

"Did she love you?"

"She said she did, but her father would have none of it. I may be the brother to Prince Henry and the son of the Duke of Anjou, but I remain a bastard. It was too much for her father to encompass."

Llelo couldn't help thinking that any father who denied Hamelin his daughter was incredibly short-sighted, but then, Llelo had been born and raised in Wales, where illegitimacy meant nothing as long as a father acknowledged a son, as Hamelin's father had done. Families came in all shapes and sizes.

Mariota's eyes widened. "So you *do* know what it's like."

Hamelin's expression turned puzzled. "Your relationship with Aelred was sanctioned by everyone, though, wasn't it? How could our situations be similar?"

"That isn't what I meant." Mariota gave a shake of her head. "I wasn't kept from my love like you were, never mind that we are both bastards. I meant that you know what it's like to be the center of someone's world. When I was with Aelred, I was the only woman he could see. There was nothing he wouldn't do for me."

Hamelin didn't reply immediately, prompting Llelo to say the one thing he couldn't help adding, "Except marry you."

Dai hesitated before translating, but he translated anyway.

In response, Mariota looked down at her hands where they rested in her lap. "Except for that."

Agnes shook her head. "I find all of this so hard to believe, beginning with that Aelred is dead!"

"If what they are saying about him and these other women is true, Mother," Mariota said, "Aelred was lies from beginning to end this whole time."

27

Day Two

Gareth

ecause she was Welsh and young, Gareth was glad for Bronwen's sake that she was seeing the truth of Aelred before he damaged her forever. More importantly, he was glad that Aelred had died before she'd fallen pregnant. While Bronwen had sworn to Gwen after their conversation with Joanna that Aelred had never touched her, it might have been only a matter of time. Illegitimacy wouldn't have mattered if Bronwen lived in Wales, in terms of the child's own station, but this was Scotland, in a castle ruled by a Scottish king with deep English and Norman roots. The rules of England and Scotland applied to her as long as she lived here.

The fact that Aelred hadn't given any of his women a child appeared to be, in no small part, his only redeeming quality, as well as an indication of the fundamental mercenary nature of his interactions with them. He hadn't desired women physically. He'd just wanted their money. It was hard to see how he could have pursued these women so single-mindedly for so many months if he didn't actually care for them or enjoy their company, but the fact that he took their money and triple-timed them indicated a cold-bloodedness Gareth had rarely encountered before. They would see when Llelo returned with Mariota if this was true of her relationship with Aelred as well.

Gareth was also struggling to reconcile Joanna's account of the man as compared to everyone else. While some of those on duty had clearly had too much to drink last night, in celebration of the return of a few of their number to Carlisle Castle, the information he'd elicited was too consistent to truly question.

To everyone but Joanna, Aelred was the spitting image of Douglas's description: *dumb as a post*. And while not going so far as to call him *sweet* as Bronwen had done, even the men Gareth had interviewed acknowledged that he was never mean. He was just unreliable and thick, to the point of perhaps being touched in the head. The garrison captain confessed that he'd taken on Aelred only because he felt sorry for him, knowing he had a betrothed in his village, and that the king was going to need men to fight his upcoming war. It didn't much matter if a man could think as long as he could hold his ground, spear in hand, and gut any man who came against him, which apparently was the one thing Aelred was capable of doing consistently and with some degree of reliability.

That didn't sound so *sweet* to Gareth, nor simple. But it had at least allowed Aelred a living.

These varying—and yet in many ways entirely consistent—accounts of Aelred were what had brought Gareth to the steward, asking for another audience with the king. If they had been in Wales, Gareth might not have felt the need to keep King Owain quite so apprised of his every move, but he was still feeling his way here in Carlisle. He still wanted to give King David the chance to reconsider his appointment of Gareth as leader of this investigation. Quite honestly, Douglas would have been a perfectly logical replacement.

Thus, with Gareth just behind him, the king's steward opened the door to King David's receiving room and ushered Gareth inside. As Gareth entered, his thoughts were still preoccupied with Aelred, so at first he didn't notice that the other inhabitants of the room consisted of King David, Earl Ranulf, and Godfrid.

"Lord Gareth." King David had been sitting perched on the edge of a table, and now he rose to his feet in a smooth motion. It was almost too smooth, in fact, and he couldn't disguise the momentary flash of irritation at the sight of Gareth and the steward entering the room. "Congratulations again to your son."

"Thank you. It is a great honor for him, for our whole family, and for Gwynedd." Gareth put his heels together and bowed.

As he straightened, he got a glimpse of the king looking daggers at his steward. Again, it was for only a heartbeat, but Gareth had long experience reading people's stances and unvoiced emotions, and the tension in the room was like thick smoke.

A flash of something that looked like anger had crossed Ranulf's face too, before he reverted to his usual discontented self.

In truth, there should have been nothing wrong with these two magnates meeting with Godfrid. As the brother of King Brodar,

Godfrid was representing the throne of Dublin to Scotland and Chester (now that Ranulf was here).

But Gareth couldn't help recalling all the ways Ranulf had betrayed his allies time and again, and he'd conspired more than once with Owain's treacherous brother, Cadwaladr, most recently to overthrow Owain and take over Gwynedd. Gareth couldn't help thinking that the way King David and Ranulf had reacted to his own entrance to the room indicated that a conspiracy of some sort was afoot, regardless of the contents of the treaty that was still in Gareth's pocket.

Godfrid, meanwhile, had risen somewhat laconically to his feet in a manner that belied the concern in his eyes. As he was faced away from Ranulf and David, only Gareth could see it: "Lord Gareth. A pleasure, always."

"Lord prince. I would thank you again, if I haven't said sufficiently, for assisting us in our journey."

"It was my pleasure."

Again, Gareth bowed, which he was quite certain he had not done to Godfrid in many, many years, if ever. The outward display of formality would have been disconcerting if he hadn't known it to be a guise. If any one of them, for any reason, was going to end up a prisoner in Carlisle, as some kind of hostage to their sovereign's good behavior, he could only benefit from the others remaining free.

So Gareth straightened in order to grasp Godfrid's proffered forearm. "Good to see you."

"Likewise." Godfrid's momentary tense expression before he'd smoothed it told Gareth all he needed to know about what was really going on here. Godfrid wanted him to continue to feign aloofness, and he would tell him all about what he'd been doing with David and Ranulf later.

Thus, Gareth endeavored not to twitch an eye, but to simply nod and play his part, whatever that part was meant to be and as if it was the most natural thing in the world for one of his closest friends in life to be pretending otherwise. But although they'd agreed on this ruse in advance, he was unprepared for how awkward it made him. "My apologies. I see you are in conference. I did not know. I will leave you."

"Nonsense." King David spoke as if he meant it. "There is no need for that, is there Prince Godfrid?"

"Not on my end."

"Vincent, you may leave us now." King David directed his words to the steward without looking at him.

His face pale, Vincent backed away before turning to leave and closing the door behind him. He wouldn't have reached his position without being trusted, which only went to show that everybody made mistakes at one time or another, even the steward of a king. Gareth was merely steward to a prince. He had a long way to go, both he and Prince Hywel, before either of them had the power and will of David.

Though, if Gareth were Vincent, he would be wondering if he still held his position after today. In the running of a kingdom, some mistakes could be brushed aside and some were less easily dismissed. It remained to be seen what this one would prove to be. Maybe Gareth was reading too much into a few looks.

But he didn't think so. A kingdom could rise and fall on a few looks.

King David bent his gaze on Gareth. "You have business to discuss, Lord Gareth?"

"It's regarding the death of this soldier, Aelred. I've learned quite a lot in the hours since we last spoke."

A tray with goblets and wine rested at the end of the table. The king reached out a lazy hand for the carafe. It couldn't be often that he served himself, but he did so now, and then poured three more goblets, one for each of them. "Normally I leave such matters to others, but the fact that the corpse was left in the castle's own church—" He broke off with a shudder. "It cannot be tolerated. It has unsettled my people. Regrettably, the knighting of your son was not enough to lift the mood or change the conversation substantially."

Gareth kept his expression serene, again endeavoring not to show that the king's comment had shed new light on the events of the morning. Initially, before the appearance of the body, King David had agreed to Prince Henry's request to honor Llelo and Hamelin because he hadn't seen why he shouldn't. Gareth supposed he shouldn't have been surprised that the king had an ulterior motive for moving forward with it even when circumstances had made it more difficult.

None of this did he say. There was so much left unsaid at the moment that Gareth's stomach was clenched around it. He accepted his goblet of wine from the king with a nod of thanks and then sipped it, endeavoring to mask his uncertainty in favor of a calm matter-of-factness.

Ranulf appeared resigned to Gareth's presence by now and said in an easy voice, "The appearance of this corpse seems even more strange in the light of day, my king, than it did last night."

"It is very strange." The king sat in an ornate chair set diagonal to the table and gestured towards Gareth with his goblet. "Perhaps it would be best if you returned to the beginning, for Godfrid's benefit. Since he's here, we might as well take advantage of whatever insight he may have into these matters."

Godfrid smiled graciously. "I'm always happy to be of service."

Gareth refrained from looking hard at King David for putting the cat among the pigeons—in theory, anyway. They'd had a conversation just last night that implied Gareth did not get along with Godfrid, and now the king was including him wholeheartedly. Gareth couldn't decide if he'd forgotten, was being mischievous, or it was dove-tailing with some as-yet-undisclosed greater plan.

Fortunately, Gareth and Godfrid were not actually at odds, so Gareth happily began again, repeating the information from last night, pretending that Godfrid didn't know all of it already and had actually been the one to discover some of it. For once, at least in terms of the investigation, Gareth had no other agenda other than finding his man. Once again, he elided his close relationship with Godfrid and Conall, implying that what he'd learned in the graveyard and elsewhere was his own discovery. He also didn't mention Godfrid's close relationship with the priest. That was Godfrid's own story to tell—or not—and Godfrid made no attempt to correct the record.

The king's brow was furrowed. "How many men do you believe yourself to be looking for?"

"It's hard to say, my lord. Someone buried the body initially. That man may or may not be the one who unearthed it."

"Or killed Aelred." Godfrid gestured with his goblet in a casual manner, as if discussing the merits of a new horse. It was nice that, by including him in the conversation now, neither of them had to pretend going forward that he didn't know all the details.

"Surely the man who killed him is the same one who buried him!" Ranulf said.

Gareth didn't quite shrug, thinking it might be viewed as rude. "Perhaps, but perhaps not. Aelred was struck on the head, but he could have fallen rather than been pushed."

"And then was buried illicitly by one man and unearthed by another?" King David said. "Why?"

Gareth allowed himself a small smile. "As to motive, it may well involve money and women." And he explained about the three women in Aelred's life and the money he'd borrowed from two of them that they knew of so far.

Ranulf laughed outright. "There's a surprise." He was being facetious.

Gareth managed a laugh too. "We are waiting on the arrival of the third woman, Mariota, to whom everyone agrees Aelred was officially betrothed. Our newly dubbed knights were sent to her village to bring her and Aelred's mother back to Carlisle to identify the body once and for all."

King David had been listening to Gareth's recitation with interest, and now he studied Gareth over his cup. "What can I do?"

"The church's priest asked me to ask you if you would object to burying him in the churchyard. The sooner he returns to the ground, the better everyone might feel. We were thinking sunset would be an appropriate hour to inter him. One of Father Dunstan's parishioners died last night, and she will be buried at the same time."

"Why would I object? He's the victim here, isn't he?"

"So it seems. He *was* a liar, however. Certainly he appears to have multiple women convinced he was their betrothed. He died unshriven."

Ranulf and David exchanged a long look. The look was long enough, in fact, that a sudden cold feeling rose in Gareth's belly that had unclenched a little during his recitation. "My lords? Do either of you know something about this death that you haven't said? I would be grateful to hear it."

Ranulf immediately made a dismissive gesture. "I do not."

King David added smoothly, "Our concerns have to do with the timing of our own endeavors and the way a lack of resolution of this investigation might affect it. As it stands now, we might need to defer our own discussions—" here he made a gesture towards Gareth, "—until tomorrow."

That was an unintended consequence of this investigation, but perhaps not unexpected for all that. There was a great deal going on under the surface at Carlisle about which Gareth was uncertain. At the moment, the only thing he was sure of was that he was merely skating over the top.

"I will tell the priest." Gareth bobbed his head.

As he turned to go, Godfrid said from behind him, still in that somewhat lazy voice. "I should depart as well. My wife is with child, and she has not been well this morning. Yesterday was a very difficult day for her."

"Travel can be a problem for a woman in her condition," Ranulf said sagely.

"I suggested she not travel with me, but we are newly wed, and she has not yet settled comfortably in Dublin. It was better to bring her."

"A happy wife makes for a happy home," King David said.

Ranulf's eyes narrowed. "I had heard it was a happy husband who made a happy home."

"I'm surprised at you, Ranulf." The king laughed. "As Prince Godfrid appears to be aware, anyone who thinks that's the case is doing everything all wrong."

28

Day Two

Godfrid

The two men extricated themselves from the clutches of King David and Earl Ranulf, leaving the room together while attempting—Godfrid hoped successfully—to give the impression that they were doing so only because they'd chosen to leave at the same time and were going in the same direction. Taking long strides, they left the keep, then the inner bailey, and made for the gatehouse that would take them outside the castle entirely. Their upcoming conversation would be best held far from the prying eyes and ears of anyone who wasn't the two of them.

"Do you know already why I was in that room with them when you arrived?" As they wended their way through the city streets, Godfrid decided he needed to speak first.

King David had kept up the traditional role of Carlisle as a royal borough in that it was a market day, where residents of surrounding villages and farms came into the town to sell their wares.

Many here remained English, imported years earlier by King Henry to populate his new holding, but under David they were no longer privileged citizens in the way they had been before.

"While I obviously can't be versed in the specifics, perhaps I can guess at some of them."

"Please guess." It wasn't fair of Godfrid to put his friend on the spot this way. Really, he was the one who'd offended, even if inadvertently, so he should be doing the talking. But he felt somehow that he needed to know the shape of Gareth's heart. If he was angry at Godfrid, or distrustful, this whole matter needed to be approached differently.

"Obviously they wanted something from you—and by *you* I mean Dublin—and have offered you something tantalizing in return. Ranulf might want to use your people to overtake Gwynedd, but I can't see it as being a high priority right now. Besides which, they have Cadwaladr for that." Gareth let out a chuckle that sounded genuinely amused and then nodded as if he was answering a question in his own mind. "They want your men. In the past, Dublin could always be counted on to seek profit above all else, and as payment they are dangling the possibility of helping Dublin overthrow Leinster."

Godfrid laughed. "You're good; really, you are."

"Do you know if they've offered Conall something similar, say help with keeping the High King at bay or maybe overthrowing the O'Connors entirely and putting Diarmait himself on the throne of Ireland?"

"They say not yet and maybe not ever. It probably depends upon whether or not I seem truly amenable to their plans."

"So that's it, then? Men for men?"

Godfrid glanced at his friend. "You've come this far. Can you guess the rest?"

Gareth's eyes narrowed. "I thought there might be a catch to all this. They want a foothold in Ireland, clearly."

"I don't think it's King David, actually. *Ranulf* wants a foothold in Ireland, you mean."

"A third of England isn't enough for him?"

"He has ambition."

"You're not wrong about that." Gareth's walk had slowed as they approached the cathedral precincts. "Is it just because you're here that they decided to stick their fingers in the fire?"

"But I'm not just here, am I? *They* invited *me*. This offer isn't the result of a happy coincidence." Godfrid eyed the gatekeeper, who was watching them. "The salient issue is what they want the men of Dublin *for*."

Gareth stopped walking entirely and turned to him. "Am I wrong? Is it to overthrow King Owain?"

"No, though you're not far off on the source of inspiration. They want us to abduct, and kill if convenient, King Stephen's son Eustace."

Godfrid had genuinely surprised Gareth, which in Godfrid's experience wasn't easy to do.

"And they call *us* barbarians."

"I would have said that epithet has been used more often to refer to Danes than the Welsh."

"Some might become confirmed in their assessment if you do this." Gareth let out a sigh. "I suppose I can't blame them for hoping for it. You did ambush Anarawd for Cadwaladr."

"And profited handsomely from it."

"Only after King Owain made him pay you, of course."

"I had thought of that," Godfrid said in a mild tone. "I brought up with them the fact that, even if we performed this service for them, it still wouldn't guarantee the defeat of King Stephen or King Henry's crowning."

Gareth was thinking hard. "With Ranulf and David, you would have no leverage to ensure payment. I can't see you landing a fleet on one of the western islands like you did on that beach near Aberffraw to force Owain's hand."

"In truth, many of those peoples were ours not so long ago. We might be welcomed." He shook his head. "But we don't actually want a war with Scotland."

"Still, David and Ranulf do hold extensive territories and have many men at their disposal. Payment could be made unconditional and not reliant upon their victory, only yours."

"You sound as if you think we ought to agree to it!"

"I'm thinking you should." Gareth put out a hand. "Not because of the overthrowing Leinster part. That's between you and Brodar. Really, if they want this done, they ought to pay you in silver for your work, not in men, and not have it conditional on their victory at all or on Danish hopes of independence."

Godfrid was gaping at his friend. "What are you saying?" The words came out loud enough that the gatekeeper heard and glanced at them again.

Gareth took his arm and began walking with him around the wall of the monastery towards a lesser gate located on the side. It would be watched too, but not by the same man, who was surely wondering by now what was so important that Gareth and Godfrid had to talk about it in the street rather than coming inside the church precincts.

He ought to know what it should have been about—the death of Aelred—and Godfrid hoped he would assume it, even if he was now very curious as to what new revelation had caused Godfrid to speak so loudly. Truly, he had never been this surprised by a conversation either.

Now Godfrid reduced his tone to a hoarse whisper. "You can't be serious!"

"I'm very serious." Gareth stopped under a tree that grew a few feet from the church wall. He tipped his head towards it, and Godfrid stepped right up to the wall and peered over it.

Then he returned to Gareth, shaking his head. "Nobody is there." Godfrid had to be the one to look, since he was taller than Gareth, who though six feet himself, was not quite tall enough to see over this wall. The church wall within the castle precincts was much lower.

"David and Ranulf have conceived a plan to murder King Stephen's son. They believe that, with Eustace dead, Stephen would have no choice but to acknowledge Henry as his heir. It was one thing for England's barons to support a woman on the throne over Stephen. She was old King Henry's daughter. But these magnates are starting to look at our young Henry as the true heir to the crown. He is named for his grandfather; he is an upright and noble young man—intelligent, capable, and full of fire. Even if they don't want Stephen overthrown, many see the sense in putting Henry on the throne when Stephen is dead."

"Why not just kill Stephen himself?" Godfrid threw up his hands.

"Did you ask them that?"

Godfrid slumped a little. "They said he was too well guarded."

"Stephen's death would just put Eustace on the throne anyway, and then the war would truly be renewed in force, with these two vibrant young men, each with their supporters, at each other's throats. Eustace is definitely the better play."

"How can you even be suggesting that I murder the Prince of England?" Godfrid felt shaken to his core by this conversation, as if his honest and upright companion had been replaced by someone else entirely.

Gareth laughed outright, and Godfrid's blood would have risen if his friend hadn't then immediately explained. "I intend no such thing! Godfrid, I don't want you to agree to this plan so you can murder Eustace. I want you to agree so David and Ranulf don't seek someone else to do their dirty work. I don't want you to abduct Eustace in order to murder him. I want you to abduct him in order to save him."

29

Day Two

Gwen

Gwen shouldn't have been surprised that the afternoon's task of speaking to Aelred's women had fallen to her. At the same time, she was beginning to feel as if she kept ending up with the short end of the stick. Despite the assumptions of the men around her, she didn't know that she was all that much better suited to dealing with the level of emotion in the room than her husband was. She didn't even have Cait with her at the moment, since she was lying down with Gwen's own children for a nap. She did have Dai, who had made himself as small as possible on a stool just behind her, ready to translate as needed.

Since Gareth was having another look at the body with Lachlann, and Godfrid and Conall had set themselves up to observe the comings and goings of Carlisle's inhabitants in the great hall (each on opposite sides of the hall, of course, as if they didn't like each other), they had the guesthouse common room at the cathedral monastery to themselves. Gwen had decided it was a better place to meet than anywhere in the castle or, heaven forbid, the church where Aelred had been found. Anyway, even now Aelred's mother, Agnes, was being cared for there by Father Dunstan. She had taken one look at the body and turned away. Gwen wouldn't have had her see the body at all, but she'd insisted, and Gwen herself had been in no position to gainsay a grieving mother.

Agnes hadn't come apart so much as become quiet and pale. And then determined. She and the priest were sorting out the funeral arrangements, such as they were. And then her intent was to remain the rest of the day in the church, praying for Aelred's soul.

That was fine by Gwen. The more she listened to these women talk, the more she despaired at the depths of human greed and willingness to deceive others in the pursuit of it. Having Aelred's poor mother a part of that would just have made it worse.

Maybe there was irony in that. Although Gwen dealt often in murder, certainly the basest of actions, the damage Aelred had inflicted on these women—damage they might not be recovering from any time soon—hurt her too. And made her grateful all the more for her loving husband and children. They had their problems, and who was to say if one could ever truly know what was in another person's heart, but the depths of hell to which Aelred had been willing to descend in order to deceive people he supposedly loved appeared to Gwen more trouble than it could possibly have been worth. She could marvel at the effort involved, even as she despised him for it, never mind that he was dead.

At least the women weren't fighting among themselves anymore. They had spent the last quarter of an hour talking quietly to each other, almost reminiscing about him as if they were at a wake. By now, they'd had some hours to adjust to their new reality, even Mariota. It was she, in fact, who seemed the most accepting of Aelred's death.

During a lull in the conversation, Gwen risked a small intervention. It was fine if they wanted to talk, and she was happy to listen, but she had a few, specific questions that needed answers. "Just to clarify, Joanna, you did not know about either Bronwen or Mariota?"

Joanna shook her head. "I did not."

"You didn't even suspect?"

"No."

"Still, you knew Bronwen to talk to?"

"Yes."

"But neither of you ever discussed the man you loved and learned he was one and the same man?"

"I didn't discuss Aelred with anyone but Jonet," Bronwen said before Joanna could answer.

"He asked me not to," Joanna added. "I told you that."

"You did, and I'm sorry to bring it up again," Gwen said, "but I am still trying to understand how Aelred could have kept this great a secret from everyone—from all of you—in any community, even one as large as Carlisle."

Bronwen's expression turned a bit fierce. "I'm not a fool. I knew about Mariota. Who didn't?" She shot Joanna a searing look, as if daring her to justify her ignorance.

Gwen put out a hand, ready to stop her from rising to her old form, but Joanna didn't reply with anger. Instead, her shoulders sagged. "I should have known that someone like Aelred could never be interested in me, but all I could think about was my good fortune in finding someone to love."

Gwen looked at her curiously. Joanna was a lovely woman, and while she was almost thirty, she was nowhere near past her child bearing years. "I'm sorry to ask about what may be a sensitive topic, but had you never had suitors before?"

"I did." She made a waggling motion with her head. "Of course I did. My father is well off, and I am not unattractive."

Here Bronwen pulled a face, prompting Gwen to shoot her a hard look. She subsided.

Joanna shrugged. "All of them were more interested in my money than in me. It took me some time to discover this, of course, being young myself. My father had the full use of his faculties then, and he explained to me what was happening in no uncertain terms. It was he who refused the first of them." She sighed. "As time went on, I began to see that all of them were either young and spoiled or old and grasping, and I would be better off without any husband than with any of them. Besides, I was happy."

Bronwen made to scoff again, but stopped herself before Gwen had to.

Joanna dabbed her cheek to sop up an errant tear. "For ten years or more I was content to run my father's shop. And then I met him."

"Aelred," Gwen said.

"Yes. He was sunshine in a world I hadn't known was gray."

This time Bronwen didn't object, just said softly. "I felt the same." Then she canted her head. "But the way you speak of him is so unlike the Aelred I knew. Are you certain we are talking about the same person?" As the idea rose in her mind, she straightened in her seat, her eyes on Gwen. "Maybe we are not! My Aelred was sweet and simple. You speak of yours as if he were the cleverest man you knew. That just isn't possible."

The issue had been on Gwen's mind for some time. Once all the women had looked at the body, however, she'd had to put it aside, especially once they heard about Aelred's accident from Llelo and Dai. That said, if the crack in his skull was from the old injury, the cause of death was back in doubt.

Within moments of his return to Carlisle, Llelo had pulled her aside, anxiety in his face, to tell her Dai's news about Gwalchmai, Gwen's own brother, who had been suffering ever since he'd been coshed on the head back in December. Gwen had known something was amiss with Gwalchmai, to the point of speaking to her father about it. He'd noticed the changes too. But from what Dai reported, their mutual plan to let him be and not expect too much from him might actually have been the right one.

By that light, perhaps Aelred too had slowly recovered over time. But everyone had been so fixed in their opinion of him that only Joanna had been able to see the improvement.

"He *was* the cleverest man I ever met." Joanna looked around at the other women, bewilderment in her face. "How could you not know it?"

Out of the blue, Mariota gave a loud snort.

"Mariota, do you have something to say?" Gwen asked.

Mariota's eyes were on her hands, which were folded in her lap. She looked at them for so long, in fact, in contrast to her very obvious snort of derision, that Gwen was afraid she was about to start weeping. So far, she had been the most composed of all of them.

Then she looked up.

Suddenly, her face transformed from that of the demure woman they'd seen so far to someone entirely different. Or some-*thing* even. Her eyes blazed, not with anger but with what appeared to be triumph. "He told me everything. I knew about the shopkeeper." She snorted now in Joanna's direction and then turned her attention to Bronwen. "And the ----"

Up until now, Dai had been translating the Gaelic the women were speaking, since it was a language Gwen understood poorly. But the word Mariota had thrown at Bronwen—so forcefully it had to be an invective or a curse—had sounded like *cwddiss*, followed by what Gwen could only describe as a sneeze. Her limited understanding of the language had the first part as *sheep*.

Gwen glanced at Dai, who was frowning. "I'm sorry, Mam. I don't know that word."

"We can guess, though, can't we?"

And the guess was further confirmed by the fact that it prompted Bronwen to surge to her feet, angrier than ever before, which was saying something. "You *bitch*!"

Mariota laughed, not offended and reveling in the other woman's anger. "You are all such fools. Aelred didn't love you. He never loved anyone but me. Why did you think he told me about you?"

In keeping with their previous tendencies, Bronwen's ire was practically exploding out of her ears while Joanna merely looked sad. Dai, fortunately, knew enough to stay still on his stool and simply keep translating.

"Why?" Gwen, on the other hand, was more curious than ever.

At first impression, Mariota was one of the most beautiful women Gwen had ever seen—and Gwen was friends with Godfrid's wife, Cait. But as Mariota's mouth twisted up and her eyes narrowed, she resembled less an angel and much more the *Gwiddonod*, the grey witches of Welsh legend, who cast spells over people and animals. Here was the true Mariota.

"Why?" In Mariota's mouth, the word was transformed into a cackle. "Neither Aelred nor I was content with our station, and why should we be, born as we were with no family, no trade, no wealth?"

"So you conspired together to do ... what, exactly?" Gwen said. "Fleece as many women as Aelred could seduce into giving him money?"

Mariota shrugged. "That and other things."

"What other things?" Gwen was determined to keep Mariota talking until she pried the whole story out of her.

"It started after he hit his head. In a single instant, he went from being the cleverest man in the village to a complete dolt. It was beyond bearing, really. The worst of it was that he knew he couldn't think, but he couldn't push past the pea soup that his mind had become. People would look to him, expecting intelligent thoughts and clever phrases to come out of his mouth, and he had nothing to give them."

"What did you think at the time?"

"I was worried about him. Of course, I was. And I knew I couldn't stay with a man who wasn't going anywhere and would never do anything interesting again. That would be absurd." She snorted for perhaps the tenth time since she'd started talking.

"But you didn't leave him?"

"No." Another snort.

Gwen was already tired of this new incarnation of Mariota. It was just too bad that so far she hadn't confessed to anything that might warrant overt sanction on the part of anyone in authority.

"It was too soon to tell what he was going to be like down the road, and it was worth it to me to put up with his near-idiocy if he would eventually recover his senses."

"Which you're telling us he did?" Gwen spoke mostly to keep Mariota talking.

"The first level of dimness lasted a good week, and then his mind began to work again." She gave her head a shake. "In that week, he realized that people had already begun to treat him differently. He had always been the one to do the sums, to keep the accounts, to read the letters—everything that the village required, really. He would get a few coins for it in most cases, but it wasn't a princely amount by any means. All that stopped during that week, and he knew all of a sudden what it was like to be a fool."

"But instead of resuming his former status, he decided to continue as if he hadn't recovered?" This was from Bronwen, who was staring at Mariota as if she'd grown an extra head.

Mariota tossed her hair. "I admit I was initially skeptical when he told me about the possibilities for deception. But then he continued to pretend, deceiving the entire village, including his own mother. Nobody looked at him twice. It was as if he wasn't there at all." Mariota smiled in satisfaction. "You have no idea where an invisible man can go, what he can see, how he can make his fortune."

"We truly don't," Gwen said. "If you would tell us—"

Mariota cut her off. "People paid to keep their secrets. And it occurred to nobody that the quiet voice in the dark demanding payment might be poor, stupid Aelred."

She was describing blackmail, an unsuspected aspect of this investigation before now. Suddenly, as a motive for murder, it had leapt to the front of the line. The length and breadth of the scheme took Gwen's breath away, and she suspected they hadn't learned the whole of it yet.

Mariota smiled beatifically, a sharp contrast to the evilness of her words. "Did or did not the village headman say Aelred was touched in the head?"

"He did," Dai translated and then answered for Gwen.

Mariota looked at Bronwen. "You thought so too."

"He was sweet—"

"He was a sweet fool. You knew it, and you loved him for it. He never asked anything of you but your love ... until he asked for your money."

Bronwen's face was pale against her dark hair. "Yes."

"And you—" Mariota swung around to look at Joanna. "You would not have loved a fool, but you also were more inclined than Bronwen to keep your relationship with Aelred a secret. You liked that it was secret. With you, he could be more himself. And then you gave him money too."

Like Bronwen and Gwen, Joanna had listened to Mariota's recitation of her crimes and deception with an open mouth. "Yes."

In all the years of investigating murder for Prince Hywel, Gwen had never heard of anything like this. "Does Agnes know?"

"Don't be ridiculous." Mariota gave one last snort.

"What was the overall plan?" It was time to bring the conversation back to specifics. "We know he never intended to march to Worcester, since he had arranged for a letter to be delivered to Joanna and tokens to Bronwen. What was supposed to happen that didn't because he died?"

For the first time, Mariota looked pensive. "You're right that the plan was never for him to march to Worcester. Instead, he was going to leave the castle the night before, and either that night or the next, he would come for me, and we would leave forever."

"But he didn't come." That was actually straight from Dai, who made the comment unprompted in the moments after translating Mariota's story.

"The first night, I didn't worry. And then I didn't worry again because the king's messenger, that Brian MacGregor, pulled me aside when the army marched through the village the next day and told me not to worry, that all was well. He showed me the tokens Aelred had arranged for Brian to bring back to Joanna and Bronwen. Then a month later, Brian brought a letter from Aelred telling *me* he was arranging a place for us in Newcastle and would come to fetch me soon." Her brow furrowed now. "But how could he have written that letter if he was already dead?"

This was a different Mariota yet again, younger and less confident. It was occurring to her only now that Aelred had intended to betray her too.

None of the other women helped her along her journey. Gwen still wasn't quite sure she was all there yet, even as Mariota put a finger to her chin and asked, "What I am also wondering is why there are only three of us here."

Joanna managed to speak first. "What do you mean by *only three of us?* Is someone missing?"

Mariota spread her hands wide. "Last time we spoke, months ago now, of course, Aelred came to me all excited. It was shortly before he was due to depart from Carlisle. He told me he'd found another—" She stopped and frowned. "That's all he said: *another.* I always assumed he meant a woman, but now I'm wondering if maybe the person was a man."

"What are you talking about?" Gwen was hesitant to even voice the question.

"I don't know why he wouldn't tell me who it was, but he was very excited not to have to feign affection this time or threaten anyone." Mariota shrugged elaborately. "This particular fool simply wanted to invest in his venture."

30

Day Two

Llelo

Llelo stared down at Aelred's body. He'd been left to his own devices for the first time since they'd arrived at Carlisle, and he supposed it could be viewed as odd that this is what he'd chosen to do with his time. He was a knight!

He could hear the squires practicing in the yard. Hamelin had graduated to overseeing them, and he'd invited Llelo to stand beside him as an equal. Llelo himself could perhaps have used a little practice with his sword.

But he'd turned him down, politely, of course, and with regret.

He'd done so in order to examine Aelred's body. The women were coming in a moment to wash and prepare him for burial, so Llelo was running out of time to pinpoint what had been bothering him about it. He held up his father's sketch, which instantly brought to life the scene in the church. In so doing, Llelo realized in a sudden flash of insight what had bothered him about Aelred from the start: the body was very dirty.

"What are you doing?" Prince Henry spoke from the step outside the door. "I thought your father had already done that."

"He has. He did. But—" Llelo broke off, a little intimidated to have Prince Henry asking questions that he himself didn't have answers to. He knew only that he had to ask them.

"But what?"

"I needed to look again."

"Why?"

There was no getting away from the prince. He had been enthusiastic about investigating the murder that first evening, and Hamelin had taken part in it today, but the prince himself had been busy with matters of state that demanded his attention—not to mention sleeping and eating to make up for the night he'd spent in the cathedral before his own knighting.

Endeavoring not to sigh, Llelo handed the prince his father's sketch.

"This is very good!" The prince looked up from his perusal. "Is it yours?"

"My father did it."

"Ah yes. I remember. But why are you giving it to me?"

"It isn't so much what you see there specifically, though my father did a wonderful job rendering the scene, it is what I'm reminded of when I look at it."

"Which is what?"

"How dirty the body was. Everyone has commented on the fact that the person who put the body in the priest's chair brushed the dirt off his face, but nobody has thought about the fact that it was dirty in the first place.

Prince Henry gave a little laugh. "It was buried in the ground. It's to be expected."

"That's just it, my lord. I don't think it is."

Prince Henry looked from the sketch to the body and then back to Llelo's face. "Why do you say that?"

"Maybe I'm imagining what isn't there, but I can't get past the fact that, while we unearthed the cloth in which we think Aelred was wrapped, when he came out of the grave, he wasn't still wrapped *in it.*"

It wasn't an obvious conclusion, he knew, which was why he hadn't said anything about it up until now.

Prince Henry didn't seem to think it was obvious either because his eyes narrowed. "Of course the man had to have been wrapped in it when he was put in the ground, else why would it have been in the grave in the first place?"

"Thus, my point. But *there* was the cloth. *There* was the body. Why wasn't he still wrapped in it when he came out of the ground?"

"Maybe he was."

Llelo shook his head. He'd seen many burials, and he'd also been present on a few occasions when a body had been disinterred. Sometimes the wrappings decayed along with the body. That wasn't true in this case.

He motioned the prince closer. "Although Aelred hadn't been buried long enough for anything but the body itself to decay, dirt is so embedded in Aelred's clothing and skin that it might not come out even after a hundred washings. It's also impossible to separate the dirt from the waxy substance that coats his body on the skin that's exposed, like his face and hands."

"So the question you're asking is: if the person who unearthed Aelred's body unwrapped it before taking it into the church, why is the body dirty?" Prince Henry said.

"Yes."

"Well ... maybe he wasn't wrapped in the cloth."

"Then why is it in the grave?"

"It has blood on it. Burying it with the body was an easy way to hide the evidence of cleaning the church."

Some of Llelo's fears eased as Henry rationalized them away.

"Your father told us the gesture of cleaning the corpse's face was a sign of respect and an indication that the person who'd buried the body and the one who unearthed him were not one and the same."

"We still think that has to be the case."

"So maybe all is as it seems."

"Maybe. And when you say it like that, it seems perfectly reasonable, especially given the oddness—utter madness, really—of this investigation. When we catch this fiend, we can ask him." Llelo sighed. "But what if my alternate explanation is the correct one? Maybe I'm reading too much into this. It's possible my imagination has run away with me, but what if the one who buried him *did* wrap him in the cloth?"

Prince Henry frowned, prompting Llelo to explain further:

"Aelred has dirt under his fingernails, the few that remained attached anyway."

"You can't be saying—"

Perhaps it wasn't courteous to a prince, but Llelo interrupted him. "According to everyone who knew him, even before his accident, Aelred was never one to do hard labor. He was fastidious, to use the sophisticated word of the village headman. His fingernails would always be clean."

Prince Henry was still frowning, so Llelo finished the thought. "I can't get out of my head the idea that it was Aelred himself who pulled aside the cloth that wrapped him.

"I thought nobody could survive a wound like his," Henry said.

"But Aelred did—at least the first time." Llelo moved to the end of the table on which Aelred's body lay and showed the prince the corpse's injury, at which he himself hadn't looked closely until just before Prince Henry had come in. "My father should be here too to look again. I am not the expert he is, but it seems to me that the cracks look this way because they occurred before he died—long before. If they were as fresh as we had initially thought, from only moments before Aelred died, the edges would be sharper. But do you see how they're filled in, like when my father rubs his fingers along a line drawn in charcoal in one of his sketches?" At Prince Henry's nod,

Llelo continued, "The wound may very well be far older than we thought. A year older, in fact."

Prince Henry gazed first at Aelred's head and then at Llelo. "You think this damage is from when he was hurt in his village a year ago?"

"It would make sense, given the severity of the injury. If that's the case, this is not the wound that killed him three months ago."

"I am still confused, then. There was blood on the cloth."

"I'm not doubting that the blood came from Aelred. But what if he was felled this time by a lesser blow that merely knocked him out for a while, but was made much worse by the underlying injury?" It was Gwalchmai's experience with being bashed on the head that had put this thought in Llelo's mind and kept him from taking the nap he desperately needed. "What if Aelred didn't die in the church at all? What if he was unconscious when he went into his grave? *What if Aelred was actually buried alive?*"

31

Day Two

Conall

King David gestured graciously to Conall that he should enter the mews, a stone building built into a portion of the new curtain wall in the outer bailey. As Conall watched, the king's falconer carefully set one of the falcons, a smaller one, obviously a juvenile, on the perch near the king.

King David stroked the bird's feathers. "If he is to be trained and work for me, then I need to be the one to feed him."

"Of course." Conall fully entered the room, noting the high ceiling—higher than perhaps would be normal—to accommodate the birds' need to flap their wings, even while constrained to their perches by leashes.

"Do you have falconry where you come from?" King David fed the bird a dead mouse, which it consumed in a single swallow.

"Yes, my lord. My uncle is a great hunter." He tried not to be offended at the surprised look on King David's face that Diarmait was a connoisseur of the sport of kings.

As David smoothed the feathers on his falcon's head, Conall waited to be told why he was here. He would have much preferred not to be. His friends would be meeting in the guesthouse common room soon, and he wanted to be with them when they did. He had the sense, however, that if he gave any sign that he had somewhere else to be, the king would keep him longer, just because he could. Or maybe he would dismiss him, thinking better of what he had to say. Either way, Conall saw the merit in cultivating patience.

It wasn't as if the entire day so far hadn't been a pointless waste of time. Maybe they were wrong about something untoward going on at Carlisle Castle. Maybe their subterfuge about what close friends he, Godfrid, and Gareth were was unnecessary. He'd just spent a fruitless few hours in the hall separated from Godfrid, who would have made the time pass much more pleasantly. As it was, in the brief moments they'd been able to speak together, Godfrid had said that he had something important to tell him.

Conall had a feeling that something had to do with why King David had summoned him now.

Fortunately, the king didn't make him wait. With a wave of his hand, he sent the falconer away so he and Conall were alone. "You have spent many months in Gwynedd, Lord Conall. I would know what you make of King Owain's resolve."

Of all the things Conall expected David to ask him, this hadn't even been on the list. He'd assumed their interactions would have had to do with Leinster, some ploy to get Diarmait to allow Normans on his lands. If it ever happened, it would be over Conall's strong objections and maybe his dead body.

"His resolve, my lord?"

David made an impatient gesture. "Is he committed to this alliance?"

"He took back Cadwaladr, didn't he?" Conall had answered a question with a question, which was an indication he was stalling. He wondered if the king knew it.

King David gave him a small smile. "He caused that much trouble?"

"Cadwaladr did. He does." Conall focused a little more intently on the king's face. "His actions led to the death of King Owain's son and heir, Rhun."

David grunted. "I understood that to be an accident."

"Is that what Cadwaladr said?"

It was another question, but this time the king merely moved on. "I am concerned about his desire for independence."

Conall had no idea what was happening here, but he kept answering the best way he knew how, taking the *his* in the king's sentence to mean Owain not Cadwaladr. "Owain is a king. All kings want independence." And then he added, in something of a gentle voice. "As I'm sure you know."

David barked a laugh. "You have me there." There was a pause, and then he spoke more softly too. "I am concerned about my nephew's desire for this alliance between us and Owain Gwynedd. Henry wants it a little too much."

Conall was trying to breathe evenly. "Why do you think that is?"

"It's this Gareth. He admires him—a little too much too."

"Gareth appears to be, on the whole, an admirable man. He has earned some acclaim in his own country."

"And in this one." David was watching the falcon instead of Conall, stroking its head. It seemed content with the attention. "Wales will be a thorn in Henry's side from the moment he takes the throne. He does not believe it now. He thinks that this alliance with Owain will keep the Welsh kingdoms at bay. He is wrong." David swung his head around to look directly at Conall. "Do you agree?"

Conall gazed steadily back. *This* new turn to the conversation was more familiar. He couldn't have been a diplomat for as many years as he had without knowing how to answer difficult questions. "I do. Owain will honor the treaty for only as long as it benefits Gwynedd."

"And after that?"

"Gwynedd is not the only kingdom in Wales, and Owain not the only king." Conall gave a little tsk. "Certainly Cadwaladr is no true ally to you or Ranulf any more than he is to Owain."

David was watching the hawk again and didn't reply immediately. Conall sensed he had only confirmed his suspicions. In truth, Conall could do nothing else.

"Do you trust him?"

"Owain?" Conall said the name and then continued without waiting for an affirming nod or shake of the head on David's part, "Kings are not to trust or distrust. He is effective."

"High praise indeed." David didn't challenge Conall's assessment, just nodded in a way that might have been a dismissal. "You will sit with us at the funeral mass? I have asked Gareth and Godfrid as well."

"Of course, my lord. It will be my honor." Conall couldn't escape quickly enough. As he walked away, he gave a sigh of relief to think himself mostly intact. That last question, *do you trust him,* had been treacherous indeed, spoken casually but with an intensity not accorded any of the others. It was in Conall's mind that *it* had been the real reason David had called Conall to him in the falconry.

Do you trust him?

Conall had spoken of Owain, but he was quite certain that David had really been asking about Gareth.

32

Day Two

Gwen

Late in the afternoon, Gwen's family and extended family gathered around the table in the guesthouse common room. These people had assembled in this manner, whether in a monastery or a castle, more times than she could count. And here they were again, in the midst of an investigation unlike any they'd encountered before. Every death was different, of course, but very often the motives for murder, if that's what this was, remained the same: greed, love, fear. Which of those described this death—or if, for once, it was about something different—had yet to be determined.

To attempt to determine it was, in fact, why they were here—that and to look ahead to what came next.

So everyone in turn laid out what they had specifically been party to learning, from the events of yesterday once Aelred's body had been discovered, to Gwen's conversations with the three women, to Llelo's latest thoughts. Llelo even recounted his experience in the chapel with the illicit couple, one of whom appeared to be Margaret, a suspicion Llelo now confessed to the others for the first time. He'd already told his parents. None of them could see how her infidelity was related, but they also didn't want to leave anything out.

"The questions before us that we must answer, then," Gareth said, "are multifold: first, *why was Aelred killed?*"

"Because he was a bad person," Dai said instantly. "I'm not saying he deserved what he got, but he was a grifter, and he came to a bad end because of it."

It was one answer, and not one that any of them were going to argue with.

"All right, then," Gwen said, "*how* was he killed?"

"Llelo had me reexamine Aelred's head," Gareth said, "and I think he is right in his observations. The bones of his skull show evidence of healing. With what we know now, it's very likely that he incurred that wound a year ago, when he was struck on the head by a beam at his village's barn raising."

Cait bit her lip. "So how did he actually die?"

"That is another good question," Llelo said softly.

"Which brings us to the person who can answer it." Conall's chin was on his fist. "That person being the one who buried him."

"Why did he die? Who buried him? Why was he unburied?" Godfrid was grumbling now. "We are no closer to any of those answers than when we started!"

"We are closer," Llelo said. "Dai has an idea. More than any of us, except perhaps for Mam, I think he has been witness to the conversations that have brought us to this point."

Gwen made a motion with her head. "Somewhat unusually, I have talked only to women. I have a few pieces of the puzzle. I'm happy to have Dai begin."

"It's as if we have before us the carved figures from a chess set," Dai began. "Here is Aelred. Here are Mariota, Bronwen, and Joanna. Here's the priest. We have a shadowy figure of the one who buried him and the one who left him in the church. We have Margaret who found him and Lord Douglas who was Aelred's commander and Brian MacGregor who brought messages from him after he was dead, though he claims not to have known that at the time. We have his fellow soldiers, the pawns, let's say, who move around the board—or rather, the castle—without seeing anything amiss. We have those he blackmailed, however many they may be. Everyone has a place on the board, but it's as if we have come into the game in the middle, with nobody standing in their usual spot and only Aelred knocked off the board."

Dai stopped, and at the silence that greeted this introduction, turned red. "Or, at least that's how I see it."

Gareth was the first to speak. "That's an excellent way to think about it, Dai. We are all silent because we are so impressed."

"Now you're teasing me."

"We aren't." Gwen leaned forward to put her hand on top of her son's where it rested on the table. "Your father is being serious."

As the younger of the brothers, Dai had in the past been more outgoing and light-hearted than Llelo. Gwen was happy to see his cheerful self again, since she realized now that he'd been far more serious of late, and maybe all the way since last summer when he'd been held captive in Ireland and could have died. All the better to see his improved mood today, given Llelo's elevation to knighthood.

As heads nodded around the table, Dai colored even more.

"Who are we on this board?" Godfrid's brow was furrowed. "Not the king."

"Maybe the queen," Dai said, "but even more, we want to be the ones playing the game, and maybe the only ones who know that a game is even *being* played."

Gareth rested his back against the wall behind him. "You think we should be the one to move the pieces about."

"If we can."

"Who do you want to move first?" Cait asked.

Dai answered immediately. "It should be Aelred's other fool, the one Mariota claimed he'd acquired."

Godfrid made a grumbling sound. "If you ask me, it's Aelred who was the fool, not those who cared for him."

Gwen had been thinking much the same thing all along. "And after that, the person who left the body in the church, if the two are not one and the same."

"A woman did not unbury that body," Godfrid said, "I don't care how strong she is. She didn't dig up a dead man and carry him into the church." He stretched his arm around Cait. "Not even my beloved wife would do such a thing."

Cait turned to him, both puzzled and laughing at the same time. "What are you talking about?"

He made a gesture with one hand. "Back when we first discovered the body, I said that a woman couldn't have buried him. After some reflection, we decided that a determined woman—like you, for example—could have done it if she'd had to. But I'd be hard-pressed to find a scenario where anyone *had* to unbury a body. A three-month old corpse doesn't engender the same degree of desperation."

Cait shook her head, still laughing. "Yes, husband. Whatever you say." She patted his knee.

Gwen looked around at everyone's faces, all of which showed some degree of contemplation, but no real disagreement. "I have been wondering why this other person, this *fool*, as Mariota said, has been keeping silent all this time, and I think I understand, at least a little bit. He or she is possibly embarrassed, potentially grieving if it's a she and she loved him as these other women did, as well as angry. But as to the one who unearthed him? Leaving the body in the church sends a very specific message—to someone. The question remains *to whom?* And why not simply speak out?"

"Because he fears speaking." Cait said. "No matter his station, whether high or low, he will be censured for not speaking up sooner. And if he's the one who buried Aelred, then either he killed him or he has known about his death for months and said nothing."

Conall nodded approvingly at his sister. "If he came upon him dead in the graveyard, he would have been in no way culpable. He could have simply sounded the alarm."

"Unless he wasn't supposed to be there in that hour," Cait said. "Unless he was doing something he shouldn't have been doing."

Gwen sighed. "Part of me still wonders if the body is indeed that of Aelred, and that the one who unearthed it and left it in the church is Aelred himself. But we seem to have arrived at the conclusion that the body really is his."

"If we can be sure of anything, we can be sure of that." Gareth said.

"Then I had another thought, one we haven't discussed because I know you don't like to think your reputation precedes you, though it obviously does."

Gareth's arms were folded across his chest as he looked at her, probably knowing already what she was going to say.

She gave him a rueful smile. "Several times before, when we traveled outside of Wales, we walked into an investigation that turned out to be a much greater conspiracy than we immediately supposed. More than once, our arrival was actually an instigating force. I just have to wonder if the way the body was displayed has nothing to do with anyone here at the castle. It might be, rather, that someone—whether the murderer himself, for reasons I couldn't say, or someone who wanted to expose the death—knew you were coming and decided to place the body in your path."

33

Day Two

Conall

Gareth rolled his eyes. "If you're right, Gwen, then we have multiple culprits, perhaps not all of them villains, working at cross-purposes."

"Where have we seen that before?" Conall liked sitting around the table with his friends almost more than he was willing to admit. He'd *missed* this and hadn't known it. Their last investigation had been half a year ago, and that one, while revelatory in the end, had been somewhat disappointing. The only death had been that of a dog, and one of the primary culprits had been one of the women he'd admired most in the world.

He still admired Queen Susanna. He'd just put away the torch he'd been carrying for her all these years. *That* was something he didn't want to think about anymore. Missing bodies, betrayed women, and stolen money was much more to his liking.

"We've seen it in lots of places," Godfrid agreed, "and I'm not sure how it helps us in this moment. We need to expose this last person who gave Aelred money, who clearly doesn't want to be exposed. So how do we do it?"

Dai lifted a hand, more relaxed and confident than Conall had seen him in a long while. "Our best bet, to my mind, is to follow the money."

Conall leaned forward. "What do you mean by that, son?"

"We know that Aelred borrowed money from Joanna and Bronwen. He was also a blackmailer. Who knows what other schemes he was carrying out in the dark. Mariota was happily supportive of everything he did, but since she had no money of her own, it doesn't seem that he took any from her. To the contrary, he was supporting her and his mother. So, *what happened to the money?* Aelred is dead. Where is the money he took from everyone?"

The others eased back from the table. While Conall himself had witnessed Joanna going through Aelred's things, and Gwen had told him Bronwen had done the same, up until now, none of them had been thinking about the money beyond the fact that Aelred had taken it from these women.

"Was no money found among his things, either at home or at the barracks?" Conall asked.

Gareth gave a slow shake of his head. "Not that we've heard."

"So what does the board look like now?" Conall asked. "Where's the money? He couldn't already have paid off the tavernkeeper in Worcester, if that was ever his plan, not with dying when he did."

"I agree it's unlikely—unless the man came to Carlisle to receive it?" Gwen said.

"More likely that scheme was just what he said to Joanna to get her to give him money," Conall said.

"I think we can pretty much guarantee he wasn't planning to become a trader either," Gareth added.

Llelo's brow furrowed. "How does a man make money without working for it? A sack of coins is all very well and good. I wouldn't say no to it. But it is merely that: a sack of coins. It makes a man temporarily rich, but it will eventually be spent, won't it?"

"In order to become truly wealthy, a man has to spend his money on something that will make him more money," Conall said.

Gareth nodded. "I am learning that lesson as steward to Prince Hywel. For example, if he cares for his tenants, they work harder in the fields, produce more crops and herds, and then he has more money to reinvest."

"So what was Aelred investing in if not ale or a wagon?" Dai asked.

Silence fell around the table, into which Conall spoke again. "There's another way to make money, far more risky of course, but one that any lord knows well."

They all turned to look at him, at which point Conall shrugged. "Two ways, actually, but they both amount to the same thing: investing in someone's else's venture, which appears to be exactly what Bronwen and Joanna thought they were doing—or outright gambling."

Gwen wrinkled her nose. "So the money could be gone. Whether lost quickly or slowly, it just could be plain gone."

"Yes." Conall was genuinely sorry to say so. "I don't care how clever Aelred supposedly was. Ventures are ventures because they're risky. And gambling is for fools."

"Told you he was the fool," Godfrid said, again under his breath.

"Except," Gareth chose to ignore the mumbling, "Aelred might not have had time to spend or gamble all of his money away—and he did end up dead, remember? Bronwen and Joanna both say they gave him their contributions within days of his death and supposed departure for Worcester. What if he was meeting the person to whom he was entrusting his money—"

"—or the person to whom he owed money," Conall said.

"Or blackmailing yet another person for money," Gwen added. "He could have met more than just Brian MacGregor in that graveyard."

"That person then killed him and buried the body to hide what he'd done." Conall sat back in his seat. "I like it."

"So how do we find the money?" Llelo asked. "If the killer took it, it's as good as gone."

Cait stood abruptly. "I will go to the inn to speak to Mariota right now. If she knows something about it, I will discover it."

King David had arranged for overnight lodging for Mariota, her mother, and Lachlann at a nearby inn.

Gwen looked up at her. "If she will tell you the truth."

"She will."

Conall knew his sister, and he could see that she had taken Mariota's deception and mockery of Aelred's other women as something of a personal affront. He sometimes forgot that her first husband had not been an honest man and had consorted with other women while married to her. Although her embarrassment at being displaced had eventually turned to relief, she was the only one among them who had personal experience with a man such as Aelred.

"I will come with you." Godfrid stood too.

Cait grinned at him. "You can be appropriately menacing when you wish, my love, but if you come, I want to hold you in reserve."

With Godfrid and Cait gone, Dai turned to the remaining companions. "I want to find the killer, but that may not be the same thing as finding the *fool* who gave Aelred money. That person is going to want it back, don't you think, now that Aelred's dead? Knowing the identity of that person could go a long way towards discovering what happened when Aelred died."

Conall's eyes lit. "We must set and spring a trap!"

Gareth laughed. "You are possibly enjoying yourself far too much."

Conall couldn't help smiling. "Mock all you like, but I know exactly what trap to set, where to set it, and when we need to do it." He looked at Dai, whose idea this all had been. "It's time to move the pieces on the board."

34

Day Two

Cait

Although Gwen's description of the way Mariota had transformed from a sweet young thing to a scheming vixen was perfectly credible, Cait had volunteered for this duty in part because she wanted to see it for herself. Her own failed first marriage had ended childless with the death of her husband, making her first impulse to sympathize with Mariota's plight. Before Mariota had confessed her role in Aelred's schemes, she'd been the wronged woman in this, more than any of the others.

And while Aelred had been toying with the affections of Bronwen and Joanna, it did seem he was less a womanizer than someone who always intended to fleece them for money. Mariota and Aelred had been betrothed before the accident. Part of Cait still wanted to give her the benefit of the doubt, and to see this new incarnation of her as an aberration. Maybe when she came to her senses she would return to her former self.

Or not.

As Cait and Godfrid approached the inn, they could hear shouts coming from the yard behind it. The front door of the inn was on the street, but a side gate led to the rear, and they passed through it to find Agnes and Mariota standing with their village headman, Lachlann, screaming at each other. Or rather, Mariota was screaming at Agnes, who was cowering before her.

"I don't understand." Agnes shook her head repeatedly.

Godfrid reached the two women in a matter of strides, getting between them and speaking to them in Gaelic. "Stop this at once." It was Irish Gaelic, but he'd been in Scotland just long enough to bend his ear to the Scottish way of speaking, which, as Dai had earnestly explained earlier in the day to Cait, a native speaker, had all the same words but pronounced them differently.

Agnes looked up at him, tears streaming down her face. "What has she done?"

"That is what we are here to find out." Godfrid glanced back at Cait, tipping his head towards Mariota as he did so. "Lachlann and Agnes, you're with me."

"Yes, my lord." Lachlann sprang towards Godfrid like a mouse released from the clutches of a cat.

Since interviewing Mariota had been her plan all along, Cait glided forward—not with an understanding expression, but with a rather more imperious one, what her husband called her *Irish princess look.*

"Come with me." The statement brooked no argument.

With Godfrid herding Lachlann and Agnes towards the inn's common room, Cait led Mariota the other way, back into the street and then towards the river. She remembered seeing a path along it that would afford them the necessary measure of privacy Cait required for this conversation.

"I'm sorry you had to witness that." Mariota skipped a few steps to keep up with Cait's pace. "I don't know what came over me."

"You are grieving." Cait chose to be magnanimous. "And the one you loved betrayed you. Anyone would be angry."

"So you do understand!" Mariota put a hand to her heart. "Nobody else does."

"My first husband betrayed me with many women. I was humiliated and angry long before I was relieved." Cait had come to the inn thinking of all the different ways she might elicit from Mariota the information she wanted. Though she had been imperious before, that Mariota had instantly apologized for flaying Agnes meant Cait might be better served now by showing her vulnerable side.

"What happened to him?"

"He died."

"How?"

"A fall from his horse."

They had reached the path and turned on to it, walking side by side. Cait glanced at Mariota, trying to see her face, which was partially hidden by a fall of hair that had come loose from the bun at the back of her head.

"You must have dreamed of that day many times," Mariota said.

"It gave me independence and my own wealth." While true, saying so out loud gave Cait an unpleasant feeling in her stomach, like she'd murdered her husband. Truthfully, she had dreamed of that too, and suddenly she realized that Mariota was thinking the exact same thing. While Cait had been talking, the woman's pace had slowed, becoming more of a saunter; the tension in her shoulders had eased; and her head had come up.

And when she spoke next, her voice sounded almost *happy*. "It really is a beautiful day. It's the first day of the rest of my life."

This version of Mariota had been what Cait had been aiming to see, even if she hadn't intended to convey that she herself was a murderess. "How so?"

"Aelred is gone. I spent the last three years of my life thinking about him and living with his mother. Now I have nobody. Like you, I feel free."

Cait wanted to ask if she was saying she had Aelred's money too, but it wasn't quite time for that question, so she took a guess. "Was that what you were telling Agnes?"

Mariota gave a little snort, a somewhat delicate one, as if she was trying to rein herself in at the last moment. "Agnes and Lachlann want to go home. They are soft on each other. I think they always have been, even before Lachlann's wife died last year." She'd been speaking normally, despite the snort, but now her voice hardened briefly. "They should just get on with it and get married."

"Why haven't they?"

Another snort. Gwen had told Cait about Mariota's tendency to make the sound. "Agnes didn't want to abandon me."

"Why didn't you just tell her that she should marry him?"

Mariota's face took on an expression of puzzlement. "Because then I'd have to live by myself, and there would be nobody to do the cooking."

Her selfishness was breathtaking.

Cait wet her lips. "You could have lived with both of them—"

Mariota cut her off before she could finish her sentence. "Not with them sniffing around each other all the time. I told Agnes months ago to send him away, and she did—for a while—but it's obvious he's back, probably to stay."

"That's what you were fighting about?"

"They wanted to go home. I want to stay here in Carlisle. As I said, there's nothing for me back in the village." All this was said without emphasis, as if it was the most natural thing in the world to abandon everything she had ever known and embark on a new adventure alone.

Cait thought a moment before replying, wanting to say just the right thing to keep the conversation going. "Although I am not from Carlisle, I am a princess. My companions are in favor in David's court. Perhaps I could help."

Mariota looked her up and down, assessment in her eyes. "I do appreciate that, believe me I do, but I think it's best if I make my own way." Her expression momentarily spasmed into something Cait might call *crafty*—even avaricious—before the look was gone a heartbeat later. "I've already spoken to the innkeeper, who hired me on the spot—and not just to serve in the common room, though he said he would be happy to put me to work there too. I can read and write, you see. Aelred taught me." She paused and then said, somewhat musingly again. "I suppose that means he did leave me something after all."

They were getting close to the topic at hand. "I'm glad to see that you are already setting your feet on a new path."

"Exactly. Carlisle is the perfect place for me."

Cait walked along another twenty feet or so before she asked, "Perfect for what, exactly?"

"As a base to search for the money."

It was a relief Mariota had come straight out with it, though Cait was now feeling ashamed that it was because she'd convinced her that she was an ally. "You are referring to the money Aelred took from Joanna and Bronwen—and maybe this other, unknown person?"

"What other money would I be talking about?"

"Could he have already ... given or gambled it away?"

Mariota snorted yet again. "Aelred didn't gamble, and the money was for *us*. He would not have given it away." She glanced at Cait. "Are you sure your husband didn't find any money in the graveyard?"

"Is there something special about that graveyard?"

"It was where he was buried and ... he often met ... people there."

By *people* Cait was guessing Mariota meant *people from whom he extorted money.*

"Godfrid has not found any money."

Mariota scoffed. "Would he say so if he did?"

Cait's step faltered at the casual maligning of her husband's honor, and then she kept walking since Mariota didn't slow her own pace—nor apparently notice Cait's hesitation. "He would."

"He is a prince, after all, and in no need of a few silver pennies, not when he has the favor of so many kings."

"Did you love him?"

"Who?" Mariota glanced at Cait. "Aelred?"

"Who else?"

This was the true Mariota. There was no pouring the wine back into the carafe on this matter. Aelred's death *had* set her free.

"Of course, I loved him. He and I thought as one, which is why it is so irksome that I can't seem to figure out what really happened to him and where he put the money. How could he put himself in a situation where he could be killed? It simply doesn't make sense. He was smarter than that."

"It is something of a puzzle," Cait agreed. It was also the exact same thing her friends had just been discussing in the guesthouse.

"And then there's this last person." Mariota was thinking hard now. "Who *is* he? Does he have the money? I'm starting to think that he might, which is the reason he has not come forward."

"If it's a woman, she could be married," Cait offered, "or simply embarrassed to be one of four."

"We *have* to make him show himself." As if struck by the conviction, Mariota came to a complete halt.

Cait wanted to say, *You do realize that even if we recover the money, none of it will belong to you?* But it would do no good. Cait was starting to wonder if Mariota was actually a strange kind of simple, like Aelred had been pretending to be. Either that or her sense of morality was so stunted she couldn't understand that Aelred's stolen money could never come to her.

So all she said, was, "How?"

"I don't know." Mariota's hands were clenched into fists. "But that too is why I must stay. Given time, I will find him—or her."

35

Day Two

Gareth

With her description of her conversation with Mariota, Cait displayed a heretofore unsuspected capacity for mimicry, and the way she dramatized Mariota's flouncing off down the path had the rest of them breathless with laughter. It wasn't funny, really, but it was a light moment in an otherwise somber investigation.

And like Mariota—and Dai, whose initial idea it had been—Gareth agreed that following the money might be the best way to sniff out the ones responsible for Aelred's death, burial, and unearthing. If Aelred had brought his money with him the night he died, the person who killed him, or buried him, or unearthed him, one and the same or three different people, would know what had become of it.

Finding the money would be like pouring cream over a honeyed cake.

As they approached the entrance to the churchyard, Gareth patted Gwen's hand as it rested in the crook of his elbow. "You know what to do?"

"You do realize you've asked me that three times in three different ways since we left the guesthouse?"

"I know. I know. I'm sorry."

"It isn't like you to be nervous."

"I think it's exactly like me to be nervous. I normally hide it better."

Gwen shook her head. "You've fought in battle; you've faced down kings and princes; but somehow this little trap we're setting has you tied in knots?"

"It's all about who's responsible, Gwen. You know that. When I'm the one doing things, then I have control over the proceedings."

"You *think* you have control." But then she nudged him with her shoulder so he would know she was teasing. "But now it's your wife who is doing the work, while you, Conall, and Godfrid stay at the front and look official and severe with the king and Prince Henry." She paused. "Do you always worry about me?"

"Yes." It was good to admit it, because as soon as he did, he felt a little of his tension ease. It wasn't gone, of course, but he could see why Gwen was looking at him with something like amusement.

"I will be doing nothing more than spreading rumors! Nobody is going to hurt me in the church or the graveyard. There is nothing to this job. As you well know, I have done far more dangerous things in the service of Prince Hywel and our investigations than this."

"So we think. But someone hated Aelred enough to bury him without telling anyone. By gossiping about it with the residents of the castle, you are exposing yourself as someone who knows something that could get him caught." Gareth corrected her because she truly was looking at this with far too cavalier an attitude. "Someone who may even have buried him alive."

"You're right. You're absolutely right." Gwen drew in a breath. "That does put something of a different light on things. My love—" she put a hand on his arm, "I promise you I will be careful."

"See that you do." He growled the words, knew he was growling, and did it anyway. "And if you are not, you have Llelo watching your back."

"Because you are a very wise husband." Gwen came up on her toes to give Gareth a quick peck on the cheek.

Then they separated, Gwen to mingle amongst the crowd and Gareth to march up to the front of the church near the altar where he would be sitting in the vicinity of King David. He was quite certain that Gwen's last comment had been said just a little bit condescendingly. He supposed he deserved her gentle teasing.

Truly, he would have much preferred to stand at the back, observing, but the whole point of him being up here was so Gwen could spread her rumors: namely that they had found a map among Aelred's belongings that pinpointed where Aelred had kept his private stash, located in the graveyard near where they'd found his body buried. King David had given permission to search for it. Since they knew this stash to contain Aelred's ledger, where he recorded the names of everyone from whom he'd taken money, they would soon know the identity of the last person to see him on the last day of his life.

None of this made the least bit of sense, of course, but it was the best they could think of to give a shove to whomever had last seen Aelred. To prevent Mariota, who was just looking for the money, from upending their plans, Cait had actually sought her out and told her the truth, never mind that it served to make her feel special to be included in the scheme. Gareth had little pride when it came to solving mysteries.

Gwen wasn't the most naturally catty person in the world—far from it—but nobody here knew that, or knew her at all, in truth. And gossip being what it was, he had no doubt that the news of what tomorrow was bringing would spread throughout the castle like a fire in the stables.

Cait and Dai, meanwhile, would be busy with a similar story on the opposite side of the crowd. They could speak the native Scottish tongue, so their audience would be slightly different from Gwen's.

They were taking a risk in deceiving King David. It had been Gareth's job to ask him with utter sincerity about digging up the graveyard in their quest for Aelred's stash. When he'd spoken to the king, Gareth had implied that there was more to this than he was telling, but that he didn't feel he could share all of the details at that time. He had also deliberately spoken of the plan when the king was surrounded by his advisers. Given that these men had included Lord Douglas, Lord James, Prince Henry, and Earl Ranulf, as well as David's steward, Vincent, Gareth was quite confident the information would be disseminated among the nobility in a timely fashion. In truth, that request alone might have been enough to spread the news to everyone of what they were planning, but it was too important to leave to chance.

While Gareth had no evidence Aelred had mingled with gentry—thus the rumormongering currently underway in the church—by the time they were done, every resident in the castle, and maybe Carlisle, would have heard what they were up to. Most would know before Aelred was put into his grave.

Gareth settled onto the bench between Godfrid and Conall. It was a tight squeeze, because the church was packed with people. The king and Prince Henry, along with his aforementioned advisers and Mariota and Agnes, were in the row ahead, also shoulder to shoulder. The crowd was large, less because of Aelred, than because of the family and friends of the woman at whose bedside Dunstan had sat the night they'd found Aelred's body. She was to be buried at the same time as Aelred. Most of her family lived in town. This was all to the good for Gareth's purposes. The crush in the church also allowed him to sit with his friends without giving the impression that they *were* friends.

"I am wondering if he hid the money in the church," Godfrid said in a murmur as the priest's voice rose in a chant in Latin.

Gareth didn't turn his head and spoke in Welsh out of the corner of his mouth, "You forget that this trap is a ruse. There is no money."

"Isn't there? He had money, and he hid it somewhere."

"You truly are a Dane, my friend. I like the idea of treasure as much as the next man, but as we discussed, more likely, the person who buried him took it, and it's long gone."

Godfrid subsided, but a glance in his direction revealed him looking speculatively around the nave. Gareth marveled at the way giving voice to the very idea of hidden treasure had sparked the imagination even of someone who should know it wasn't real.

Then again, Llelo had been curious enough—and concerned enough—about the state of Aelred's body to look at it on his own. Perhaps Gareth should be trusting his companions' instincts more rather than less.

Dunstan, bless his heart, was well into the Latin service. Gareth understood his words, but tuned him out nonetheless and said to Conall, out of the other side of his mouth, "Our Danish friend is drooling over the treasure. What do you think?"

"I'm not drooling—" Godfrid had overheard.

"The priest's lectern," Conall said immediately. "It was being stained at the same time as the choir stalls, wasn't it?"

The trio's eyes focused on the priest, who was standing above them in the lectern. It was a definite possibility, though Gareth had gone over it and found no secret hidey-hole.

"Then we have the choir pews themselves," Gareth said. "They are raised up. Underneath there must be room for sacks of money."

"I confess to have poked around both places," Godfrid said. "Short of taking either apart, we can't know for certain. But Father

Dunstan assured me they were already completely built before Aelred died. That's why they were being stained."

"Under the altar, then," Gareth said, "or within it."

"I looked there. I know you did too." Conall was gazing down at his hands in a guise of prayer. "As you probably saw, it has a cupboard in the back. But if Aelred hid his money behind that little door, it's gone now. All it contains are communion dishes and more altar cloths."

"Keep thinking," Gareth said.

Godfrid grumbled deep in his chest. "Has the king really agreed to allow us to dig up the graveyard?"

"As long as we don't touch any actual graves, yes."

"It's your dream come true, Godfrid," Conall had an amazing ability to speak without moving his mouth. "Buried treasure!"

But Godfrid shook his head, suddenly much more sober. "When it comes to it, greed is a terrible vice. Look at what just the idea of treasure has done to me, who has no need for it. I'm thinking now that I would rather pay Joanna and Bronwen back out of my own pocket than taint this castle any further with a single one of Aelred's corrupted coins."

36

Day Three

Conall

Godfrid was crouched on his low stool, appropriated from Dunstan's house for this occasion. "I have something to tell you, and you're not going to like it."

Conall glanced at his friend. "How long have we known each other, Godfrid?"

"A few years."

"I would have thought that was long enough for you not to be worried about what you can and cannot tell me."

They had found a spot near the corner of the churchyard wall. From their position, they could see both the front and rear gates from the bailey into the yard and the front and rear doors of the church itself. Llelo and Dai were posted together on the opposite side of the church, with instructions to hoot like an owl if anyone tried to clamber over the wall. All were making sure they kept hunkered down so anyone in the bailey couldn't see them.

Gareth and Gwen were in the guesthouse with the rest of their family, alert to any attempt to sneak inside and rifle through Aelred's things, which they had retained to protect Agnes from the same problem. Nobody was allowed to go about alone anymore.

Here at midnight, poor Godfrid had to be missing the companionship of his wife, who was tucked up alone in their bed. Instead, he was having to make do with his wife's brother.

"I knew I could trust you very shortly after our initial acquaintance," Godfrid admitted—somewhat grudgingly, Conall thought. Something significant was bothering him.

Conall adjusted his attitude accordingly. "Just tell me. Can it be worse than I imagine? Is it something between you and Cait?" He shifted on his stool. "Is something wrong with the baby?"

Godfrid put out a hasty hand. "Nothing like that. Thank goodness, nothing to do with Cait. At least not overtly."

Conall subsided. "So it's a matter of state. I knew things weren't quite right since your meeting with King David and Earl Ranulf this morning. Did they offer you suzerainty over Leinster instead of the other way around?"

Godfrid gaped.

Conall laughed to see Godfrid's aghast look. "Of course they did."

His friend made a dismissive motion with both hands. "Actually, merely independence."

Conall gave a low chuckle. "*Merely.*"

"If it makes you feel better, as recompense there was talk of offering King Diarmait enough forces to overthrow the O'Connors and become High King."

Conall raised his eyebrows. "This afternoon, I spoke to King David in private. All he wanted to hear about was Gwynedd. How is it that I have heard nothing of this?"

"Maybe they've been busy."

"Of course. That must be it." Conall shot him a wry look. "What did they want in exchange? Fighting men, I assume."

"Yes, but not for what you think. They want my brother to stage another raid like the one we did at Cadwaladr's behest when we ambushed King Anarawd of Deheubarth."

Conall let the silence between them lengthen as he absorbed that bit of information. "I admit to having struggled with the fact that you and Brodar agreed to kill Anarawd. Didn't the mission give you pause?"

"Our king at the time had agreed to the terms, as had my own father, and we served them, doing what our people have always done best. We gained wealth for Dublin. And, of course, I did not know the people of Gwynedd as I do now. It would be a very different matter now."

"It would be a betrayal." Conall knew his tone was somewhat accusing. "One might argue it was then too. Your people are kin to King Owain, as are mine."

"In our defense, we didn't see the raid as much more than a lark. We were merely waylaying the King of Deheubarth. He was betrothed to Owain's daughter, but not yet married." Godfrid was explaining, but he was neither cowed nor apologetic. "One war is much like another, and Prince Cadwaladr was very convincing as to how Owain was depriving him of his birthright. He insisted that the outcome of this particular raid would reset the balance of power in Gwynedd."

"It did that all right, and put him in his place."

"I will not apologize, Conall. You know as well as I why we did what we did. If nothing else, I was doing as my father bid me."

"And if you had known what you do now?"

"I might have argued against the mission a little more forcefully." Godfrid chuckled, even as Conall struggled not to take offense. It was rare for any matter to come between them. In fact, he might even say that they'd avoided talking about matters like this—and specifically this matter—in all the years they'd been friends. "Yes, you are right. My people long for the days we went *a viking* and made our wealth by taking what we could. We built Dublin on such wealth. There's no denying it. Just because we raid far less now does not mean we have forgotten how." He waggled his head. "I don't have to remind you that many of us gained greatly at Cadwaladr's expense, including myself and my brother."

"I suppose we can't regret that part of it." In that instant, Conall decided to let the conversation end. His own people had suffered at the hands of the Danes for generations. But Danes had also suffered at the hands of the Irish, with the result that Dublin had become subservient to Leinster. It was pointless to litigate the past, never mind go to war with each other over it. "Who does King David and Ranulf want you to ambush?"

"Eustace, King Stephen's son."

Conall reared back. "Lord have mercy!"

"You might well call upon him."

"You refused, of course."

"I did not."

It was Conall's turn to gape.

Godfrid's lips twisted. "I'll have you know it was Gareth's suggestion to agree."

"By all that is holy, why?"

"If we do not agree to the plan, who else might they ask who will have fewer scruples than we do? Gareth is of the mind that we should abduct him rather than kill him—and if we must make a profit off it, then we can simply sell him back to his father."

Conall let out a gasping laugh. They were trying to be quiet, though in the heat of the conversation he'd almost forgotten why they were in the graveyard. "I did not see that coming."

"Nor I," Godfrid admitted. "I feared taking the offer to my brother and feared not taking it."

"You can't not take it," Conall said flatly. "We both know that."

"But now I have told you about it, and I will tell my brother I have done so. It will force his hand and narrow his choices, which he won't like."

"You knew before you married Cait that doing so might split you in two," Conall said gently. "I know your loyalties are with Dublin and with your brother, always, but you also know that an independent Dublin can never be again, not with the O'Connors breathing down your necks."

"Your necks too." Godfrid bobbed a nod. "I will never like it. But I do believe that an overlord we know in the form of King Diarmait is better than one we also know in the High King."

Conall gave a low laugh. "And when the High King dies?"

"We will deal with his heir when there is one."

"I don't look forward to seeing you alienate King David and Earl Ranulf."

"Their power base is very far away from Ireland, and neither can do anything to us at this time. Besides, they are moving on York within days, far too soon for me to get back to Dublin, convince Brodar of the sense of the plan, raise my forty men, and return. In addition, only King David and Earl Ranulf were in the room when this was offered to me. Prince Henry does not appear to be a party to this plan, and I suspect that is because he would not approve."

The very idea of abducting King Stephen's son raised the hairs on the back of Conall's neck. He'd come to see that the alliance these three magnates had forged was based on very little, which meant that it could fall apart as quickly as it was conceived. "Ranulf and David want it to be *fait accompli* before Prince Henry learns of it."

"I imagine so—" Godfrid broke off at a noise that had both of them shushing the other. Fortunately, they had been talking in whispers for the latter part of their conversation.

A soft patter of feet came from the other side of the wall, evident through the still night air. The sound disappeared into the distance, and then the gate at the far end of the graveyard, farthest from the church entrance, creaked loudly enough for the person opening it to freeze in position. Such was the perfection of their current location that, in the moonlight, they could see the figure of that person hesitating halfway through the gate.

Then the figure slipped into the graveyard, leaving the gate open, and moved towards the place where Aelred's body had been found (rather than where he was currently buried). The person held a lantern low to the ground, which gave off a small circle of light. The intruder then bypassed the grave and set to work at the base of the closest tree.

Conall and Godfrid glided through the moonlight towards the form. Conall signaled with one hand that Godfrid should circle around to the left, keeping close to the church wall and out of the intruder's line of sight. Thus, they both crept closer.

Then, when they had each achieved a distance of ten paces away, Conall stopped and straightened. "Lady Margaret, so interesting to find you here. By your presence, we can only conclude that you were the last person to give Aelred money. Was it of your own volition or was he blackmailing you?"

37

Because Gwen and Cait had done most of the interviewing of the women in the castle up until now, it was only fair that this new interview with Lady Margaret was left to them as well. But as Gwen reached the church, where Gareth had detained Margaret, her husband looked at her warily—like he didn't quite believe this was going to go the way they hoped.

"When are you going to learn that I can take care of myself?" she said.

"I know you can. I'm just not always good at letting you."

She laughed. "I do love you."

"You love me because I let you do whatever you want." The words came out a bit petulant. He'd been grumpy quite a bit lately. She knew why. They'd come here to sign a pact, which King David had kept putting off, in favor of an investigation that was like riding a horse that hadn't yet been tamed. He feared being bucked off at any moment and taking her with him.

He should know better, really he should. But she gave him the benefit of the doubt, in that he had been under significant pressure throughout their sojourn to Carlisle Castle. He'd told her about King David's offer to Godfrid, as well as Conall's awkward conversation with him.

To her mind, these forays were merely one layer of the complicated intrigue that seemed part and parcel of life in any court, not just King David's.

It was a foreign court, though, and one they were supposed to navigate in such a way that they were always serving Gwynedd's best interests. That King Owain's signed document remained in Gareth's pocket was making them all wonder if David, Ranulf, and Henry genuinely wanted Gwynedd in their alliance at all.

Margaret sat in the first level of the choir stalls, staring at her hands. As Cait and Gwen approached, she looked up. There was a pinching around her mouth and eyes that revealed her tension, and it looked like she was gritting her teeth as well.

"I did nothing wrong."

That Margaret chose to be combative at the start did not come as a surprise to Gwen, which was why she had brought a carafe of wine. Without bothering to reply, she poured wine into a cup and handed it to Margaret, who took it and drank thirstily.

When she'd drained the cup to the dregs, Gwen refilled it.

Margaret had already told Godfrid and Conall that she had given money to Aelred willingly and that she wasn't being blackmailed. But then she had refused to speak to the two men about it further. Thus, Conall had sent Dai to fetch Cait and Gwen.

"Tell us about the night you met Aelred in this church," Gwen said.

With two cups of wine in her, Margaret replied without belligerence. "He was alive when I left him. That's all I can say."

Her words had put the ending before the beginning, but she was right that how the evening had ended for her was the most important matter. Gwen was glad she'd admitted, both in the graveyard and just now, that she'd met with Aelred. It hadn't been a given that she would.

"What was your relationship with him?"

"Purely financial."

She answered very quickly—too quickly to Gwen's mind. "Really?"

Margaret made a dismissive motion with one hand. "Of course I was attracted to him. No woman with eyes could fail to be attracted to him. But he wasn't interested in wooing me. Besides, he was a common soldier. It would have been unseemly." She looked down her nose, offended by the very thought.

It wasn't that she was wrong either, but the way she made the comment exposed, as little else could have, Margaret's lack of morality: it wouldn't have been wrong to have a relationship with Aelred because she was a married woman; it would have been wrong only because he was a commoner and she a noblewoman. And, of course, Gwen knew from Llelo that she was currently having an affair with someone else.

Cait had taken over the management of the wine and poured Margaret her third cup, while Gwen asked her next question. "What was the nature of this financial arrangement?"

"He was a peasant, but he was the cleverest man I had ever met. I invest in many ventures. His was to provide ale to the men in Worcester in excess of what they would receive from the king."

That was the same story Aelred had given Joanna. It might even be true, though Gwen was still disinclined to think so. To truly know the answer, they'd have to track down the tavern keeper in Worcester. If he existed.

"How much money did you give him?"

This new question flustered Margaret more than any of the others, and she took a moment to reply. "Not such a great sum for me, much more for him. Two hundred pence."

At a penny a gallon, that would buy two hundred gallons of wine from Anjou, but far more ale, especially if the tavern keeper made it on site. It was a considerable amount of money to anyone but a nobleman. Even then, the castle clerk would never be casual about mislaying that amount of money while doing the castle accounts.

"When did you give it to him?"

"We met in the church the night before he was due to leave for Worcester. It appears now that it was also the night he died, though, as I said, I did not know it then."

Gwen had been assuming she'd been lying about Aelred being alive when she'd last seen him, but her reiteration of her position was said in a normal tone, without any defensiveness.

"Please talk me through exactly how that meeting went."

Margaret sighed, as if the story was so dull it was tedious to tell it. "We had agreed to meet in the church as I was finishing tidying up."

"Did you leave flowers?"

"Yes, as always. It was early in the season, but I had a few crocus and winter iris. I left them in a vase on the table." She paused, frowning.

"What is it?"

"Normally I throw away the previous day's flowers when I come the next day. I did that when I put these new ones in water. But now that I think about it, when I came the day after, the flowers were already gone."

"You remember that?" Cait asked. "That day particularly?"

Margaret made a rueful face. "I remember wondering if Aelred had taken them to give to his latest conquest. I thought it impertinent, but at the same time typical for him. He thought normal rules didn't apply to him."

"How did you meet Aelred in the first place?"

"We met here, in the church." Margaret made a gesture to indicate where she now sat. "His shifts as a soldier prevented him from coming at regular hours, and one day he was here when I arrived. He was polite and so very charming. We soon started talking. He was unlike any man I'd ever met." Her voice was wistful. "I have heard others say he was a dullard, but they were very much mistaken to ever think so. At one point, he confessed to me that he made them think so on purpose. He found being underestimated both amusing and useful."

Whether or not she admitted it to herself, it looked to Gwen as if Margaret had been in love with Aelred, at least a little bit. Or perhaps, she simply missed the companionship. Everybody needed someone to talk to.

"So you came to the church with flowers and met Aelred," Gwen prompted.

Margaret nodded. "We prayed together, I gave him the money, he said he was going to stay a while afterwards, and I left. It was time to get back to my husband."

"And did you—get back to your husband?" Cait spoke for the first time, while handing Margaret her fourth cup of wine. The carafe was all but empty.

"Of course." Margaret was confused that Cait would ask the question, but Cait knew about the affair, which they had deliberately not charged Margaret with as yet. While it was perfectly plausible that Aelred had been blackmailing her about it, they had no evidence to support the idea. Margaret wasn't going anywhere, and those questions could be asked later, once more important ones had been asked. "Well, I suppose not right away, as he'd already left by the time I arrived back at the hall."

"Was that usual for him?" Cait asked. "To leave so early?"

"Not so unusual that I thought anything of it."

"Was he in your rooms when you reached them?" This was Cait again.

A 'v' formed between Margaret's brows. "Come to think on it, he wasn't. He came later, waking me from sleep. He said he'd taken a walk on the battlement to clear his head of wine. *That* was unusual.

He likes his drink, does my husband." Without irony, she tipped the cup to drink the last of her own wine. "Why are you asking?"

"We are just looking to clarify everyone's movements that night." Gwen made a dismissive motion similar to Margaret's gesture earlier. "What were you doing in the graveyard with a shovel?"

Margaret allowed the change of subject, giving Gwen a sardonic look. "As if you have to ask."

"You could have lied."

"We're in a church!" Margaret sniffed. "Besides, as I said, I wasn't doing anything wrong. The money was mine to do with as I please, and you didn't need to know of it. If I chose to invest in a venture in Worcester, that was my business." But then she sighed one more time. "My husband, however, will not understand and will be upset both by my friendship with Aelred and the loan. The only thing he might agree with is my desire to get my money back!"

Now she sat up straighter in her seat. "May I go now? Lord Carr is a deep sleeper, but even he may notice I've been gone for some time and wonder."

Gwen made an instant decision. "You may return to your room, but please do not leave the castle. We will have more questions in the morning."

"Where would I go?" A moment later, Margaret was flitting out the door.

Cait began to pace towards the high altar and back, her hands on her hips. "How can we believe her, knowing about her tryst in the chapel?"

"Admittedly, she's had three months to make up a story, but she does not seem devious in the way of Mariota. Selfish, yes. Focused entirely on her own wants and needs, yes. But I'm having trouble seeing her murdering Aelred and burying him in the graveyard."

"She was pretty quick to pick up a shovel tonight."

"But according to Godfrid and Conall, her efforts were ineffective at best. She barely knew which end to use!"

"I'm interested in her admission that Lord James came to bed late that night." Cait tapped a finger to her lips. "My first husband didn't love me and had many extramarital relations, but that didn't mean I could do as I pleased. He would not have countenanced a friendship with another man, much less an affair. I was his property."

Gwen frowned. "It was in my mind that James was with another woman that night, which was what made him late to bed, but you're suggesting that *Lord James* killed and buried Aelred?"

"All I'm saying is that, if my first husband knew I was meeting a commoner in the church most nights, it's what he would have done."

38

Day Three

Gareth

It seemed an impossible question to ask Lord James, especially on a hunch that wasn't even his: *Did you follow your wife to the church that night and murder the man you thought was her lover?* Gareth had dealt with some fraught, politically delicate issues in the past, but this was worse than most.

To bolster his courage, he was sitting in a back corner of the great hall, watching the proceedings at the high table, which weren't momentous in any fashion, other than that Gareth had something to ask that he didn't know how to. Lord James was a nobleman and an important member of King David's court, if only as a representative of an even more lofty member, Hugh de Morville. With Margaret having come into her estate after the death of her father, James had become even more important in his own right.

Llelo slipped onto the seat at the end of the table, cradling a cup of warm mead to his chest as the steam from it rose towards his face.

Gareth narrowed his eyes at his son. "Where'd you get that? I've had only ale since we got here." He looked morosely into his empty cup.

Mead was the lifeblood of Wales, but for all that the Scots and the Welsh shared ancestry, those in Carlisle appeared to have adopted English tastes. Of course, when Carlisle had been taken over by King Henry earlier in the century, he'd brought in English settlers to occupy it, many of whom remained—as well as their tastes—despite the change in governance.

Llelo poured half of what was in his cup into Gareth's. "You have to know the right people to ask."

"And you do?"

Llelo grinned. "Not me. Dai."

"Of course." Gareth laughed too.

At that moment, Lord Douglas entered the hall and made a beeline for where Gareth and Llelo were sitting. Putting his palms flat on the table, he leaned heavily onto them. "I hear you have the murderer in custody?"

Beside Gareth, Llelo stiffened. He didn't speak, however, so Gareth replied, "I wouldn't say that as yet, but we know more than we did yesterday."

"But someone came to the graveyard to look for the money? You know who killed Aelred?"

"Lord Douglas—"

"Who is it?" His voice was demanding.

"I cannot say anything until I've had a chance to speak to the king."

Douglas subsided. "Of course." He gave a slight bow. "If I can in any way be of service, please don't hesitate to ask."

Even as Gareth bent his head and said *thank you*, he considered the various questions he hadn't yet had a chance to ask Douglas, namely, his true relationship with Aelred.

So, as Douglas stalked off, Gareth looked at his son. Llelo, however, was staring rigidly after Douglas. "He was the man in the chapel with Lady Margaret."

Llelo would never make any accusation, especially not such an embarrassing one, if he wasn't certain. Still, Gareth had to ask, "You're sure?"

"I'm sure, not that it matters, does it? That has nothing to do with Aelred."

"Doesn't it? Margaret does, especially if they were having this affair before he left for Worcester. Besides, I was thinking just now that various people among those we've interviewed implied that Douglas had more interactions with Aelred then he admitted to us ..." Gareth's voice trailed off as he considered the implications, which were legion.

"I'm sure their affair dates back to that time. I heard them speaking about it." Llelo met his father's eyes. "The addition of Douglas gives us two men connected to her with a stake in her behavior with Aelred. Either could have followed her that night."

"Or both."

Llelo let out a short laugh. "Lord Douglas was very quick to identify the body. At the time I thought we were lucky he arrived when he did. And if you think about it, it was his identification that set us on the path we have followed ever since."

"That makes him *less* likely to have killed him rather than more." Gareth tapped a finger to his lips. "If he hadn't said anything, we might never have known Aelred's identity, or it would have been quite a bit more difficult to discover it."

"You'll have to speak to him." Llelo put his head into his hands. "Or I should, since I'm the one who thinks he heard him."

"You can leave that task to me. Yours will be slightly more difficult." Gareth tipped his head towards the high table, still full of noble diners. "Once I talk to Douglas, if it goes the way I think it might, you should be the one to talk to Lady Margaret."

"Me!" Llelo was aghast. "We're plucking at straws! What if I'm wrong that she was with him?"

Gareth knew his son. "Are we wrong?"

"No." Llelo's shoulders sagged. "She'll deny it, no matter what Lord Douglas tells you."

"Maybe. Maybe not. We did not tell her husband where she was last night. She may believe us when we say we don't want to expose her secrets if they have no bearing on Aelred's death."

"But do they?"

"It's time we found that out, don't you think?"

Lord Douglas hadn't quite made it to the high table, having been waylaid by Vincent, the castle steward. Gareth approached closely, standing at Douglas's right elbow while he waited for the conversation to end. The two other men appeared to be discussing the quality of the ale served to the soldiers, which Gareth hoped was merely a coincidence and not related to Aelred's supposed venture in Worcester.

As the steward moved away, Douglas turned to Gareth. "Did you need something already?"

"Yes." Gareth didn't quite take Douglas's elbow, but he did urge him towards a side door that led out of the hall and then into the courtyard. King David had constructed another great hall within his new keep, but his people still ate and lived their daily lives in the free-standing structure in the inner bailey. It was larger, warmer, and more accessible to general comings and goings. "I have a question for you, one you do not want me to ask or you to answer with anyone watching."

Douglas came along somewhat stiff-leggedly, but not protesting, so Gareth didn't actually have to drag him through the inner gatehouse to a quiet corner of the bailey near the stables. The sun shone down, and the clouds had been swept away, making the day warmer than it had been earlier that morning.

Finally, Douglas dug in his heels and came to a complete halt. "Ask."

It was a command, which might not have sat terribly well with Gareth under other circumstances, but since he wanted to ask anyway, he went ahead with his question. "It has come to our attention that you are having an affair with Margaret Carr."

Douglas's expression turned so still he could have been a block of wood. "Is there a question in there?"

Gareth bobbed a nod. "Good, you don't deny it. There were witnesses to your liaison in the chapel two nights ago."

Now Douglas's face drained of color. "It was dark—"

"But not empty."

"What do you want? I am not a rich man."

"Blackmail? Is that what you think this is about?" Douglas's assumption was so unexpected, Gareth gaped at the man for a moment before shaking his head. "You misunderstand. I'm not Aelred. The person who overheard you is scarred potentially for life, but I have no real interest in your relationship with Margaret except as a means to an end. I want to know if it is that relationship which prompted you to dig up Aelred's body and sit him in the priest's chair in the church within hours of your return to Carlisle."

39

Day Three

Llelo

Llelo hesitated outside Margaret's door, his hand raised to knock but reluctant to do so. This was a true job of an investigator. Part of him was honored that his father had given it to him, and the rest of him was mortified to tell Margaret what he knew.

But then he decided that she didn't need to know *how* he knew, and his father was right that if he told her Douglas had confessed to being her lover, then that might be enough to get her to talk. She had talked to Llelo's mother already, and the experience might be fresh enough in her mind—and the consequences so far minor enough—that she would be willing to do it again. And maybe talking to someone as young and potentially as unthreatening as Llelo would be easier than talking to his father. Llelo suspected that this was another reason his father had sent him. Though it was now too late to do so, Llelo wished he'd enlisted Hamelin, who had been as much a witness as he.

So he knocked.

After a count of three, he heard footsteps, and then the door was opened by a serving girl. Llelo shouldn't have been flustered, since it was no surprise that Margaret wouldn't answer her own door, but the two of them stared at each other for a moment, and then the girl dropped into a curtsey. "Sir Llelo. I'm Jonet."

Llelo had just managed to stop himself from bowing his head to her, which would have been odd and inappropriate, but her manner with him was more like that of a friend. He remembered her name from Dai's recounting, and Llelo could see why Dai had been happy to talk to her. She was a very pretty girl.

"I was hoping to speak to Lady Margaret."

"Tell him to come in." Lady Margaret's voice came from within the room, confirming in Llelo's mind yet again that she had, in fact, been the woman with Lord Douglas in the chapel.

Jonet stepped back and allowed him entry, and Llelo moved past her to find Lady Margaret sitting near an open window through which warm air was blowing.

Margaret indicated the door with a tip of her head. "You may leave us."

Jonet's lips twitched for a moment, but she curtseyed and then obeyed, closing the door behind her and stopping the easy flow of air.

Llelo had remained standing, but now Margaret flapped a hand in his direction. "Don't loom over me like that. Pour yourself some wine and sit. Pour me some too while you're at it. I can see you are here at your father's behest and have more questions. I imagine I'm not going to like them." She paused as she studied him. "I'm interested that he sent you instead of coming himself."

Rather than replying right away, Llelo did as she asked. When his mother had questioned Lady Margaret, copious amounts of wine had been poured down her throat, and Llelo supposed he preferred insobriety to having her sob into his chest. It was still very odd to him to know what he did about her relationship with Lord Douglas. They were both twenty years older than his parents. He would have thought that made them old enough to know better.

Llelo accepted the straight-backed chair Margaret indicated, took a sip of the very good wine, and said, "We have learned from Lord Douglas that you and he have been lovers."

Not unexpectedly, Margaret recoiled and in the process slopped some of her wine out of her cup and onto her hand. But then, just as abruptly, she settled back into her seat.

She mopped and took a large swallow of her drink, after which she said, in a totally calm voice, "He said that?"

"Yes, Madam."

"Why?"

"Because my father told him he already knew so there was no point in lying."

Margaret's face contorted into a moue. "I don't believe you. Why would you even think to ask him such a question?"

Llelo wavered in his own mind, noting she was asking her own questions instead of answering his, but then he sighed and felt he had to confess, just as his father had done to Douglas, "Because you were not alone in the chapel two nights ago."

According to Gareth, Douglas's face had paled at this news. Margaret flushed to the roots of her hair. "No."

"I'm afraid so."

"Who?"

"I cannot tell you that."

"Whoever it is, they're lying."

"Then why, when confronted with the fact, did Lord Douglas admit it was true?"

Margaret looked down at her hands. "Even if it is true, which I'm not saying it is, why does it matter?"

"Because of what happens now."

She frowned. "What happens now?"

Llelo stood and held out his hand to her. "You need to come with me." He paused and said gently. "You may want to finish the wine in your goblet first."

40

Day Three

Gwen

King David's receiving room felt crowded, but maybe that was more because emotions were running high than because too many people were in the room. They were in the keep, in the king's private audience chamber rather than the more public space off the great hall, and not even all that many people were present: Gareth and Gwen, King David, Lord Douglas, Lord James, and Lady Margaret.

Conall, Godfrid, and Cait had recused themselves even before Gwen had suggested they stay behind at the monastery. They'd also left Llelo, Dai, and Hamelin out of it too. All of them had contributed to the investigation, which had allowed them to reach this point, but the situation had become far more fraught than even an hour before.

For his part, the king sat relaxed in a padded chair that bore a passing resemblance to a throne, in that it was large and square and slightly raised above the other chairs. The king was a tall man, so it actually fit him better than a lower chair would have. Given David's general lack of flamboyance, that could be the primary reason he was in it.

The lords James and Douglas were seated with Lady Margaret on the left side of the room, each in their own more utilitarian chair. Gwen herself sat in the window seat built into the opposite wall, and Gareth stood in the middle of the floor. Unusually, he wasn't wearing his armor but was dressed in the attire of a diplomat: a long, blue robe belted at the waist. When he'd arrived in the keep, he'd removed the matching mantle and left it with his sword in the entryway.

Now he stood with his legs spread and his hands behind his back, having just related as fully and succinctly as possible the results of the investigation so far. Much of this information he perhaps wouldn't have shared with the three members of the nobility, who were also their suspects, but he had decided that their reactions could be informative. And they needed to know what he'd discovered to understand what came next.

For most of Gareth's recitation, the two lesser lords had looked nothing more or less than bored. They cared not at all for the women in Aelred's life and the various schemes in which he'd ensnared them. Lady Margaret had spent that quarter of an hour staring down at her hands. So far, Gareth hadn't even touched on any of her activities, including her midnight sojourn in the churchyard, other than her role in the discovery of Aelred's body, which they'd all witnessed anyway. He furthermore hadn't mentioned her loan to Aelred nor her affair with Douglas. It wasn't so much that Gareth was drawing out his explanation as laying the groundwork, very deliberately, for the denouement. By the time he presented the pertinent details, nobody would have any doubt he spoke the truth.

Gareth now said, "Which brings us to our more recent discoveries—"

"Look here, Gareth." Lord James interrupted him with something of a braying tone, even as he put out a hand to the king. "Pardon me, my lord, but I am a busy man, and my presence here appears to me to be a shocking waste of time."

Gareth simply gazed at the king, waiting to be told to continue or to stop. They weren't here to argue the details of the investigation but to expose them and were investigating at all only because King David had asked them to.

Gwen really could have walked away at this point, as strange as that might seem. She would be happy to see justice done, but Aelred was dead, and no amount of investigating was going to bring him back. She wasn't sure either that uncovering the truth was going to do more than make a great many people unhappy, but such was the way with unnatural death.

The king made his continuing desires known. "Lord Gareth is here at my request, James, and I would ask that you hear him out."

Lord James didn't want to subside, but he did.

Lord Douglas then shifted in his seat. "I suppose it's time for my part in this."

James's head swung around. "Yours!"

Douglas, however, was looking at the king, who nodded his approval. This time, Gareth hadn't kept the king in the dark, and he knew everything Gareth did. So Gareth backed away from the middle of the floor, towards Gwen, though he didn't sit, allowing Douglas to take his place in the central position. Gareth had been prepared to finish the story. It was interesting that Douglas felt honor-bound to tell his part himself.

"I fear, my lord, that much of what has happened is my fault." He bowed to the king. "It was I who disinterred Aelred and put his body in the church."

King David already knew this, since Gareth had told him so to gain his permission to have this meeting in the first place, but the shocked reactions from Lord and Lady Carr were illuminating.

Lord James leapt to his feet, practically foaming at the mouth. "By the bones of St. Brendan, sir! How could you!"

Margaret, for her part, stared at Douglas with a completely white face, her lips bloodless. Gwen worried in that moment that she might faint. "*You* killed him?"

Douglas chose to respond to her, despite how much quieter her tone had been compared to her husband's. "I did not."

Some of the color returned to Margaret's face, but Gwen was already crossing the room with a goblet of wine she'd brought to the proceedings expressly for this purpose. Lady Margaret undoubtedly was salving her grief at her father's loss, and her boredom and un-happiness in her marriage, with too much wine, but this was not the moment to chastise her with her excesses. While drinking away her life wouldn't have been Gwen's means of coping with unhappiness, she couldn't really blame her for it.

Margaret took the cup, sipped it, and said, "I didn't either."

"I know." Lord Douglas remained turned towards her. "The murderer is Lord James."

"What?" James Carr had already been on his feet, but now he reared back. "What are you talking about? *I* did not murder Aelred."

Douglas was insistent. "You killed him, and you buried him."

Gwen hadn't resumed her seat after giving Margaret her wine, instead finding a place next to her husband. They had cooked up this scene with the help of their friends and the king, and it was going better than any of them had expected, with the three aggrieved parties—Margaret, Douglas, and James—turning on one another.

"Oh no." James shook his head back and forth vehemently. "I buried him. I admit to that, but that was only because he was already dead."

Douglas took a step towards him. "I *saw* you!"

"You couldn't have!" Lord James shot back.

"You dragged him out the vestry, wrapped in a shroud, and buried him in that newly turned grave from which I recovered him two days ago!"

"I did not kill him!" Lord James punctuated each word with a stabbing finger.

"If not you, then who?" King David asked into the silence that followed this vehement denial. "Why would you, James, take it upon yourself to bury a dead man you stumbled across in the church rather than giving him a proper send off? And Douglas, if you believed Lord James had killed Aelred, why did you not come to me to accuse him at the time?"

Douglas was the first to reply. "I couldn't. It would have been my word against his."

Lord James's mouth had been opening and closing like that of a landed fish. Gwen was holding onto Gareth's elbow, the two of them hardly daring to move or even breathe, fearing to disrupt the scene before them.

Margaret's hand was to her mouth. "James thought *I* killed him."

Lord James swung around to face his wife. "Of course I thought you killed him. You *did* kill him. I followed you to the church and then witnessed Aelred's arrival shortly thereafter. Half an hour later, you hurried away. I waited for Aelred, thinking I would confront him about his relations with my wife, even if I was loath to do so. That's why I didn't come into the church itself when you were both there. It was horrifying, what the two of you thought was acceptable behavior inside a church."

Gwen could only agree, given what Llelo had witnessed between Margaret and Douglas inside the chapel in the keep. Clearly, the idea had precedent.

James continued, "But he didn't come out. Eventually, I couldn't wait any longer and entered, to find him dead on the floor by the choir. *You* killed him."

"I didn't!" Margaret shivered. "He was alive when I left. I swear it!"

"Margaret, we already know that you gave Aelred money." King David's voice was heavy. "Tell us the truth now."

"He was your lover!" James was beside himself with righteous anger and spoke before Margaret could. "He was probably blackmailing you, and when he wouldn't stop no matter how much you paid him, you struck him on the head and killed him."

"No." Open-mouthed, Margaret was looking from one man to the next to the next. "That isn't what happened. Don't you think if I killed him I would have taken back the money I'd given him? I didn't take it because I didn't kill him. Besides, we weren't lovers." She paused. "My lover then was Lord Douglas."

Gwen and Gareth had withheld that information even from King David so as not to embarrass Margaret if they didn't have to, but it was something of a relief that she told this particular truth herself.

Lord James swung around to face Douglas. "You!" In truth, nobody could blame him for being upset, no matter what he'd done himself.

"Me." Douglas was standing with his hands on his hips. "You didn't deserve her."

Gwen was finding herself believing Lady Margaret that she hadn't killed Aelred and thought she deserved her support in the face of the disbelieving men. "To sum up, the order of events as we understand them is that Lady Margaret, by her own admission, met with Aelred to give him money for one of his ventures, such as Gareth related earlier. She says he was alive when she left. This meeting was witnessed, at least in part, by Lord James." She met his eyes. "Why were you following your wife?"

"Because I knew she had a lover, and I wanted to know who it was."

"Why did you then bury Aelred?"

"Because I wanted to protect her!"

"You wanted to protect yourself." Margaret spoke not quite as much under her breath as she might have done had she not drunk several cups of wine in rapid succession. "You didn't want to risk me being put on trial for murder. If convicted, I would forgo my inheritance from my father. All that land and wealth. You needed me alive and at your side at least until then."

The stunned look on Lord James's face was enough to confirm that Margaret knew her husband well.

Gwen turned to Lord Douglas. "Why were you in that churchyard?"

His lips were pressed together, apparently reluctant to answer, but then he seemed to realize he had no choice and, by this point, had nothing to lose. "I came to the church hoping to speak to Margaret, with no idea she was meeting someone else—this Aelred—that evening. As it turned out, I was delayed and arrived in time to see her leaving. I would have waylaid her, but in my approach to the churchyard, I spotted James hovering by a large sarcophagus. That was unusual enough behavior that I decided to watch him instead. If he'd got wind of our relationship, I certainly didn't want him to see me with her. And then the evening grew very odd indeed."

"Why didn't you tell anyone about Aelred's death and burial?"

"As I explained, I saw all the ways that might go badly. At the very least, my accusation of James might have ruined Margaret, which was the last thing I wanted. Even if she'd been having an affair with Aelred, which I had no knowledge of, he was now dead, and the field was clear for me. Perhaps I should have confronted James in the moment, but I was too shocked to do so, and once the body was buried, how could I possibly account for my actions, or lack thereof? If James played things right, he could even have denied everything and insisted that I killed Aelred. Besides, we left the next morning for Worcester, and I didn't return to Carlisle until now."

Gwen actually found herself sympathetic to his plight. Gareth had said he seemed competent, and she gave him credit for honesty, even if too long after the fact. "So why unearth him now?"

"Because I could not stand to see Margaret at James's side for even a single hour, knowing what he is and what he has done."

"Or was it because my father is dead, and I've inherited his fortune," Margaret said softly, to no one in particular. "With James hanged, you and I would be free to marry."

King David had heard her too. "Is that the real reason, Douglas?"

"No, my lord. On my honor." Douglas turned to Margaret. "I knew Lord Gareth was a renowned investigator. It was inevitable with his arrival that he would be called to the scene. I thought it likely I would too and, one way or another, the truth would come out. Everybody knows that no murderer is safe from Lord Gareth." He went down on one knee before her. "I love you."

Margaret remained looking down at her hands. "I broke it off with you the very night I found the body."

"You'd had a shock, one I should have anticipated."

"You left the body for me to find."

"No." Douglas shook his head. "I assumed you'd already come to the church and gone again. Normally, you would have, so it would have been Father Dunstan who discovered his body, not you."

"You'd only just returned," Gwen said. "We intended to be in Carlisle a few days at least, so why the need to unearth him *that* night?"

"Everyone was busy with the knighting ceremony. And the fact that I'd just arrived back in Carlisle meant nobody expected me to be in any particular place at a particular time. It was the one evening I wouldn't be missed."

"You said you were informing those who'd lost loved ones in Worcester of their loss," Gareth said.

"I did do that. It didn't take as long as one might think."

Gareth was looking at him thoughtfully, nodding. "I'm guessing you also knew the schedule of the guards and when that area of the castle wall would be vacant."

"I might have even left some ale in the guard room, to celebrate the return of some of their number." Douglas admitted this without apology.

"This is absurd." Lord James had recovered enough to revert to his haughty tone. "It is Margaret, not I, who murdered Aelred. It is she who must hang."

"I didn't kill him," Margaret said softly. "He was alive when I left him."

"You are lying," James Carr said. "I know what I saw."

Gareth stepped again into the middle of the floor. "Or perhaps you don't."

41

Day Three

Gareth

King David leaned forward. "Explain, Lord Gareth, if you would."

Gareth spread his hands wide. "For argument's sake, let's assume Margaret is telling the truth."

"She isn't," Lord James cut in.

"Enough, James," King David said. "Let Lord Gareth speak."

Gareth bent his head to the king in respect before continuing, "All along, we have known only that Aelred is dead. We thought we knew how he died—a blow to the head—but even that turned out to be an old wound." Now he looked directly at Lord James. "Why did you think he was dead?"

Lord James snorted in derision. "Because he was lying on the floor by the altar in a pool of blood!"

"What did you do once you found him?"

"It was just as Douglas said. I took a cloth that had been left on the floor, wrapped him in it, and put him in the ground."

This was essentially what Gareth had envisioned. He turned to the king. "Would you accompany Gwen and me to the church?" He gestured to the others. "Everyone?"

"Indeed." The king stood and processed out the door.

"What are you thinking?" Lord Douglas said in an undertone to Gareth, for whom he'd waited. "What do you think happened?"

"Just come."

Douglas shook his head. "Did I really get it so wrong?"

"We all got it wrong," Gareth said.

They arrived at the church to find Father Dunstan on his knees in the second row of the choir stall, hammering away at a floor board. At their arrival, he looked over, put down his tools, and hastened forward. "Pardon, my lords. I didn't see you there!" He brushed off his hands. "I was just addressing an errant nail. They do tend to work themselves out over time."

"No need to apologize, Father Dunstan," King David said. "You had no way to know we were coming."

The priest bowed again. "How may I be of service?"

King David gestured in Gareth's direction. "Tell us why you've brought us here."

Having Father Dunstan present was a good fortune Gareth hadn't known he was missing. The seven of them gathered in a loose semi-circle between the altar and the choir stall. "Please show us exactly where you found Aelred's body, Lord James."

James gave a little sniff, but he complied, pointing to a spot to the left of the altar as they faced the entrance to the church.

"Was he face up or face down?"

"What does it matter, man?"

"Lord James." King David's voice didn't even contain a warning tone, but it was a warning nonetheless.

"On his back, his arms flopped wide."

"You said blood had pooled beneath him?"

James shuddered. "I will never forget it."

"Where was it coming from?"

"A wound." He gestured to the right side of his own head. "It wouldn't stop bleeding."

That was where Aelred's skull showed damage, indicating to Gareth that the old wound had been reopened.

Lord James was still speaking. "There was blood *everywhere!* It was as if Margaret had stabbed him in the head. The blood was pooling on the dais and dripping down to the floor."

Gareth could see now why he thought Aelred was dead, but he also knew that head wounds bled excessively, and liquids spilled on the floor (milk, water, wine, or, in this case, blood) could look like more than was actually there.

James frowned as he relived the memory. "He was holding a cloth. I didn't think about it at the time, but I would say now it came from the altar."

"Which hand was it in?"

"The right. I used it to wipe the blood from the floor."

"Was that the same cloth you wrapped him in?"

"No, for that I used one of the drop cloths for the choir."

Gareth had already guessed that. The one they'd found had blood on it, but not in the quantity James was describing.

"What did you do with the altar cloth afterwards?" Gwen asked.

"I-I-I burned it," James said.

Gwen's eyes narrowed. "Why? Why not simply bury it with the body?"

"I forgot about it in getting the body to the grave, which was already covered over by the time I came back to clean up. I took the cloth with me when I left and stuck it in one of the kitchen fires. At that hour of the night, the fire was still bright." He shrugged. "It was gone in a matter of moments."

While the nobleman had been speaking, Gareth had been keeping an eye on Father Dunstan, who had been listening to this conversation with evident alarm. Now the priest said, "Oh!"

"Father?" Gareth turned to him.

"That was the morning the altar cloth went missing."

James frowned. "Why was it on the floor in the first place?"

"It wasn't on the floor when I was talking to Aelred," Margaret said softly, having listened to her husband's answers with utter calm. "It was on the altar as it was supposed to be. If it had been on the floor, I would have put it back."

"I didn't remove it!" James was indignant.

"No." Gwen spoke for the first time. "Aelred did it himself when he hit his head on the corner of the altar. He must have tripped coming up the step and grabbed the cloth in an attempt to arrest his fall."

42

Day Three

Gwen

King David actually laughed. "You're saying he wasn't murdered?"

"I'm saying the head wound was an accident." It wasn't quite the same thing, but nobody noticed, so relieved were they at her conclusion.

The solution to the mystery had come to Gwen as she'd observed the interactions of everyone in the nave, at which point she had finally managed to put herself in Aelred's boots. She'd avoided doing that up until now, because she'd come to detest Aelred and everyone else involved in his death. Not a single one of the participants came off well, with the possible exception of Joanna, who just wanted to be loved.

In regards to Aelred, on the other hand, the more they delved into his life, the more clear it became that he *could* have hurt someone so deeply that they followed him to the church. After he finished his conversation with Margaret, that person could have killed him and taken the money.

Father Dunstan had remained a prime candidate, despite Godfrid's love for him. Except, like Margaret, he said he hadn't done it. Gwen believed him, just as she believed Margaret, though the good father seemed unsettled about *something* today, beyond witnessing the conversation currently underway in his church.

For his part, James was liking being on solid ground again. "Why can't Margaret have pushed him?" He really didn't like his wife. He'd also lived for the last three months convinced she was a murderer.

Gwen turned to Gareth and was pleased to see him nodding and stepping in. "She says she didn't, that he was well when she left. We are taking everyone at their word at the moment, for argument's sake. Which means, however, that we must also take you at yours."

"Of course." James harrumphed.

Gareth's expression turned rueful. "Then, if we do that, we know that Aelred was alive when you came upon him, not dead as you say he was."

"What?" Margaret had been standing a little apart from the men. Her head hadn't even come up when Gwen had explained why she wasn't guilty of murder.

"We learned three important things from my son's examination of the body." Gareth held up one hand to tick them off his fingers. "The first is that Aelred had dirt under his fingernails. According to those who knew him, he was fastidious. He would not willingly have gone to meet Margaret with dirty hands."

"I don't see why this matters," James was offended for himself still and wasn't noticing the roundabout way Gareth was getting to his point, "or how you could even tell when he looked like a dried apple."

"Bodies, even ones buried as long as Aelred's, can tell us many things. Among these is the second thing we learned, which is that the damage to his skull occurred long before his death." At everyone's puzzled looks, Gareth hastened to explain. "Aelred was hit on the head by a beam during the construction of a barn in his village. It made him simple, for a time, while the wound healed. When I saw the body, I made the assumption that such grave damage had to have been the cause of death. But my son pointed out that the edges of the wound were blurred, as if they'd healed over time, which is also in keeping with Aelred's slow recovery."

Gareth paused as everyone digested these two important points.

"Those are the first two of Llelo's discoveries. You said three things," the king prompted.

"Yes, my lord." Gareth looked at Douglas. "When you dug up the body, was it still wrapped in the cloth?"

Douglas's narrowed eyes indicated he was wary of answering, but he couldn't think why he shouldn't or why it mattered. "Only from the chest down. I pulled it all the way off him rather than allow the end to trail on the ground into the church, since the grass was wet."

James frowned. "That doesn't make sense."

"No, it doesn't." Gareth was relentless now. "But even without that evidence, you yourself gave us all the information we needed to determine that he was alive when you entered the church."

"How?"

"Aelred's head wound wouldn't stop bleeding. You soaked the altar cloth in it. Men who are dead don't bleed."

King David was looking at Gareth and ignoring the way James's mouth opened and closed with no sound coming out. "You tell me truly?"

"It is a known fact, my lord," Gwen said. "The moment the heart stops beating, blood stops flowing."

Gareth made a motion with one hand. "The fact that Aelred was bleeding when you came upon him, and continued to bleed, enough to soak the end of the cloth in which you wrapped him, tells us what we need to know."

"Which is what, exactly?" King David said.

"Aelred was alive when Lord James found him. And he was still alive when Lord James put him in his grave. Aelred woke up enough to pull the cloth away from his face before the dirt James was throwing over his body suffocated him."

43

Day Three

Godfrid

"Godfrid, my son!" Father Dunstan came out of the vestry to see who had opened the door to the church.

The bright sun of another lovely afternoon shone onto the floor as Godfrid strode down the nave towards the altar. Although Dunstan attempted to head him off, Godfrid reached the altar and was past it before he could. "Father, would you sit with me?"

Without waiting for an answer, Godfrid moved towards the choir stalls, climbed into the second row, and sat.

Father Dunstan hesitated before smiling again and saying, "Of course."

Godfrid scooted over so the priest could sit next to him, with perhaps a foot between them.

And then Godfrid simply waited.

After a significant pause, Father Dunstan asked, "Was there something you wanted, son?"

"You know what I want."

"I truly don't."

Godfrid turned his head. "Father, I am not the boy you once knew. I have some experience with deception."

"What are you talking about, Godfrid? I am not deceiving you."

"Perhaps not me." And he told the priest of his meeting with Ranulf and King David. It was a significant chance, but it was worthwhile to illustrate his point. "When a great king is asking me, with apparent sincerity, to murder the son of another king, you can perhaps understand why I'm not so trusting as I once was, even of you.

"You did ambush a king before. You can see why he might think it nothing to you."

"I can, and I can't blame him for wanting it. I can blame him for asking."

"Ah. The same way you took Cadwaladr's wealth and despised him for it." Father Dunstan relaxed against the back of the stall. "Raiding churches and villages, encouraging the local magnates we conquered to turn traitor to their own people as an avenue to peace, was a way of life for our people for many generations."

"That doesn't mean it was a good way to live."

"Not in the eyes of God, perhaps, but we survived by doing it." Dunstan's lips twitched. "And grew rich."

"We did."

"But you don't yearn any longer to go *a viking?* That is not the man you are now?"

"It is not." Godfrid knew it in his heart, to the point that the words reverberated in his chest: *it is not.*

"King David and Earl Ranulf have vast resources to hand. They could help Dublin overthrow Leinster."

"Maybe they could. Maybe we could even win. But once in Ireland, would they ever leave? Gareth has warned me more than once to be wary of gifts these Normans offer with one hand while stealing your most valuable possession with the other. If they came in force to Dublin to help us overthrow Leinster, would we simply become puppets of Ranulf or David as we presently are of Diarmait? What's to stop them from carving out kingdoms for themselves in the same way they have done in Chester or Carlisle—or Pembroke?"

"I confess to have never considered the situation in that light."

"David and Ranulf have been enemies for years, but the—" Godfrid fought for the word, "—glee with which they offered me this deal and heard my general acceptance cannot help but give me pause."

"The Normans were once Danes too, son, you know this. Their blood is our blood; they just conquered a different kingdom."

"So you're telling me I should view them as Danes." Godfrid tapped a finger to his lips. "David is merely Ottar with a finer weave to his robe."

"Or Thorgest or Rolf," Dunstan said, naming the founders of Dublin and Normandy respectively. "King Stephen too. This is a family squabble between them, exactly like what went on in Denmark that made our ancestors decide to pursue their fortunes on other shores in the first place."

Godfrid found himself relaxing against the hard wooden back of the choir stall, and the pair sat in companionable silence for a moment. It wasn't enough, unfortunately, and not really why he'd come to the church today. Thus, Godfrid felt compelled to add, "As I was saying, I am not unfamiliar with intrigue. As I sit here, dear father, your heart is beating faster than it should, and you are tapping your foot in a most uncharacteristic manner."

Dunstan immediately stopped, but it was too late.

"I came here torn in my own mind as to whether I should challenge you or leave you in peace. But I cannot let sleeping dogs lie, as my father used to say."

"I have no notion what you mean."

"From your attempt to cut me off before I reached the altar and your obvious reluctance to sit where we are sitting now, it is clear you are hiding something. I am not Gareth, but he has taught me a little of what he knows. When a man is so obviously intent on *not* looking at a certain spot, that is most definitely the spot where one should look.

"It was really quite by chance that it even occurred to me you were hiding anything at all. I was passing by the chapel, thinking I'd stop and speak to you, when I heard hammering coming from the interior. I thought that was odd, but I didn't turn in the gate because, at that moment, King David strode from the gatehouse with Gareth, Gwen, and our suspects in tow. I made myself scarce. Afterwards, I asked Gareth about the noise, and he said you'd been hammering down some flooring." Godfrid lifted one foot and dropped it with a *thunk*. "Right here, in fact."

Dunstan was looking at his hands. "What do you want from me, Godfrid?"

"The truth would be nice."

Dunstan let out a sigh. "I didn't know about any of this three months ago when I found the coins inside the cupboard in the altar. It was a fortune! I assumed someone had left it there as alms for the church."

Now that Dunstan was speaking, Godfrid was almost sorry he knew the truth. "But you didn't tell anyone, I'm guessing, and you moved it."

"A nail had come up that very day, just as I told the king. I am happy to handle these things myself at times. Leaving the money in the hollow underneath the row made sense at the time. I needed to keep it safe."

Godfrid wanted to chastise him, but decided he wouldn't, that they'd come this far, and there was little to be gained by being antagonistic. "May I ask why you didn't tell anyone?"

"I meant to!" He put his hand on his heart. "Truly, I did. But somehow ..." He shook his head. "The garrison left that day, as did King David, and it didn't feel right to tell only the castle steward."

"What have you done with the money, Father?" Godfrid said gently. "I'm guessing there's a little left or you wouldn't have been hammering earlier."

"I didn't keep it for myself, Godfrid! What do you take me for?"

Godfrid didn't become defensive in return, but simply asked, "Then what?"

"I have been doling it out, penny by penny, to the poor and needy, the widow and the orphan." Dunstan hung his head. "I will make restitution."

"Is there any left?"

"Half."

"Half being a hundred silver pennies?"

"No." Dunstan's brow furrowed. "Half being five hundred. And a beautiful brooch."

Godfrid laughed. And then he laughed again. Here he had come to chastise his old friend and priest for not reporting the discovery of two hundred and fifty pennies, only to find it was four times that amount and not really stolen at all.

"Father, the Lord has smiled upon you. Aelred took fifty pennies from Joanna, two hundred from Lady Margaret, and a brooch from Bronwen."

"That—that's all?"

"That is all."

"Where did the rest of the money come from?"

Godfrid's cheer ebbed a little. "Likely other people Aelred blackmailed or manipulated."

"I must return it to them too!" Dunstan was more horrified by the unknown people Aelred had harmed than by those who were known.

But Godfrid himself suddenly felt better about the course he needed to follow. "I will tell Gareth, as well as King David, that you had an idea that Aelred had hidden his money in the church, and you have found it. You don't need to say when you found it or the original amount. We can at least make full restitution to those who trusted him here in Carlisle. I leave the rest to you, Father, to make amends in whatever manner you see fit."

Hope filled Dunstan's face, along with determination, evident by the new set to his chin. "I will have to confess."

"And do penance, I'm sure. But not to me, not to the king—and certainly not to Aelred."

44

Day Three

Gareth

Gwen smoothed Gareth's mantle along his shoulders. "Are you ready for this?"

A warm day had become a warm evening, but even so, it was important that he look his best, and that included sweating under the decorative mantle of his office. "Am I ready to commit our king to a treaty with men I know to be dishonorable?"

"Yes. That."

"No. But do I have a choice?"

"You do not. King Owain agreed to this, even if it meant taking his brother back into his favor, for the chance to rule all Wales."

"And when King Stephen learns of it?"

"As I'm sure he will, it will not be the first time that Gwynedd has chosen to fight against him on Maud's side. And it isn't as if Stephen has made more than a half-hearted foray in King Owain's direction. Stephen can hardly blame our king for taking sides when one side offers him nothing and the other everything."

Gareth let out a breath. "I suppose King Stephen himself has had his own ethical missteps."

"He is the King of England. He can do as he likes."

"And pay the price, as he has done with Ranulf, and as he may well do with the Danes if Brodar prefers King David's deal to what I suggested."

"If he does what you want, David and Ranulf will call them traitors. They might even convince Henry of that in time. The Danes could pay dearly in the future for following your advice."

"As might King Owain and Prince Hywel. Nobody can see the future, Gwen, not for certain."

"So we do what we can with the information we have and what we are given."

Gareth tightened his sword belt at his waist. "Which means, in this moment, allying ourselves with a passel of feckless foreigners."

"It will not be the first time, my love." She grinned. "Perhaps I should drape a lavender satchel around your neck, so you don't have to hold your nose."

Gareth laughed, genuinely, as he knew Gwen meant him too, and further steeled himself for the upcoming encounter. After all, this was what he'd come to Carlisle *for*.

So it was with some surprise that their arrival at the castle was not greeted with significant fanfare. In fact, while the mood in the outer bailey could be described as subdued, in the inner bailey it was all but grim.

"It's as if the castle is about to be put under siege," Cait said in an undertone. She was feeling well enough—likely had forced herself to feel well enough—to attend tonight's feast.

"You might not be far off." Gareth put out a hand to a passing servant, who otherwise would have hustled by them with hardly a sketch of a bow. "Where is the king?"

"In the hall, my lord. I believe he is awaiting your arrival."

That sounded a little more promising. A guard pulled open the main door, and they all entered in a group, with Gareth slightly in the lead.

Though the usual number of people were eating at the tables, Gareth and his family appeared to be late, as most were well into their dishes. Like the people they'd seen in the outer bailey, everyone was hunkered down, focused on their food and their ale, and few looked up at Gareth's arrival. He was starting to feel self-conscious in his finery.

King David's steward hurried down the length of the hall to greet him. "My lord, the king requests that you dine with him tonight on the dais." He made a gesture to encompass Gwen, Dai, Llelo, Conall, Godfrid, and Cait. "All of you."

The high table had been arranged so guests could sit on all four sides, accommodating twenty people with room to spare. Neither the Carrs nor Lord Douglas were present tonight anyway, and their spaces were filled by Prince Henry, Ranulf, Hamelin, and other advisers.

This wasn't turning out to be the evening Gareth had imagined—and worried about—for months. He had assumed that the actual signing of the document might take place in a more private space, but his understanding was that Gwynedd would be feted somewhat more than was currently occurring.

They all bowed to King David, who bent his head in return and gestured for them to sit. Gareth found himself to the king's right, which admittedly was a place of high honor. Prince Henry sat on the king's left, With Ranulf one space down. Although the young prince looked up as Gareth sat and lifted a hand in greeting, his focus, as with everyone else in the hall, was on his food. In fact, he appeared to be shoveling vegetables and meat into his mouth with surprising speed.

"My lord—" Gareth began.

King David put up a hand. "Do not trouble yourself in wondering why our agenda has changed. I will tell you. We have just received word from our spy in Stephen's court that he has heard of our alliance and, more importantly, of our imminent attack on York. His army is already halfway there as we speak."

"Your king's assistance is no longer required, I'm afraid." Ranulf dabbed the corners of his mouth with a cloth. "We do not have the men, even with your spears and bows, to counter the number of men Stephen is bringing to the defense of York. And our men can't reach the city before Stephen's anyway."

"Though we are grateful, of course, for your presence here and all you've done," King David made haste to add, while shooting a glare at Ranulf.

"So ..." Gareth looked from one to the other. "That's it? It's over?"

"Not over." Prince Henry's tone was grim. "Just deferred, for now." Then he made what might have been an apologetic motion with his head. "Please pardon my elders' abruptness. It is a product of extreme disappointment. I myself will be leaving for Normandy in the morning."

"You have a spy in your ranks, my king," Ranulf said, not as much under his breath as he might have. That he hadn't already left Carlisle indicated his part in the alliance still held—for now.

He didn't look at the Welsh contingent when he spoke either, indicating nobody was blaming them—a small consolation. Of course, for King Stephen to already be marching to York meant he had heard of the planned attack weeks ago, and that knowledge had nothing to do with Gareth and Gwen.

"I am aware, Ranulf," David said repressively.

Ranulf tore into his chicken with his teeth, oblivious to David's censure.

"So ..." Gareth felt a bit at sea, "we are simply to return home?"

"We remain united and confirmed in our goals. King Owain, is, of course, a valued member of our coalition." Prince Henry shot a piercing look in Ranulf's direction, not any more happy with him than the king was.

Ranulf appeared finally to realize that his comments had not been well-received by his fellow conspirators, but all he did was wave a hand, as if dismissing their concerns. "Chester has no argument with Gwynedd."

"But we dare commit nothing to writing until we have rooted out this spy," King David said, addressing Gareth's real question. "It is for Gwynedd's own benefit that we don't formalize our agreement at this time. We would not want Stephen to turn his wrath on you."

"I repeat, a truce with Chester still holds." Ranulf took a long gulp of wine and stood. "I'm off." He bowed to King David and Prince Henry. "My lords." A moment later, he was gone.

Gareth hated to bring it up, but he had to ask, for Prince Hywel's sake if nobody else's. "What of Prince Cadwaladr?"

"The king's brother?" King David frowned. "What of him?"

That he would behave as if he didn't know that participation in their rebellion was contingent upon Owain's acceptance of Cadwaladr in his court was disconcerting—and uncharacteristically disingenuous.

"What say you, my lord prince?" Gareth directed his attention to Prince Henry.

The prince bent his head graciously. "Your king may, of course, do with Cadwaladr as he sees fit. None of us will object, not even Ranulf."

Gareth felt as if he were seven years old and floundering in a pool of water that had suddenly become too deep.

Conall came to his rescue. "We appreciate your candor, my lords." He gestured down the table to his companions. "We will also depart in the morning."

King David smiled gently at Gareth. "I can't say that I am pleased by the outcome of the investigation you conducted, but I am grateful for your service, and I will not forget it." His eyes went around the table too. "As you can see, Lord Carr is not here. He has been given stewardship of lands in Halkirk, for which he has already departed. Meanwhile, Lady Carr has retired to her father's estates. *Her* estates."

Halkirk was the absolute northernmost region of mainland Scotland and an area David was working hard to control. Since it was as far from Carlisle as it was possible to get and still be within the king's domains, it was the opposite of a plum assignment. Carr had been lucky to survive this week with so little consequence. In fact, he'd been lucky to survive.

While Gareth appreciated the king's thanks, that appeared to be that.

After the meal ended, the family walked back one last time through the streets of Carlisle, which were as quiet and subdued as the castle bailey had been.

"I'm not looking forward to telling King Owain and Prince Hywel that they accepted Cadwaladr back into their midst for no reward," Gareth said.

"Maybe the alliance really does hold for now. That could be good for all of us," Conall said, though not without a rueful glance at Gareth.

They all doubted it, but nonetheless, Gareth said, "We can hope."

Gwen reached out to clasp his hand. It was so like her to know the extent of his turmoil without him having to articulate it. "In the words of Abbot Rhys: *Give over to God his due.* If ever there was an event over which we have no control, it is this one."

"And just think!" Godfrid's head was up. "Tomorrow we'll have the sea air in our faces!"

Cait laughed. "You, my love, will always be a Viking."

Gwen bent forward to look past Gareth to Godfrid. "I saw you speaking to King David before we left. By the look on your face as you walked away, he still wants you to *go a viking.*"

"He does."

"Which makes me wonder," Gwen said, "if making this offer to you was the entire point of this journey all along."

Historical Note

One of the pleasures of writing historical fiction is when events in the past become the basis of a story. Prince Henry was, in fact, knighted by his great-uncle, King David of Scotland, on May 22, 1149 at Carlisle Castle. As soon as I became aware of this historical tidbit, I knew I had to write a story around it and invite Gareth, Gwen, and their friends to come along.

The alliance between Ranulf, Henry, and David is also a matter of historical record, along with the fact that it fell apart almost immediately upon its conception. Just as in *The Faithless Fool*, King Stephen got wind of the alliance's plans and marched his men to York before his enemies could gather. His plans foiled, Henry returned to Normandy, where he was named Duke of Normandy by his father and was soon embroiled in new conflicts in France. He did not return to England until 1153, after his marriage to Eleanor of Aquitaine.

But that's a different story.

The role of Cadwaladr in these proceedings is more obscure, though he was returned to King Owain's favor around this time. He didn't keep it, as one might suspect, and that is definitely a story for another time.

About the Author

With over a million books sold to date, Sarah Woodbury is the author of more than forty novels, all set in medieval Wales. Although an anthropologist by training, and then a full-time homeschooling mom for twenty years, she began writing fiction when the stories in her head overflowed and demanded that she let them out. While her ancestry is Welsh, she only visited Wales for the first time at university. She has been in love with the country, language, and people ever since. She even convinced her husband to give all four of their children Welsh names.
She makes her home in Oregon.

Thank you for continuing this journey into the Middle Ages with me! Please don't worry that this is the last *Gareth & Gwen Medieval Mystery*. There will be more! If you'd like to know as soon as the preorder for the next book is available, feel free to subscribe to my newsletter at
www.sarahwoodbury.com